Tsunami Warning

A Sylvia Avery Mystery

BOOK SIX

Jan Bono

Sandridge Publications
Long Beach, Washington

Beware!
Jan Bono

First Printing, Spring, 2021

Printed in the United States of America
Gorham Printing, Centralia, WA 98531

Cover Photo: Tery Pierson, Long Beach, WA
　　　　　　5th Generation Peninsula Girl

Sandridge Publications
P.O. Box 278
Long Beach, WA 98631

http://www.JanBonoBooks.com

ISBN: 978-1-7356589-1-9

DEDICATED

to Dr. Hook and the Medicine Show
for without them
I might never have discovered
Sylvia's last name

OTHER BOOKS BY JAN BONO

Sylvia Avery Mystery Series:
Book 1, Bottom Feeders
Book 2, Starfish
Book 3, Crab Bait
Book 4, Hook, Line, & Sinker
Book 5, Oyster Spat

Health and Fitness:
Back from Obesity:
My 252-pound Weight-loss Journey

Collections of humorous personal experience:
Through My Looking Glass: View from the Beach
Through My Looking Glass: Volume II
It's Christmas!
Forty-three stories and three one-act plays
Just Joshin'
A Year in the Life of a Not-so-ordinary
4th Grade Kid

Fiction:
Romance 101:
Forty-two Sweet, Light, Delicious,
G-Rated Short Stories

Poetry Chapbooks:
Bar Talk, Chasing Rainbows, and
Fisher Girl, Fisher Wife, Fisher Poet

A number of Jan's books are now available as eBooks at Smashwords.com. Find them at:

http://www.smashwords.com/profile/view/JanBonoBooks

NORTH BEACH PENINSULA

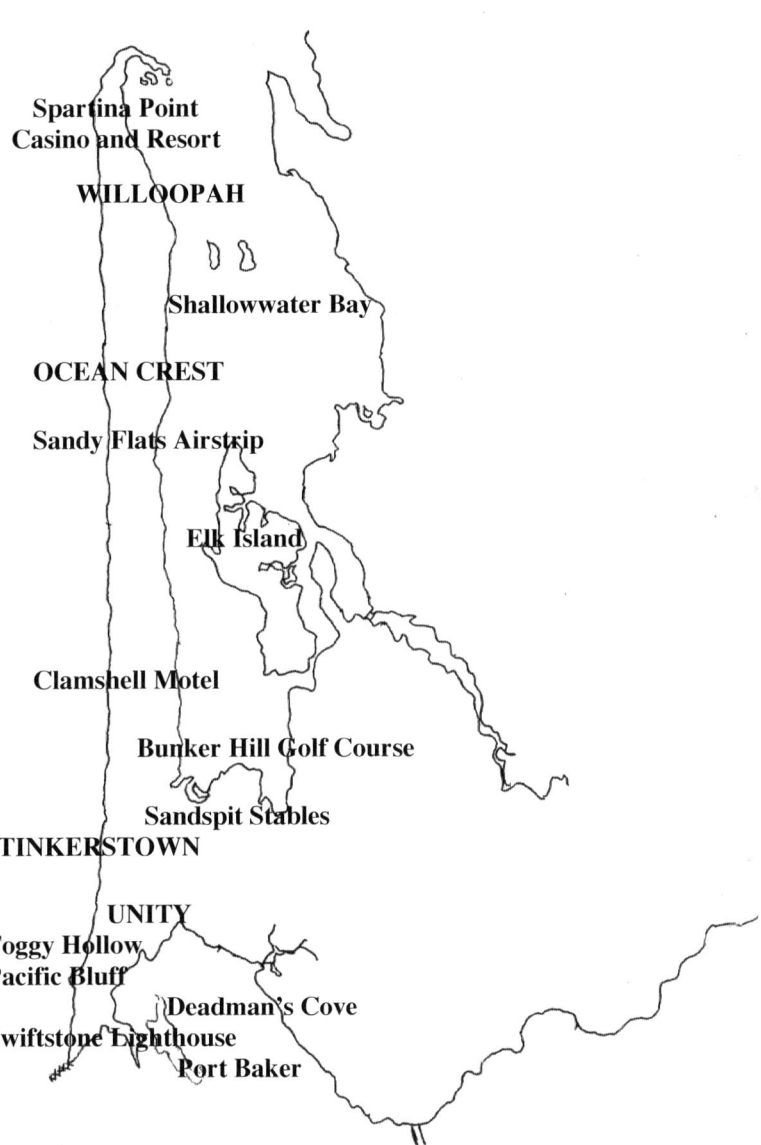

Spartina Point
Casino and Resort

WILLOOPAH

Shallowwater Bay

OCEAN CREST

Sandy Flats Airstrip

Elk Island

Clamshell Motel

Bunker Hill Golf Course

Sandspit Stables

TINKERSTOWN

UNITY
Foggy Hollow
Pacific Bluff

Deadman's Cove

Swiftstone Lighthouse

Port Baker

TSUNAMI WARNING

CHAPTER 1

I could see dozens of fish swimming far beneath me, just going about their own business, oblivious to my pain. I closed my eyes, and the darkness drew in tight around me, at once both comforting and terrifying. I inhaled deeply and my body involuntarily shuddered.

I was lying face down in the Pacific Ocean, my arms and legs outstretched, and limp. Salt water filled my ears and made the world around me eerily quiet. The constant rise and fall of the waves lulled me into a sense of security rather than danger.

Was this what it was like to be dead? To be suspended in a dark floating eternity and to feel absolutely nothing?

It's not true that in times of presumed imminent demise your entire life flashes before your eyes. Sometimes it's just one distant memory. Or maybe not so distant, as in my case it had only been five and a half months. Nevertheless, that one memory seemed to run on a continuous loop whenever I let my guard down. The same scene, over and over and over and over.

The vivid memory constantly haunting me took place last New Year's Eve, when I'd kicked off my high-heeled shoes and run from the dance floor with panic-filled eyes. Like a scared rabbit, I'd darted blindly this way and that, hoping to outrun the

7

circling eagles with outstretched talons.

Of course, there'd been neither circling eagles nor outstretched talons in the casino ballroom that night—just two men who truly loved me, both on their knees, both holding ring boxes.

It was the stuff most women dreamed of, what romance novels were filled with, and what the Hallmark corporation thrived upon. And yet that scene caused the bile to rise harshly in my throat, and I had hiked my ballroom gown up around my knees and run for the parking lot while imagined fire-breathing demons hotly pursued me.

Still floating supine with my eyes closed, I took another deep breath, mildly surprised to realize my lungs filled with air and not water. Of course, I could change that in a heartbeat…

"No!" my internal voice screamed. "No! Don't you dare!"

I shook my head to clear it and opened my eyes. The fish were still peacefully swimming below me. Their colors were vibrant and alive. And so was I. I kicked my feet and scooped water with my hands to pull myself upright in the ocean.

The island of Molokini was right where I'd left it. The *Cherokee Rose*—the boat that had brought me here—was still quietly idling nearby. The two dozen snorkelers I was supposed to be wrangling this afternoon all seemed to be doing fine, despite my inattention to them.

I felt a little guilty about taking these few minutes to myself, but since I hadn't heard Captain Rick sound the foghorn alarm, I knew they were having fun paddling around among themselves without my constant hovering.

As long as one of those seniors didn't suddenly go into distress, need to be physically hauled to the boat and given oxygen, this job was beyond a doubt the best gig I'd ever had. Since I started working here in January, we haven't had to use the cardio defibrillator even once, and I'm grateful. Of course, knowing how to use it is one of the reasons Captain Rick had hired me.

The fact I'm CPR certified, can swim fairly well, and have had extensive experience working with the elderly made me a shoo-in for this job. Of course, it's a bit of an embellishment to equate hanging out with the geriatric belly-dancing members of *The Veiled Rainbow* as working with the elderly, but it's not like I'd fudged on a formal resumé.

It was actually my new landlord's recommendation that sealed the deal. Turns out she's Captain Rick's twin sister, and he's trusted her good instincts his whole life.

"Lee! Lee!" someone suddenly called out, waving her arms up over her head. "Lee! Over here! Come look! There's a sea turtle!" A small group had gathered together in their bright Hawaiian swimming attire. Clustered as they were, they looked like a bobbing bouquet.

It still took me a moment to realize the woman had been calling out to me. My name was not Lee, it's actually Sylvia Lee Avery, but I'm currently living under an assumed name. That's right—I was a woman on the lam.

Dutifully, I paddled over to the group, counting the bodies in the water as I neared them. Twenty. I looked up at the boat and Captain Rick held up four fingers. Four of the snorkelers had already worn themselves out and returned to the *Cherokee Rose* without waiting for last call. The captain made a sweeping circular motion in the air with his index finger. Time to round them up and climb back aboard.

The chatter and camaraderie as the boat made its way back to Lahaina was easily 10 times as loud as during the outbound trip this morning. The senior citizens always reminded me of a bunch of high school kids returning from a field trip, excitedly sharing their individual snorkeling adventures. I pulled a pair of shorts and a tank top on over my swimsuit and smiled as I set refreshments out on a table on the lower deck. These older tourists would likely be as ravenous as teenagers, too.

After attending to the passengers, I climbed up to the wheelhouse. "Looks like another successful trip, Captain," I said, as I handed him a cup of sparkling pineapple juice and a macadamia nut cookie.

Captain Rick smiled and winked at me. I could almost recite his customary response along with him: "Any day we take a bunch of elderly mainlanders out on the ocean, get them into water, let them paddle around gawking at pretty fish until they tucker themselves out, then get them back safely on board, I'd say the trip was indeed successful."

I loved standing on the bridge with Captain Rick. The wind in our hair, the towel-wrapped tourists sharing their stories and eating refreshments on the deck below us—it was all so perfect, I wanted to stay up there and bask in the satisfaction of a job well done. But before we got back to the dock, I had some chores to do, or I'd be stuck on the boat half the night doing them.

I climbed down, refilled the pitchers of juice and platters of cookies, and set to work collecting the flippers, masks, paddle boards, and foam noodle floatation devices. I sprayed the inside of the masks, and put the equipment away in its proper place, securing the cupboards with latches after making sure everything was accounted for.

The optical masks were always a surprise to those "of a certain age" who were afraid their eyesight would prevent them from seeing any fish in the water. But these special masks worked so well we'd never had a passenger sidelined because of his or her near or farsightedness.

I smiled as I thought about the ladies of *The Veiled Rainbow*.

I bet they'd have a great time on one of these excursions. Thinking about them made me nostalgic and sentimental and sad. I briefly wondered if maybe it was time for me to get my fanny back home and start making amends before it was too late to make things right with some of them.

"Lee! Would you mind taking a few photos for us?" My self-reflection was interrupted by the passengers gathering together on the front deck. I was only too happy to oblige them by becoming their designated photographer. With the captain on the bridge at the top, the name *Cherokee Rose* painted on the beam below him, and a group of happy, satisfied customers beaming smiles all around, it was better advertising than anyone could wish for. In a matter of minutes, these photos would be out on the internet, going viral—at least among their friends and family.

Word of mouth was the best advertising you could ask for, and most of the passengers were return clients bringing new friends with them. Today it was a private party, celebrating someone's retirement, and they all knew each so other well it was like one big, happy family.

Captain Rick's rather unusual business model was truly unique, and what kept many of them coming back year after year.

For one, he never left port until mid-morning, because "tropical fish don't care what time you get there, and we're on vacation, so what's the rush?"

For two, although his boat could probably hold 40 to 50 passengers, he chose to hold the trip roster to between 20 and 30.

And for three, he catered to seniors only, so they'd feel less self-conscious strutting around the deck in their bathing suits.

After I finished taking photos with the various phones and cameras handed to me, someone asked about the name of the boat.

"Yes, Captain Rick Abrams is part Native American, but the

boat's name is more of a nod to his southern upbringing. *Cherokee Rose* is the State Flower of Georgia, where he and his twin sister grew up."

My practiced answer always got the inevitable follow up question, some variation of: "He has a twin sister? Does she live in the islands?"

"Yes, his sister, Yvonne Abrams, also retired to Maui," I answered. "But neither are fully retired. She's the one you talked to when you booked your reservations, and she bakes the banana bread, macadamia nut cookies, and other goodies you've enjoyed today."

Murmurs of appreciation rippled through the crowd. I refilled the pitchers and platters one final time, and went back to restoring order to the floatation devices. After that I started hosing off the back deck and readying the bumpers for tying us up dockside.

While I worked, I considered how fortunate I'd been in finding such a great place to live and a wonderful job so quickly upon arriving in Maui. It must have been fate. Or maybe I'd had enough good karma points saved up.

Yvonne Abrams owned a charming home just a few blocks from the port docks on Wainee Street. She and Rick had wisely chosen not to live together, as they feared that would be just too much togetherness, but they were great business partners.

It was Rick who had placed the ad about renting out Yvonne's spare bedroom on craigslist—the very one I'd seen on my flight from the mainland. I called from the airport, found out the room was still available, then hopped on a bus from Kahului to the dry side of Maui. By eliminating the need of a rental car, I didn't need to use my legal ID and credit cards. Technically, I was a 55-year-old runaway, and I didn't want to be easy to find.

Yvonne Abrams turned out to be a powerhouse of positive

energy. A little on the chunky side, she had thick, curly gray hair, and a big, boisterous laugh. I liked her the moment I met her, and apparently, she liked what she saw in me right away as well. She had given me a short tour of her home, told me about my kitchen and laundry privileges, informed me no overnight guests were allowed, and then told me how much the rent would be.

I paid her for six months, in cash, right up front, and she didn't even blink. She just tucked the money in her bra, said I could call her Evie, and gave me a house key.

It was a lovely place to live, if you didn't mind not having a view, no lock on the bathroom door, and sharing the house with seven cats. The location was central to the entire town, and everything you'd ever need was pretty much within walking distance.

I was still on mainland time that first morning. I had awakened early, fixed a cup of coffee, and taken it outside. Surrounded by a towering lush green hedge was a tiny back yard, just a patio table, four chairs, and two chaise lounges, making it ultra-private. I sat down on one of the lounges and was immediately covered in cats.

Two black and gray tabbies, two tuxedos, two that defied such descriptions, and a single calico magically appeared and had busily checked me out. I'd felt instantly at home.

Evie found me that way a short while later and said she was happy to see the cats had so readily accepted me.

"I'm used to having cats around," I told her. "My mother has three, all named after her deceased husbands."

"Gracious!" Evie had said. "When I first got here, I visited the local shelter. They had seven cats available, and I couldn't decide which one, so I brought them all home." She'd laughed. "Always figured I'd turn out to be a crazy cat lady. And since there were seven, I just made it simple and named them after the seven days of the week."

We'd had a good chuckle, and then Evie had suddenly turned serious. "Does your mother know where you are, dear?"

"My mother?" I echoed, stalling for time. How had Evie known I'd been sitting here wondering what kind of person would just disappear without at least telling her mother where she was going, or at least let her know she was okay?

I tried dismissing Evie's question. "I'm an adult, Evie. I didn't need my mother's permission to relocate in Hawaii for a while."

She must have sensed my inner distress. She got up, went inside, and returned immediately with the pot of coffee and a fold-over pamphlet.

"Here, Lee," she'd said, handing me the pamphlet with one hand and refilling my coffee cup with the other. "Since you paid me for six months, I'm assuming you've got some things you want to sort out that might take some time. This might help you find your answers while you're here on Maui."

The pamphlet was a meeting schedule for the island's Alano Club.

"But I don't drink," I started to protest. "Well, not really. Maybe just a little once in a while—but only on special occasions. Mostly."

Evie just smiled, and the way she smiled told me she might know something I didn't know, like when someone offers you a breath mint, you should always take it.

"Well, I guess it couldn't hurt," I said slowly. "I really don't have anything else to do."

"Alcoholics Anonymous is a good place to meet good people," Evie had said. "Those 12 steps are guidelines for living, whether you have a problem with alcohol or not." She paused. "And they won't judge you for past mistakes—love and tolerance is what they're all about. Everyone is welcome, and made to feel safe."

I nodded mutely, and decided I might as well check it out, since I didn't know anyone except Evie on the island and could use a few friends. And like I'd already said, it couldn't hurt.

Thankfully, she didn't continue along that line of conversation, but had abruptly gone in a whole 'nother direction. "Are you going to be looking for work, dear?" she'd asked.

I told her I hadn't really thought about it, but realizing my money might not last forever, I told her I'd probably look for something part-time so I didn't end up living on the street.

"That's good," said Evie, nodding. "Living on the street is universally frowned upon, even in the Aloha State." Then she'd tilted her head and seemed to look clear through me. "Can you swim, dear?"

Little did I know my answer to that simple question would open the door to the best part-time job *ever*.

Now I looked up from my boat-cleaning chores over to the shoreline to calculate how much time I had before we tied up at the dock. Red, right, returning, Rick skillfully followed the navigational lights and traversed the narrow channel leading to the inner harbor.

The *Cherokee Rose* tied up in a spot along the second line of boats, facing away from land. It was only marginally cheaper to rent a space back there than among the prime docking spots, where boats were lined up like hungry tiger sharks, packing the tourists in with their big flashy signs and decorated registration booths along the shore.

I always loved helping the passengers disembark. When I offered my hand to help them step from the boat to the dock ramp, they often squeezed it tight and told me how much fun they'd had and how they'd be sure to come back soon.

At the end of the ramp was a small table where Captain Rick

stood, shaking hands, passing out his business cards, and asking each of them to do a short online survey so he could improve his service. To which they almost always responded there was nothing that needed improved. The small, three-legged table next to the captain held a discreet tip jar for those especially happy with our service.

When the last passenger left us, Captain Rick picked up the tip jar in one hand, the table in the other, and joined me on the back deck. As was our comfortable routine, I split the last of the decaf coffee between us and waited for him to count up the tips.

The money was divided three ways: for the captain, for the boat maintenance fund, and for me. I didn't mind. I made a pretty decent wage, as well as having the time of my life, so the abundant tips were just the sprinkles on the frosting of my cupcake.

Captain Rick scooped up each of the equal piles and put them into 5" x 7" manila envelopes. As he handed one to me, he asked, "Have you been doing any serious thinking about returning to the mainland?"

His question caught me off guard. Had he known how homesick I'd been as I'd cleaned the equipment? Was he that intuitive? Perhaps it ran in his family.

"You trying to get rid of me?" I hedged.

He smiled, and pushed his *Cherokee Rose* ball cap back on his head an inch or two, reminding me of Sheriff Donaldson, back home. "I'm not in any rush," Rick said. "You're one of the best deckhands I've had, but when you signed on, you said it was temporary. I was just wondering if you had any idea when your time here would come to an end. I don't need you to give me two weeks' notice or anything, but I hope you'll let me know as soon as you've decided."

A fair enough request, but it made me uneasy. I nodded. "I pinky swear to do that, Rick. But as of right this minute, I have no plans to leave."

He nodded, and picked up his two envelopes. "Time to call it a day then."

We walked back along the dock, then turned and followed the sidewalk along the front side of the marina until we got to where it joined the appropriately named Wharf Street in front of the Old Lahaina Courthouse.

There we parted ways, Rick heading for his pickup, and on to his condo a few miles outside the town's city limits, and me cutting through the infamous Banyan Tree Park, which was a beautiful shortcut between the marina and a multiple-level mini-mall of eclectic shops.

If I had a dollar for every picture I'd offered to take under that Banyan Tree, I'd be a wealthy woman. But I felt it a privilege to take those photos. That way everyone in the party could be in at least one picture, just like the photos I'd taken on the boat that afternoon.

Banyan Treats, my favorite ice cream shop, is at the corner of the park and Front Street. On afternoons when I haven't already filled up on banana bread and cookies, the place is irresistible. Forcing myself not to indulge in a triple scoop of macadamia, pineapple, and coconut ice creams every day, I was happy when I succeeded in walking on by.

Next door to the ice cream shop is *Bad Ass Coffee of Hawaii*. After I arrived last January, I quickly learned Hawaii is the only state that grows their own coffee, and they are quite proud of it! The barista at *Bad Ass* knows me pretty well now and makes my one cup of excellent java each day as soon as she sees the whites of my eyes, regardless how long the line in front of me is. Special treatment like that is definitely one of the advantages of being accepted into the inner circle of local workers in a tourist-filled town.

Today, after a full day's workout on the *Cherokee Rose*, in which I'm sure I burned enough calories for my ice cream treat, I was pretty worn out. I thought I'd just go straight home, shower, and hang out with the cats in the backyard. Even after five and a half months, I still couldn't always put the right name on each cat, but they never seemed to mind.

I stood on the street corner, waiting for a break in the traffic to cross Front Street and cut through the Wharf Cinema Center, my air-conditioned hideout on hot days when I didn't work, when I heard a decidedly familiar voice call my name.

Holy Criminitly! Instant nausea threatened to overwhelm me, and my stomach clenched as tight as a mariner's monkey's fist. The woman, who must have been sitting where I wouldn't have noticed her on one of the many benches constantly filled with tourists beneath the Banyan Tree, had not called out for "Lee," but for "Sylvia."

CHAPTER 2

Somewhere, deep in my heart of hearts, I'd known this day of reckoning would eventually come. Caught like the proverbial deer in the headlights, I froze. My feet would neither propel me across the street, nor turn me around to face the voice that had hailed me.

I'd always known, after the stunt I'd pulled on New Year's Eve, this time would eventually catch up to me and smack me hard on the nose, like when a naughty puppy needs to be corrected and/or trained to behave properly. Some might find it useful to employ a rolled-up newspaper to get the pup's attention, such as the *North Coast Tribune*.

As it turned out, on the front page of the *North Coast Tribune* on January second, the headline had read: "Former CPS Worker Turns Modern Day Cinderella." The photo showed two men in tuxedos, standing on the dance floor of the *Spartina Point Casino and Resort*, each holding a ring box in one hand and one of my strappy, glittery-gold high heels in the other.

I guess I'm what you'd call a commitmentphobe. Or maybe I just needed to sign up for a short course in polyamory, because what I really wanted was both of those gorgeous, totally sexy and wonderful men in my life, without having either one of them actually move into my house with me, or me having to move into one of their homes.

Not knowing how to answer either man's proposal, I'd run from the casino ballroom just as the clock struck twelve. I knew neither one of them could immediately follow me, as both were committed to stay until the party was over and the last guest had left. That had given me enough time to dash home, throw whatever I thought I might need, for wherever I ended up, into a couple suitcases, and head for the airport.

When I'd left the North Beach Peninsula, I hadn't a clue where I was headed. I just knew it was going to be an airplane that took me there. I needed to go far, and go fast, but first I spent two nights in a crummy motel near the train station because I needed money, and the banks were naturally closed on January first for the holiday.

On January second, I all but emptied my bank account, put my beloved Mustang into long term storage, and put the car battery into the trunk. In the interim, my phone had rung at least one hundred times, plus text messages, and I had answered none of them. None.

All my bills were paid through autopay, and my state pension deposited directly into my bank account, so I received very little mail. I had no pets to take care of, and no plants I'd miss too much if they weren't watered. What I needed was to go someplace far away to think. I needed to carefully consider my options. What, and who, did I really want? And once that was settled, was I strong enough to give up everything, and anyone, else?

After securing my car in long-term storage, and pre-paying six month's rent, I powered my phone completely off and took the city bus to the airport—destination Maui. While holed up in my motel room, I'd found out there were three carriers now with direct flights to Kahului, and it hadn't been too difficult to find one with a vacant seat, even on very short notice.

But right now—right this minute—everything and everyone I knew back home on the North Beach Peninsula was suddenly clamoring for attention. I'd learned, by attending a 12-step meeting almost every day we didn't take the boat out, that "fear" could stand for either "Face Everything And Recover," or "Forget Everything And Run."

Unfortunately, my five months in the program wasn't enough to stop the bile from surging up into my throat, and I chose the second option.

I panicked and started running blindly, not for my room at Evie Abrams' house, but for the sanctity of the Alano Club, tucked inside a secluded stand of palm trees a few blocks in the other direction. The frequent swimming had gotten me into pretty good shape, and I knew the backyards without dogs I could safely cut through, keeping off main streets and sidewalks. I dared not look back. I put every ounce of energy into running like my life depended on it.

If I'd been found walking home from work, I was pretty certain my residence had also been compromised. But how had I been found? Although I'd considered leaving my phone in the glove box of the Mustang in Portland, I'd taken it with me because I was sure I couldn't remember all the unlisted numbers in my phone, and someday I might need to make an important call. But I'd made sure to keep my phone turned off! I just kept it with me in case of an emergency. If it was off, it was off. Right? Sheriff Donaldson couldn't have tracked me down—could he?

I suspected Deputy Fredrick Morgan, one of the men I'd left holding a shoe and a ring box, thought I'd left my phone in Tinkerstown. The years of watching crime TV, and being endlessly teased about it, warned me the police were only too eager to ping someone's cell phone to find them. And I didn't know when I'd be ready to be found.

Nothing at my house gave any indication where I was going, because when I left, I hadn't known where I was going. I guess I had counted on the sheriff to play by the rules and respect my privacy, knowing he "could" trace me if he'd really wanted to—at least that was how it worked on television. But until today, I'd never given it much thought, or what I'd do if surprised by someone wishing to press the issue with a face-to-face confrontation.

I was totally out of breath when I arrived at the Alano Club. A few members were hanging out having coffee at the tables under sun umbrellas in the courtyard. I recognized my friend Tom M, having a cigarette. I wanted to shake my finger at him, as I know he's trying to quit smoking, but I just faked a smile, gave him a little wave, then hurried up the steps and into the club.

Dang! The women's bathroom was locked, so I rapped twice on the men's room and barreled in, not even pausing to lock the door behind me. Dropping to my knees, I hugged the porcelain commode, and threw up into the toilet for several minutes.

When I stopped throwing up, I assumed my stomach must be empty, but I didn't get up. I just sat there on the floor and cradled the bowl and cried and cried and cried. My head throbbed and my heart ached. Then a light tapping on the door pulled me away from my pity party.

"Occupied!" I yelled at the top of my lungs. But the door opened anyway.

Tom M came into the bathroom and closed the door behind him. From where I sat, his 5'8", decidedly thin frame towered over me, and I involuntarily shivered. He leaned his back against the door and looked at me with a combination of what I'd call pity and bemusement.

"So, Lee, what's going on? Did you drink four or five or nine too many fruity Mai Tais out on the boat this afternoon?"

I searched my mind for a quick and biting comeback, but nothing occurred to me. I just leaned my head against the edge of the bowl and started crying again.

"There, there," he said, sounding truly compassionate. He wet a paper towel, handed it to me, and told me to wipe my face.

I did as he said, then mindlessly started to hand the towel back to him.

"Eeww!" he said, shrinking back as if in horror. "I'm not touching that! Put it in the garbage can."

Again, I followed his directions. Then he crouched down, took both my hands in his, and pulled me to my feet. "Follow me."

He found us two overstuffed chairs in a quiet little area of the screened porch that ran halfway around the outside of the building. "I know you haven't been drinking, Lee. I don't think you'd resort to getting drunk just to try to drown your problems." He paused. "So do you want to talk about what's got you so upset?"

I shook my head, and reached for the box of tissues, grateful every table in the club had a handy supply of them. After a few minutes I asked, "Why does everyone called you Tom M when you're the only Tom in the group?"

"Nice attempt at deflection," he replied, and sat quietly waiting for me to open up.

"Deflection is one of my super powers." I said dryly. Then I blew out a huge breath. "Tom, I need to be honest with you—my name's not really Lee."

He nodded, but said nothing, and within a few minutes, I started pouring out my story, bit by bit. For the most part, he let me set the pace and did not interrupt, unless there was something needing immediate clarification.

I decided to start at how I came to stay on Maui, filling him in on what I thought was the root of my problems—being unable to choose which man to marry—and how I'd run away and left them both standing there on the dance floor.

Tom M, bless his heart, did his best not to smile or smirk, but

I could tell there were moments when he had to work at it, and when I quoted the newspaper headline, he pretended he had choked on a swallow of coffee.

"Former CPS Worker Turns Modern Day Cinderella?" he asked rhetorically.

I nodded. "It was quite humiliating."

"For you as much as for them, I presume," he replied. "Only you weren't there when the newspaper came out, so you didn't have to face the music, or the fallout, of your actions."

Until this moment, I had not seriously considered how either of the men felt it. "I suppose you're right." I nodded. "I took the chicken's way out."

I paused for a few minutes, before taking a different tack. "My mother and father got married on Valentine's Day," I continued.

When he started to ask a question, I waved him down. "Long side story," I said, "and not what I'm upset about today. The short version is my parents met and had a brief, but intense relationship nearly 60 years ago, and I was conceived. But my father didn't know about me until last fall, and now they've fallen in love again and gotten married."

Silently, Tom M nodded once again.

"I made a fake Facebook page," I confessed, "without friending anyone. I only used it for silently lurking, keeping up on the news from home—in case anything happened that might give me a reason to hurry back."

"Hhmm."

I wasn't sure what his "Hhmm" meant, so I plunged on ahead. "Most of my friends aren't especially computer savvy," I explained. "They pretty much keep their privacy settings on 'Public,' so I didn't think they'd notice I was reading their posts or anything."

"Uh-huh."

"No, really. Quite a few of my friends are my mother's age, give or take, and last fall when some of them wanted to sign up for online dating, they had a terrible time navigating the dating website and—"

Tom M cut me off by abruptly holding up his hand, signaling for me to stop talking. "Although I'm sure their online dating adventures are fascinating side stories, let's stick to the main event here—you were lurking on Facebook, and…"

"Yes." I took a breath as I regrouped my thoughts. "And when I found out what time my mother was getting married, I did the time zone math calculations, waited until 20 minutes into the ceremony, and left a message on Mother's cell phone wishing her good luck. I knew her phone would be off—or at least I hoped so—and just let her know I was happy for her that I was okay, but not ready to come back yet. Then I turned my phone back off."

"On Valentine's Day," said Tom M, keeping a poker face. I think he thought if he echoed my words I'd hear how they sounded. And I guess I did, but it still didn't seem like I'd done anything wrong.

"Yes." I nodded. "Six weeks after I'd left town. And as it turned out, my biological mother and father got married in a double ceremony in an historic church in Willoopah with a young woman and her beau from that same town." I smiled. "The new bride later posted a video of the wedding on her Facebook page, so it was almost as if I'd been there." I dabbed at my eyes again with a fresh tissue. "Almost."

Tom M chose that opportunity to ask a question. "You passed on being there to support your own parents at their wedding because… because you couldn't bring yourself to face the two men whose proposals you'd turned down on New Year's Eve?"

"Yes. That's right. Well, kind of."

"Hhmm," Tom M murmured again. "Kind of right?"

"I didn't exactly turn them down," I hedged. "I just hadn't... haven't... made up my mind. And I didn't think it was appropriate to address my indecision in the middle of two happy couples tying the knot, so I stayed away."

"For exactly whose sake did you stay away?" asked Tom M. "Your parents'? Your men friends'? Or yours?"

"You make it sound like staying away was a selfish thing for me to do."

"Wasn't it?"

I sighed. "So anyway, I stayed quiet after that until the young woman—Nautika—the one who'd just gotten married, and her business partner—Lorraine—who lived next door to her, launched a lunch counter at their new joint venture, the *Diamond Booi Oyster Farm*. I couldn't let that occasion go by without an anonymous card of congratulations to the enterprising Women of Willoopah, could I?

"I knew they'd know it was from me, but by then—it was March—I knew they wouldn't come looking for me. They'd be way too busy for anything like that."

I paused, and Tom M jumped in to do a short review. "So you called your mother in February, and you sent a congratulations card to some businesswomen friends in March. How, pray tell, did you commemorate April?"

"Well, there was a baby shower for Nautika in April, so of course I sent a shower gift. I sent it directly from the online company to her home, with a gift card signed, "From Your Secret Pal.""

"And in May?" prompted Tom M.

"In May, when I read Sheriff Donaldson's wife Mary Ann had finally passed away from Alzheimer's, I had to send flowers." I paused. "I had the florist enclose a 'Thinking of You' card with no name written on it."

Tom M couldn't control himself a moment longer, and his laugh shook the entire porch. "Online messages, gifts, cards, flowers—and you claim you didn't want to be found?!"

"Well, when you put it that way, it does sound rather silly."

"Rather," said Tom M. He reached his hand up to his shirt pocket where he kept his cigarettes, saw me scowl, and changed his mind about having a smoke.

We sat in companionable silence for a few minutes before Tom asked, "So who do you think finally found you?"

My eyebrows shot up in surprise. "I never said anyone found me."

"Then what's got you so upset?"

"Okay, so someone found me." I took another deep breath and shook my head. "I'm 99 percent sure it was my young friend, and new bride, Nautika."

"Ninety-nine percent sure?"

"Over the past several months she's been posting messages on her Facebook page, addressed 'To My Distant Friend.' The first one said, 'Please know that you can call or write anytime. You are loved, and always welcome'." I paused, and gnawed on my lower lip. "At least I hope that message was for me."

I took another tissue and blew my nose again. "I don't know how many other 'distant friends' she might have, but doesn't that sound like it might be for me?"

Tom M said nothing, but one of his eyebrows was raised considerably higher than the other.

"After that, there was another generic note thanking her distant friend for the shower gift. It was a little longer and said her husband—Cliff—had started working full time at the Oyster Farm and his fisheries degree was coming in handy, as her OB/GYN had told her to work a little less strenuously during her pregnancy."

I nodded with conviction. "Don't you think she meant that message just for me?"

This time Tom M also nodded. "I don't know anything about your relationship with this woman, but if it was addressed to her distant friend, then I can see how you might think, and perhaps rightly so, that it was meant for you."

"Especially since it said her father Brent was doing really well on his heart meds and was now functioning at about the 85% level of his pre-cardio event."

"And this woman—Nautika—would know you'd be interested in her father's health?"

"Absolutely." I nodded again, this time more enthusiastically. "Brent's not on Facebook, and I'd had no way to know how he was doing. He and I have known each other since high school, and last fall we became pretty good friends."

Tom M looked thoughtful. "And how did you know the sheriff's wife had died? Did someone post that on Facebook, too?"

"Oh, no, that I read in the *North Coast Tribune's* obituaries. I got an online subscription to the newspaper as soon as I got here."

"So you never really let go of anything back home."

It was a statement rather than a question, but I answered him anyway. "I always intended to return home, but I just didn't know when that would be. Now I've got a great job here, a great place to live, and I've made some great friends—like you..." My voice trailed off.

"Yes, it sure sounds like everything's 'just great' with you, alright." Tom M smiled. "So why didn't you want to be found?"

"I'm not ready to be confronted with my past," I explained. "It's not on my terms."

Tom M pointed through the window screen to a wall sign inside the Alano Club: "Life on life's terms."

"Point taken," I said. "So what do you think I should do?"

"What do you think you should do?" asked Tom M.

I hated that he said that, and rolled my eyes, a habit I thought I'd left back on the mainland. Then I sighed, expelling my breath as if I were a helium balloon giving up all my air. "I suppose I should go to Ms. Abrams' house and deal with it. But I'm not any closer to making amends to everyone than I was on New Year's Day."

"You don't know who is here yet," said Tom M. "Don't get too far ahead of yourself. Perhaps it is only Nautika who has tracked you down."

"Perhaps." I gnawed on my lower lip for a few minutes more and tried to sort things out, but my mind was a swirling bowl of mush.

"Tom?" I finally asked. "When I told you my name wasn't Lee, you never asked me what my name really is."

"It doesn't matter," he said with a shrug. "This is an anonymous program."

I smiled a genuine smile. "Thank you, Tom... For everything."

"My pleasure." Tom M stood up and extended his hand to me. "I've got my car here today, whatever-your-name-is, and I'd be happy to give you a ride."

CHAPTER 3

Parking is always a challenge on Wainee Street, so Tom M double parked in the middle of the road to let me out of the car. He idled his Outback for just a moment next to the cars parked along the sidewalk in front of Evie's home, wished me the best of luck, and drove on the moment I'd climbed out.

I stood outside the gate and stared at the hedge and shrubbery surrounding Evie's house. The knot in my stomach grew larger by the moment. I could feel the bile rising up in my throat again, and thought anxiously about finding another escape route. But where would I go? It wasn't like I had too many options. I suppose I could always go down to the harbor and hide out on the boat, but that didn't seem like a very good idea.

A car horn sounded, and when I turned, there was Tom M's car coming to a stop in the middle of the road again, after having apparently circled the block. He powered his passenger side window down. "If you want," he shouted, "I can find a place to park and walk in with you."

I shook my head. "No, thank you. I've got this." I gave him a half smile. "But how did you know I might be having second thoughts?"

"You're not the only one who's had to face the wreckage of his or her past, you know."

"Thank you. Again." I gave him the other half of my smile. "But aren't you going to tell me how sometimes we can do things together that we could never manage alone?"

"Atta girl," said Tom M, and he put the car in gear and drove off a second time, waving back at me as he did so.

I considered waiting to see if he went around the block again, but dismissed it. It was time, as I've heard plenty of people say, to pull on my big girl panties and just deal with whatever needs to be dealt with. But I wasn't looking forward to it.

So instead of taking the most direct route through the front entrance, I decided to enter the building by going around the back and using the sliding patio door to access the house. Then I'd be just steps from my bedroom. That way I could temporarily delay Evie's always intuitive interrogation for a few more minutes.

Naturally, the Universe had other plans.

I heard voices talking out at the patio as I worked my way through the lush shrubs. Even though there was a wide gravel walkway, the deep, green, leafy foliage had completely taken over and it was like wading through a jungle to navigate the path.

The dense shrubbery served two purposes. First, it dissuaded those who did not belong there from entering the backyard. Second, it provided a great deal of cover for anyone—like me, at the moment—wishing to eavesdrop on a conversation without being seen.

There were three distinct voices gathered around the patio table: two female and one male. One of the females was Evie Abrams, of course, and I was fairly certain the other one was Nautika Henry, now Nautika Evert.

The man's voice carried no hint of a lilting Indian accent, so I ruled out Kanji Kumera. And it wasn't Freddy Morgan's voice either. I breathed a sigh of relief, glad the pressure to choose between the men had not followed me all the way to Maui.

I closed my eyes and concentrated, trying to put the voice to a face, listening for any random clues dropped in the conversation.

31

Evie had a gift for putting everyone at ease, and the people on the patio were chatting like old friends. From plenty of tidbits dropped in the easy-flowing conversation, I gathered they were drinking sweet tea and eating mango pie.

Evie had just explained that she had brought her love of sweet tea, a Southern tradition, as well as her special recipe for Georgia Peach Pie, from the mainland. She explained how she'd adapted the pie recipe for mangos by precooking the fruit to soften before pouring into the pie shell.

"However you concocted this pie, it's absolutely delectable!" said the man's voice.

From my hiding place, I could picture Evie beaming with pride. "My brother says that baking is my super power," she said. "But unlike you two, I wouldn't be worth a diddly squat trying to use a computer to track down any of my friends." She chuckled.

"That was all Nautika," said the mystery voice. "She's quite the computer sleuth."

"It took the two of us putting our heads together," said Nautika. "A real team effort. No need for you to be so modest, Dad."

Dad?! Of course! It was Brent Booi who had come along with Nautika! I shook my head to clear it. It should have been a no-brainer that Brent would accompany his daughter here. I should have figured it out without any effort. My deductive reasoning must really be slipping!

"Well, Sylvia—or Lee, as you call her here—and I go back a long way. Clear to high school," said Brent. "And since we're the same age, give or take, Nautika asked me if I thought Sylvia would have completely detached from her life on the North Beach Peninsula.

"I told her I honestly didn't think Syl could do that, not with her mother and many of her friends getting up there in years, but

32

I didn't know how she'd be able to stay in touch without someone knowing she was staying in touch—if that makes any sense."

"Of course it does," said Evie. "I would have guessed she must have had a contact on the inside. Someone back at home she trusted who would feed her information as it came along."

"That was my first thought too," said Brent.

"On the other hand," said Nautika, "I dismissed the idea of having a mole to provide her with intel and immediately thought of Facebook."

"And I, on the other hand, would never have thought of Facebook!" Brent chimed in.

"Dad's kind of a dinosaur," said Nautika. "He doesn't even have an account." She laughed and then continued, "But that's okay. I kind of think staying in touch with family and friends might be more of an intrinsically female thing."

"I agree," said Evie. "My brother Rick wouldn't have any idea what's going on with our friends back in Georgia if I didn't keep him filled in."

"But Syl's Facebook account was disabled right after she left," said Brent. "The very night she left. So I thought she was through with that, and we were at a dead end."

"Then I explained to Dad that Sylvia had probably created a fake account just for lurking," said Nautika. "But it took both of us putting our heads together to figure out what name she was using on her bogus account."

"Mercy!" said Evie. "How did you go about that?"

Yes, I wanted to know how they went about that, too, but at the moment I was busy trying to shoo away Tuesday, or maybe Wednesday, from blowing my cover back behind the gigantic leaves. Whichever cat it was kept head-butting my shin, insisting I stoop to pet it and scratch its ears, and I was afraid if I didn't comply it would set up a fuss meowing.

When I tuned back in, Brent was telling Evie it was his idea that Sylvia might have used her married name—Gardner.

"So next I looked under Sylvia Gardner, or S.L. Gardner," said Nautika, "and I came up with nothing. It was Dad who suggested to look under Lee Gardner."

"Lee, spelled L-E-E, makes it look like a man's account," said Brent.

"Might I venture a guess that Lee is her middle name?" asked Evie.

"You're right!" said Nautika. "Good for you, Evie! And this 'Lee Gardner' didn't have any friends listed, male or female. A Facebook page with no friends kind of sealed the deal. We figured it had to be her."

"But I still don't understand how her bogus Facebook page helped you tracked her here," said Evie.

"This is where it gets really interesting," said Brent. "Her profile picture is a boat, so it further encouraged anyone looking at it that it was a man's page."

"And her cover photo was a line of palm trees on a beach with a little yellow lifeguard tower in the middle," added Nautika.

"The palm trees were a big clue," said Brent. "It ruled out somewhere around 40 of the 50 states."

Nautika laughed. "It only took me a minute to enlarge the cover photo and read the sign hanging from the lifeguard's tower: D.T. Fleming State Park. By using Google maps it was easy-peasy to put her on Maui."

"So I told Nautika to try that trick with her profile picture," said Brent.

"And I'm guessing you were able to read the name on the boat?" asked Evie.

"You're really good at this!" said Nautika. "Maybe you've got more than one super power!"

They chuckled, while I stood in the bushes with my face flaming red. *Good grief and gravy!* How could I have not realized someone of the younger, more Facebook savvy generation, would figure these things out? Maybe Tom M was right; maybe I'd wanted to be found all along.

"I looked up the *Cherokee Rose*, got the phone number for snorkel tour reservations, and had Dad call," said Nautika.

"And I answered the phone," said Evie. "And it didn't take much time at all for me to spill my guts." She sighed. "Rick's not going to be very happy with me when he finds out how much information I gave out without knowing why you wanted it."

"Don't worry, Evie," said Brent. "When I asked about safety for senior swimmers, I had no idea you were going to tell me about a deckhand named Lee who'd been with the boat about five months and who always got into the water with the clients and who knew CPR."

"Yep, that's me," said Evie. "Quite the blabbermouth."

The trio chuckled again.

"So," said Nautika, "that's pretty much how we got here. And today when I saw Sylvia crossing the park, I called out to her, but she took off running like she was auditioning for some kind of cross-country event at the Olympics."

"I hate to ask you to spill any more beans," said Brent, "but do you happen to know where she is right now?"

"I have a pretty good idea," said Evie. "But don't worry. I'm sure she's safe, and I'm sure she'll come home when she's ready."

"That's what we thought five months ago," Nautika said softly.

I pulled back one of the low-growing palm fronds and peeked out at the group. Nautika, dressed in an oversized purple and gold University of Washington t-shirt and Mariners ballcap, was absentmindedly rubbing her six-month, barely-showing, baby bump, and I could tell that Brent, in a brand-spanking new Hawaiian shirt, was considering helping himself to another piece of Evie's mango pie.

"So why come after her now?" asked Evie. "Why not wait her out?"

"Two reasons," said Brent. "One, we needed to come before Nautika is too pregnant to fly. Which is, by the way, one of the reasons I decided to come with her. That's my first grandchild in there, and I want to make sure nothing happens to him or her."

Evie excitedly clapped her hands. "Grandchildren are the best! I don't happen to have any myself, but I hear that it's the greatest gift ever."

Nautika told her she was due in late September or early October.

"It's a New Year's Eve baby," supplied Brent.

"Dad!" Nautika admonished him. "You don't have to keep telling everyone I was knocked up six weeks before I got married."

Brent laughed. "I don't care what the circumstances were, I'm just glad I'm around to celebrate this great, and unexpected, blessing."

It was good to see them happy about the coming addition to the family, but I was still wondering what the second reason was for them to come after me at this particular time.

As if reading my mind, Nautika returned to the former subject of conversation. "And two," she said, as if they hadn't segued into all things baby for a few minutes, "one of Sylvia's...uh... one of her friends—her very close friends—has been... is... uh, um... hhmm.... is in very deep trouble, and... and we need to convince Sylvia to come home right away. We need her help."

Hearing that someone I cared about was in trouble and needed my help, I couldn't hold back any longer. I stepped around the enormous fronds and entered the tiny backyard, clearing my throat as I walked toward the group on the patio.

"Sylvia!" Brent leaped to his feet, took two steps, and hugged me so tightly I thought he'd probably break a couple of my ribs.

Nautika had also come to her feet and had placed her arms around both Brent and me. "Group hug!" she happily called out.

Only Evie was still seated at the patio table, but her smile said just as much as their hugs.

Naturally, I was crying, but this time they were tears of joy. "It's so good to see you both!"

"Come, sit," directed Evie. She leaned over and patted the seat of the fourth chair at the table and poured me a glass of sweet tea, because, of course, she just happened to have brought an extra glass out on the refreshment tray.

"How long have you been listening? asked Brent.

He looked good, especially for somebody who'd had a heart attack in December while all alone out on Elk Island in the middle of Shallowwater Bay with no cell service.

"Long enough to know someone needs me at home."

Brent and Nautika looked at each other, neither willing to spill the full reason for coming to retrieve me. Nautika was rubbing her belly. In truth, she could pass for just a little overweight, if you didn't happen to know she was pregnant.

"You're still on the bank signature card for *Spartina Point Casino and Resort*, aren't you?" asked Brent.

My brow furrowed. What did my ability to sign checks at the casino have to do with anything? "That's a train wreck of a segue, Brent."

"Could you just answer the question, please, Syl?"

I sighed. Apparently, I wasn't going to get any of the answers I wanted until Brent first got the answers he wanted. "Yes. It takes two out of the three registered signatures to pay the bigger bills, but not the monthly payroll. Payroll is standard issue and it only takes one.

"The larger food vendors such as meat, seafood, vegetables, and linens, slot maintenance, and so forth aren't always the same amount. They fluctuate by the season or the special events that have taken place that month. Freddy liked to check the bigger invoices for all payments going out. He put me on the account as a back-up right after he inherited the casino, in case his CFO didn't work out." I scowled. "What was the CFO's name?"

"Wayne Korski," Brent confirmed.

"Excuse me," said Evie, her eyebrows knitting together in question marks. "CFO?"

"Chief Financial Officer," I replied. "A fancy name for a bookkeeper."

"Of course." Evie nodded. "It's been a few years since I've had any connection with the business world." She chuckled. "And I don't miss it!"

"Wayne is also referred to as the casino's business manager," Nautika added.

"Korski was inherited, along with the casino, from Freddy's Uncle Harry about 15 months ago," said Brent. "Freddy figured he'd give the guy a chance, and it seems to have worked out fine."

"You mean Wayne Korski is still on the job?" I asked, looking from face to face. "Then why are you here?"

A sudden realization struck me like a lightning bolt. "Has... Has something happened to Freddy?"

Brent reached out and took my hand. "Let's not go getting the cart before the horse, Syl. Wayne needs you to come home right away to co-sign some checks so he can keep the casino running. Freddy always kept a few checks signed ahead of time, but Wayne's run out of those now, and he..."

"Where's Freddy?" My voice had gone up about an octave,

and I looked quickly from Brent to Nautika and back again several times. "Somebody, please tell me! What's going on? What has happened to Freddy?"

"To be honest, at first we thought he'd finally gone out looking for you, Syl," said Brent. "He's been really depressed ever since you left."

"But when the new housekeeper went into Room 552 last week, she thought it looked a lot messier than it needed to be," said Nautika.

"At first she tried to dismiss it as a rich entitled bachelor leaving it all for his maid to clean up," said Brent, "and she almost quit. But then she wisely decided not to clean the room and called the sheriff's office instead."

"And Sheriff D took a look and decided it was time to send someone out on a quick trip to the middle of the Pacific to come get you," finished Nautika.

"So Sheriff Donaldson knew where I was?" I looked for some confirmation on one of their faces, but they both looked guilty as sin. "For how long?"

"Well," said Nautika, "Meredith would have killed me if I hadn't told her when Dad and I first figured it out. But I made her pinky-swear that she'd give you your space and not come over here so you'd have time to work things out for yourself. However, Merri didn't promise not to tell the sheriff, which she immediately did."

My heart felt suddenly too heavy for my chest. "If the sheriff knew, then Freddy must have known too, I suppose…"

"Yes, and that made him even sadder, to think of you in Hawaii without him. He'd planned to bring you here for your honeymoon," said Brent. "He knew you'd never been to the 50th state and thought he'd surprise you."

I felt the gut-punch of my failure to choose hit me all over again, and my tears welled up.

"Sheriff D hasn't released the news that Freddy's missing," said Brent. "There's been no ransom note. He doesn't want to jump to conclusions, or assume foul play, regardless of the condition of the room."

"What about his keys and cell phone?" I asked. "Are both his vehicles still in the casino parking lot? Has the sheriff watched the surveillance camera videos?"

"You must watch a lot of crime TV," said Evie, absentmindedly stroking the cat that had found her lap temporarily empty.

I ignored her comment and waited for Brent to tell me again I was jumping to conclusions without enough facts.

"His keys, cell phone and vehicles are still there," said Brent. "And nothing showed up on the security cams."

"Nothing?" I asked. "You mean there's no evidence of Freddy leaving with anyone?"

"Nope, nothing," Brent confirmed.

"Then he must have gone out by way of the far east exit," I said. "Since his vehicles are still there, he must have left with someone he knew… Or someone he didn't want to be seen with on the security cameras." I scowled, and heard my voice crack when I said, "Maybe he had a date, and left in the woman's car."

"No," said Brent. "Don't even think it. He's carrying a torch for you, and only you, and he's shown no signs of giving up hope any time soon."

"Then…" I couldn't entirely wrap my mind around the panic-filled thought that I couldn't quite put into words.

It was Nautika who finally said exactly what I'd been thinking. "Who'd be dumb enough to kidnap a county deputy?"

CHAPTER 4

Kidnapped. There it was. The word that had been rolling around in my head finally came out of someone else's mouth. Kidnapped. Freddy. My Freddy. Kidnapped.

The world around me started swimming. Brent jumped up and grabbed my shoulders just as my eyes rolled back in my head and I uncharacteristically pitched forward in a full faint. Thankfully, someone must have caught me before I fell and banged my forehead on the glass-topped table.

I came to lying on one of the patio chaise lounges. Three faces, five if you count the two cats who had managed to wiggle by Evie and take up residence on my lap, stared at me with deep concern in their eyes.

There was a cold, wet cloth on my forehead and Evie had pulled her chair over beside me. When I opened my eyes, she immediately stood up. "Have you eaten anything besides banana bread and cookies today?" she asked.

Without waiting for my answer, she asked Nautika and Brent to please excuse her for a few minutes, and went inside to "throw some sandwiches together" for dinner. Normally, I cook and clean up after myself, but right now it felt pretty good to just lie here and accept her mothering.

Mother! I struggled to sit up, but Nautika put her hand on my shoulder to stop me from any sudden movements. "Just lie still."

"How's Meredith?" I squeaked out.

"We can fill you in on everyone and everything once we're on the plane," said Brent.

"The plane?" I asked. Then I giggled and said, "The plane! The plane!"

Brent immediately got my reference to the old *Fantasy Island* TV show, but Nautika had no idea what I was blithering about and she whispered to Brent, "Her blood sugar must be really out of whack, she sounds delirious."

Brent and I looked at each other and exchanged a knowing smile. It really was nice to have someone my age around who knew what the heck I was talking about, even when it didn't seem to fit into the conversation at hand. It was almost as if we had a secret code, exclusive to our own generation, and indecipherable to the next.

"Our flight leaves first thing tomorrow morning," Brent continued.

"Tomorrow?" I echoed, looking from face to face. "Tomorrow? Why so soon? You just got here! Don't you want to enjoy Hawaii for a few days before flying back?"

"Time may be of the essence," said Nautika.

"We're not sure," Brent quickly added, "but it would be prudent for you to be nearby if there's a ransom request and a large amount of money is quickly needed."

I nodded. "Yes. Of course. I understand."

"Here we go!" said Evie, returning to the patio with a potluck summer supper of pulled pork sandwiches and fresh fruit. She put a sandwich and a few pieces of fruit on a separate plate and brought it over to me.

"Now eat!" she said, handing me a fork for the fruit. "And don't even think about getting up from there for at least 20 minutes after you finish." She had a no nonsense look on her face that made me feel both mothered and loved, and I found myself feeling incredibly grateful and blessed for her friendship.

Naturally, the fresh fruit platter sported pineapple, dragon fruit, and sliced mangos. Always there are lots of mangos available, and I once saw a man using a snow shovel to clear his driveway of the fallen over-ripe fruit. What a penalty to pay for living in paradise!

Brent speared a piece of fruit with his fork. "What's this?" he asked, sniffing it. "I've never seen a fruit like this." He took a small bite. "It looks like a chubby banana, but the flavor is more like…" He chewed another bite thoughtfully, then shook his head. "I give up."

"It's an apple banana," said Evie. coming to his rescue. "Also known as Manzano banana. When they're not quite ripe, there's an apple flavor, but when fully ripe, it tastes more tropical, like a pineapple."

"Manzana is apple in Spanish," I said. The tasty and timely food was starting to make me feel a whole lot more like my usual self, and I was happy I could contribute coherently to the conversation.

"Whatever you call it," said Nautika, "it's delicious!"

My world seemed almost normal as we conversed over dinner, as long as I pushed the panic of returning to the North Beach Peninsula the next day to the metaphorical back burner. But all too soon, Brent and Nautika left to take in a short walk along Front Street as the sun set before turning in at their hotel for the night.

"Well," said Evie, as we cleaned up the kitchen together. "What are you figuring to do?"

"I don't think I have a choice," I replied. I was almost annoyed with Brent and Nautika for being so sure of themselves that they'd only booked one night in the hotel and three tickets for the next day's flight back to the mainland.

"There are always choices, hon," Evie replied. "You didn't even have to come home today, but you did."

"That's true," I said. "Now I have to pack my suitcases, and I need to send Tom M a quick text, then I must call Rick, and…" I looked at Evie and tears sprung unexpectedly to my eyes. "And I need to thank you for all you've done for me while I've been here."

"Well, you can cross two of those items off your list," said Evie. "No need to thank me for doing what's right and proper to help another human being, and Rick already knows you're leaving."

"He does?"

"He does," said Evie. "I called him last night after your friends told me they'd be coming for you today, and he decided not to say anything to you. He told me he wanted to let you enjoy one more memorable day out on the *Cherokee Rose* before reality came knocking."

Now the tears streamed down my cheeks. "So that's why he asked me this afternoon if I'd had any thoughts about leaving."

Evie nodded. "He's sure going to miss you, Lee… I mean Sylvia…" She smiled. "Or maybe I better call you Sylvia Lee until I get used to the whole name changing thing."

"Oh don't do that!" I said. "If you called me Sylvia Lee, I'd think for sure I was in trouble with my mother!"

Evie laughed. "Nevertheless, we're really going to miss you, Sweetheart." She sighed. "But Rick and I want you to know you're welcome back anytime."

"Oh! That reminds me, Evie! We need to square up on my rent."

Evie shook her head. "We're fine. Just promise me you'll come back after the dust settles at home for a good long visit. At some point we evolved from a renter/landlord relationship into being good friends, Sylvia Lee, and I'm eager to hear what happens when you get home. I'll be curious as all get-out waiting to hear the rest of the story."

The way she'd said 'Sylvia Lee' choked me up. I really was blessed. "Thank you." I wiped my hands on a dishtowel and hugged her tight. "I'll let you know when we get home safely, and I pinky-swear to come back soon." I bit down on my lower lip. "I suppose, though, that Rick will have long-replaced me by then."

Evie nodded. "Time marches on."

I sighed. "Well, I guess I better go throw my clothes into my bags and text Tom M." I laughed. "I never did find out what his last name was."

"It's an anonymous program," said Evie. "And he was just the friend you needed." She turned me around by the shoulders so I faced the hallway to my room. "Now get going so you can catch a few hours' sleep before your friends come to collect you in the wee hours of o'dark thirty tomorrow morning."

I turned back around and hugged her tightly one more time. "Thank you, my dear, dear friend."

I sat between Nautika and Brent on the plane ride home. Nautika was on the aisle, so she could make frequent "I'm PG and gotta go pee" trips to the bathroom without climbing over either one or both of us. Brent was in the window seat.

At first, I felt cornered—as if they thought I was a flight risk— no pun intended. But then I realized they were merely being considerate. This way I could talk to each one individually without shouting across the lap of the other.

It wasn't like there was any place for me to go while we were in the air over the Pacific. I didn't even have a DB Cooper parachute with me, and I wouldn't have any land to land on anyway, so all I could do was try to relax and enjoy the flight.

I turned to look at Nautika. "Are you up on your southwest

Washington hijacking folklore?" I asked her.

She looked back at me quizzically.

"If you're referring to DB Cooper," said Brent, "you're out of luck. We already had the parachutes removed prior to coming aboard." He grinned, then quickly squeezed and released my hand. "Like it or not, Sylleegirl, you're coming home."

The familiarity in his use of my nickname caught me off guard. Until now, only Freddy and Kanji had ever used that particular term of endearment. I wasn't sure if Brent had done it on purpose, or if it was one of those things other people called coincidence, but I raised no objection. It felt nice to have someone escorting me home who seemed to genuinely care about my mental health as I contemplated my return.

I strained to look out the window as the Kahului Airport disappeared from view. The island became only a small dot in the vast expanse of ocean. My emotions roiled in every direction at once, and I took a few slow, deep breaths to prevent a panic attack.

After we were at cruising altitude, and I'd had some time to collect my conflicting thoughts, I turned to Nautika. "Ok, Nautika. Dish."

"Dish?" she asked, her eyebrows knitting together.

"Spill your guts," said Brent. "Let the cat out of the bag. Come clean. Blab. Talk. Tell all."

"Hhmm," said Nautika. "It must be another one of those generational things."

"Kids!" Brent turned his palms up and shrugged.

It hadn't been that long since Nautika had discovered Brent was her biological father, although he'd known about her since the day she was born. Funny how things worked out. To see them together now, I couldn't imagine their connection being any stronger.

"Nautika," I began again, "my mother has a Facebook page,

but she rarely posts on it. Please tell me how she's doing."

Nautika smiled. "She's doing great. She and Lester act like they're still on their honeymoon, but they are very active in social causes. It's like they picked up right where they left off about… How old are you, again?" She laughed. "Let's just say about half a century ago."

"Close enough. And nice save." I smiled. "Has *The Veiled Rainbow* been doing much dancing?"

Nautika shook her head. "Not publicly. They get together and practice now and then, but nobody really has their heart into it since Deenie passed. She was such a little spark plug."

I nodded. "Our designated Greenpeace go-getter and expert on all things environmental." I sighed. "So what about Goodie? And Patrick?"

"Goodie's been doing a lot of gardening," said Nautika.

"Patrick built her a greenhouse for the backyard," added Brent.

"Oh he did, did he?" I couldn't help but chuckle.

"Goodie's got a pretty tight rein on him," said Brent. "She only allows him space in the greenhouse for five or six of his… uh… you know… his 'funny plants' at a time."

"Patrick has turned into quite the entrepreneur," said Nautika. "His lawnmowing jobs expanded into a total landscaping business, and now he has branches in both South Bend as well as Ocean Crest."

"Yeah," said Brent. "He's been written up in several regional magazines as an expert on helping restore and increase the honeybee population."

"Nadine would be so proud," I said. Just thinking about her put a lump in my throat, so I changed the subject. "And what about Orpha? What's she been up to? Is she still seeing Grandpa BeeBops?"

"No." Nautika shook her head. "Sadly, that relationship ended poorly, and she tried to file a million-dollar lawsuit against the Department of Motor Vehicles for 'Alienation of Affection'."

"*She WHAT?!*" I realized my exclamation had come out somewhere between a squeal and a shout when the people in the row ahead of us turned around and scowled in my direction, and the people in the row across the aisle from Nautika leaned our way so they could hear the rest of the story.

Brent, with his well-modulated deep voice, took over telling me about Orpha's latest adventure. "The trouble started when Sheriff D found out Orpha's driver's license had expired some time ago."

"How many years is some time ago?" I asked.

"Let's just say in her photo she still had her glasses on," whispered Nautika.

"And that's a bad thing?" I asked.

"These days," said Nautika, "all glasses are removed for the ID picture so the facial recognition software can be more effective."

"When did they start doing that?" I asked. "I think I still have my glasses on in my photo."

"You probably renewed by mail," said Brent. "If you didn't have any tickets, they let you do that. But for Orpha, it's been over a decade, so the sheriff gave her 90 days to renew her license. When she and Grandpa BeeBops went over to the DMV in Unity, he discovered she was actually a dozen years older than him, and he broke up with her on the spot."

"The cad!" I rolled my eyes, and hoped no one on either side of me would do the math and figure out how much older than Freddy I was.

I tilted my head and whispered to Brent, "How far did Orpha get with her lawsuit?"

Apparently, my whisper was still loud enough for Nautika's sharp little ears, as she quickly said, "All the way to the front page of the *North Beach Tribune*."

That gave us a good chuckle, but it also gave me pause to consider what others might have thought of me when my Cinderella behavior had made the front page of the same newspaper.

The flight attendant interrupted our catching up by offering several beverage selections. I knew it would be mid-afternoon before we landed in Portland, and declined anything caffeinated, opting instead for sparkling pineapple juice.

"Bringing a taste of the islands home with you?" asked Brent.

"This was Captain Rick's favorite pick-me-up on the way back to port, and he made me a firm believer in the medicinal qualities of the drink. It's high in Vitamin C, and contains a great deal of the enzyme bromelain, which helps reduce pain and swelling."

Both Nautika and Brent stared at me like an open-mouthed guppy.

"What?" I looked from one to the other. "You're never too old to learn to take better care of your body."

Brent snorted, and Nautika choked on her diet soda.

"You've changed!" said Nautika.

"But only in good ways," Brent quickly added.

I let them both off the hook when I asked about Jimmy. "Is he still rockin' the Boy George spikey-haired look?"

"Absolutely." Nautika nodded. "And since he has to be onsite so much as manager of the *Clamshell Motel*, Julio moved in with him right after Valentine's Day. They're such a cute couple! Jimmy with white/blonde hair and fair skin and Julio with his black wavy hair and Mexican heritage. They're like night and day, salt and pepper—"

"Vanilla bean cake and chocolate fudge frosting," Brent interjected.

It was my turn to snort and have my juice go up my nose. I wiped my face with an airline napkin and moved on to my next inquiry. "I know that Mercedes and Sheriff Donaldson are still dating, but now that Mary Ann has passed, do you think they'll be making their relationship a little more... permanent?"

"I doubt it," said Nautika. "Merc says she's very happy just the way things are."

I nodded, sipped the final swallow of pineapple juice from my cup, folded up my napkin, tucked it inside, and handed it to the flight attendant as she walked down the aisle with a large trash bag.

My seatmates both looked at me expectantly.

"What?"

"Nothing," they both said at the same time.

"Oh." I chewed on my lip, which I seemed to be doing a lot of these days. "Are you waiting for me to ask about Kanjirappally Kumera?"

"Kanji's doing well," said Nautika.

"But you should know," said Brent, "that he and Lorraine Diamond have been spending quite a lot of time together the past few months."

I wasn't sure how I should react to that piece of information. "Oh, well, since the *Diamond Booi Oyster Farm* supplies fresh seafood to the casino, and Kanji manages the restaurant and bar, it's only reasonable they spend a chunk of regular time working together."

"It's not just about business," said Nautika.

Brent studied my face. I wasn't sure if he expected tears, relief, or something else, but I surprised myself and went with the something else. "That's good," I said. "I really hope he's happy; he deserves to be happy." Then I sighed. "I guess I just didn't expect him to replace me quite so soon."

"It's been five and a half months since you refused his proposal," said Nautika.

"I didn't exactly refuse it," I countered, "I just wasn't ready to accept it."

"Would you accept it now?" asked Brent.

It was a fair question, but I really didn't have an honest answer and fell back on my super power of deflection. I pulled a magazine from the back of the seat pocket in front of me and started flipping through the pages. "Moot point, Brent. Nothing to say here."

The final hour and a half of our flight was spent in our own quiet reflections, but as we made the wide loop to approach PDX from the east, Brent cleared his throat.

"Sheriff D has laid a few ground rules for your return," he began.

"Ground rules?" I asked. "For my return? What the hell does that mean?"

"We're not going to be picking up your car today, Syl."

"We're not?" I looked from Brent to Nautika and back again. "Why not?"

"Your Mustang is a one-of-a-kind, Sylvia," said Nautika. "It really sticks out, and the moment it's spotted on the peninsula, the whole community will know about it."

I couldn't disagree with her there. I even wondered if that, too, would be considered front page news. It briefly crossed my mind that Mother was probably keeping a scrapbook of all the articles about me appearing in print.

"You're also not going home tonight," said Brent.

"What's going on? Am I on house arrest or something?"

Neither Brent nor Nautika said anything.

"Okay." I took a breath, and in a calmer tone I asked, "So where am I staying, and why?"

"You'll be staying with us in Willoopah. No going outside, no phone calls, no internet," said Brent. "The sheriff says he will have you fitted for an ankle bracelet if you don't behave yourself."

"I'm not the criminal here!"

"Sylvia," said Nautika, "he just wants to make sure you're not the next victim, either."

"Shouldn't be longer than a week or two, tops," said Brent. "Sheriff Donaldson said he'll be out to talk with you first thing in the morning. He wants to pick your brain and see if you might shed some light on where to look for Freddy."

Freddy. Yes, that was the reason for my return. Where was Freddy? And *how* was Freddy? Although it's a small, gossipy peninsula, there have been several instances of people, along with their pickup trucks and dogs, just disappearing—forever—and I prayed Freddy would not end up being counted among them.

CHAPTER 5

Freddy was having such a wonderful dream. Contentment filled his heart, and everything in his world felt right. He was warm, and happy, and a soft breeze ruffled his hair. It was a dream he knew well, and even in his sleep he realized he was dreaming, and that he'd had this very same dream many, many times before.

He was wearing his casino tux, complete with black polished cowboy boots and a silly, floral bowtie, and he was standing with a woman dressed in white lace, but it wasn't a full-length gown. She was standing there, barefooted on a sandy beach, in a knee-length dress with lots of fluffy ruffles. They were standing next to each other and holding hands.

Freddy particularly enjoyed this next part. A man in a long, dark robe with an ivory silk stole was speaking. "Do you, Frederick Harold Morgan, take this woman—"

Freddy's groaning stomach abruptly awakened him. "Really bad timing," he said aloud. He patted his stomach. "The least you could do was wait until I got to kiss the bride."

But his stomach was unsympathetic, and growled loudly a second time. Freddy was more than hungry. He wasn't sure how long ago his stomach had started gnawing on his spine, but he knew it was downright ravenous. "Settle down," he said. He hoped his voice commanded authority. He wanted to be able to believe his own words. "I'm sure someone will come to bring us some food pretty soon."

But Freddy wasn't sure of any such thing.

"Do you happen to know what time it is?" he asked his stomach. "I mean, are we hoping it's something for breakfast or something for dinner that's coming?" He paused, as if waiting for an answer, but this time his stomach had nothing to say.

"Well, I hope it's breakfast, cause I'm really learning to like those eggy muffin sandwich biscuit kind of things, and right now I could eat about a dozen of them." This time his stomach rumbled in complete agreement.

Freddy had quite recently picked up the habit of talking aloud to himself just to have something… someone… to listen to. "You know," he continued, "if we were on a deserted island, I'd probably be talking to a volleyball instead of to you." He almost chuckled. "Would you like me to call you Wilson? Or is there another name you'd prefer? How about Spaulding?"

He vaguely wondered if his stomach even remembered that Tom Hanks' movie they'd seen so many years ago. How many years was it? Twenty? Twenty-two?

Freddy also wondered if talking to his stomach as if it were a separate entity meant he was losing his grip on reality. But that probably wouldn't stop him. He needed the company, no matter if it came from inside or outside his own head.

And while Freddy was at it, he wondered what day of the week it was, and how many days he'd been in this nondescript room with no windows. Pesky little details like that gave him something else to consider while he obsessively calculated his chances of survival.

The first time he'd awakened in this room—maybe 6 or 7 or even 8 or 9 days ago—his hands had been zip tied behind his back, and he'd been blindfolded. By sliding his hands up and down back there, he'd discovered that his belt had been removed. And by rolling around on the bare mattress beneath him, he'd discerned that his pockets were all empty. After that, by the simple act of wiggling his toes, he knew his cowboy boots were also gone.

Freddy had wondered if his kidnapper thought he might be suicidal, or if the guy had simply confiscated anything he thought could be used against him as a weapon. Weapons, of course, would only be useful if Freddy had somehow managed to get out of the zip tie restraints, which so far had only been wishful thinking.

Freddy had quickly figured out that he could probably rub his face hard enough against the mattress to pull the blindfold down. Yet he was also smart enough to know that if he did that, he could likely identify his captor in a police line-up. And if he could identify his captor, he would most definitely be killed after any ransom was paid. Maybe even before. Therefore, he made sure to keep his blindfold securely in place.

That first day, or maybe night, he'd expended a lot of energy trying to get to his feet while his hands were still bound behind his back. He figured he'd burned a heck of a lot of calories and invented several new yoga poses in the process.

Once he was standing, he had carefully walked the perimeter of the room, pacing it off, over and over, counting the steps this way and that. Eight paces one way, and a little more than six paces the other. If his math was correct, the room was roughly 20 by 16 feet, about the size of a large bedroom or small rec room. He'd also concluded there was nothing in the room to bump into, and only the mattress on the floor to trip over.

By pressing his face at intervals against the walls, he knew they were paneled, that there was only one door, and it was in the wall farthest from the mattress. By lying on the floor, and rubbing his cheek against it, he'd concluded the floor covering was cheap—probably that 70s indoor/outdoor carpeting laid over cement. That, in turn, made him wonder if the paneling on the walls was covering sheetrock or cement blocks. Was he in a basement or a bomb shelter? An older home or a derelict business?

The Clamshell Motel is cinderblock, he thought, but the ancient motel rooms all had windows, and the business didn't have a basement, which he had concluded he was probably in. Not a lot of places on the North Beach Peninsula had basements. He knew of a couple with swimming pools, so it was possible construction could be done below ground, even on a 28-mile long, and two-mile wide, sandspit between the Pacific Ocean and Shallowwater Bay.

When he had not been able to hold back any longer, Freddy had relieved himself in the corner to the left of the door, as far as he could get from where he slept. He almost gagged as the strong smell of warm urine ran down his pant leg. He had hoped he wouldn't have to do anything more in the way of relieving himself anytime soon, and his prayer had been answered.

Freddy had heard the car when it first drove up. The noise had almost startled him. Until then, his world had been eerily quiet—totally devoid of any sound he didn't make himself. It almost made him think he might be in a soundproof room, it was so still. Maybe there was just a long driveway, leading up to an isolated house in the woods.

That first time, the vehicle had sounded like a big car, not a pickup, not a van, and not a compact, certainly not a motorcycle, but something substantial and probably American made. It was just a feeling, but his ears had told him it was a gas-guzzling sedan.

Freddy had held still, and he'd heard one set of heavy footfalls descending stairs. So his deductive reasoning that he was likely in a basement was probably sound. He didn't know why that particular tidbit of information made him feel any better, but it did.

Then there'd been a pounding on the door, as with a fist, and then a voice which was completely inconsistent with the heavy banging. In a high, squeaky, and obviously phony falsetto, the voice had said, "If your blindfold is not firmly in place, turn away from the sound of my voice and close your eyes. If you do not do this, I will shoot you dead, Señor."

The "Señor" was a nice touch, thought Freddy. He didn't know exactly how he knew, but he was suddenly absolutely certain the kidnapper was neither female nor a native Spanish speaker. It seemed highly unlikely a woman would decide to imitate a woman when trying to disguise her voice. *Great detective work, Deputy Morgan,* he'd thought to himself. *You've just ruled out the entire female population and several hundred local Mexican workers. Good job!*

And Freddy had answered back, "I give you my word. My blindfold is in place, and I am sitting with my back to the door. I will not try to see your face."

Someone had entered the room, and set a bag smelling of hamburgers on the floor inside the door.

"You behave yourself, and I'll give you the food I brought. You try anything funny, and the food goes back out the door with me," said the squeaky voice. "Just sit where you are, and don't you dare move a muscle until I tell you to."

Freddy hadn't moved. And even though his salivary glands were working overtime, he'd channeled every bit of sensory deduction he could muster to visualize what might be going on in the room around him while he waited.

The door opened and closed several times, and each time the deadbolt was employed before he heard the clomping of feet going back up, and coming back down, the stairs. Freddy had heard the sound of metal banging against the door frame and imagined a folding chair being brought into the room. Then it sounded as if someone had opened up the chair and placed it in the corner he now thought of as his bathroom.

He'd been directed not to move, but he'd not been told he couldn't talk. "Is there anything there I can help you with?" he'd cheerily called out.

"You hush your mouth!" said the squeaky voice. It was still a falsetto, but now the accent sounded decidedly more southern than Spanish.

Okay, thought Freddy, *now I can probably rule out both Spanish and southern folks. We're narrowing this right down.* But right behind that revelation he had another, more disturbing thought: *What if there is more than one kidnapper?* That was something he hadn't considered before, and it deeply troubled him. What if there were several different people coming and going and all using a high-pitched, fakey-female voice?

The more he thought about it, the more he was almost certain that one person, working alone, could not have gotten him here—to wherever here was—without being seen. Someone, or some two or three, would have needed quite a bit of physical strength to carry him. At 180 pounds, Freddy wasn't overweight, but he was pretty sure it was more than one guy could carry down a set of stairs, even in a traditional fireman's carry.

After listening to a few more trips up and down stairs to the car and back, Freddy still couldn't decide if there was one kidnapper or two. But then just one man had stood in front of him, and still using that silly falsetto, he told Freddy he was going to cut the zip ties off his hands, but that Freddy must wait until he'd left the room to take off his blindfold and eat. "If you do not follow these directions, I promise I will shoot you dead, Señor."

Dutifully, Freddy had waited several full minutes after the door closed. He'd heard the man go back up the steps, and the car drove off. Still not sure if there was more than one of them, he'd called out, "I'm taking my blindfold off now, if that's okay."

When no one answered, he pulled off the mask, and discovered a small LED lantern was turned on and sitting on the floor in the center of the room. It had enough power to illuminate the entire space, and Freddy quickly took in the rest of his surroundings.

He discovered a metal folding chair next to the mattress with a stack of *New York Times* newspapers on the seat. He jumped up and went to the door. He knew it was a long shot, but he tried to turn the knob anyway. He was not surprised when the knob didn't turn, but he knew he'd keep trying to turn it after every visit—if there were any more visits.

He found a light switch on the wall next to the door and flicked it up and down several times, but the overhead light remained dark. Had his kidnapper purposely removed the overhead light source to further control Freddy's atmosphere? Then why give him the little lantern?

In the corner where he'd peed, there was now an ancient camping-type potty chair with a bucket underneath the cracked, padded toilet seat. Freddy nodded. "Okay. So the guy's not going to make me crap my pants. Maybe he's got one small compassionate bone left in his body." There was no toilet paper, so Freddy assumed that was the primary purpose of the newspapers.

Then, and only then, did he pick up the bag of food and eagerly began eating. There were two burgers, two bottles of water, and six or eight of those energy power bars inside the bag. Freddy smiled. He recognized the burger wrappers. His kidnapper had brought him two mini-tsunami burgers from the *High Tide*. And as he had hoped, Freddy could now confirm he was still on the peninsula!

A while after he'd eaten, he'd used the porta potty, fashioning a small amount of make-do wipes from his burger bag and food wrappers, saving the newspapers until after he'd had a chance to read them. But he didn't read them the first day. That first day he'd turned off the lantern, thinking he'd better conserve his ration of light, and sat in the darkness thinking about everything he'd learned during his kidnapper's visit.

The second day, the sound of a distinctly different car pulled up to the house. This one sounded less substantial. Lighter, somehow. More like a small foreign car, maybe. So it was still possible there was more than one bad guy–or gal. Or perhaps it was just one guy pretending to be two. It was something to consider, and Freddy collected and tucked away those bits of information to think about while he passed the time.

And so a routine had been created. Once a day, someone arrived with food. That was a good sign, as it meant his captor, or captors, needed him alive. Some days he got several McMuffins, or other breakfast sandwiches, and some days it was mini-tsunamis, or a footlong sub. But Freddy wasn't particular. He'd even gotten a roll of real toilet paper, and a stack of semi-current magazines that had the address labels carefully cut off.

But today, or tonight, no one had yet come, and Freddy's stomach went from a growl to a roar. To take his mind off his hunger, he went over the facts of the case, as best he knew them, for the umpteenth time.

What could this guy, or guys, want from him? What was the motive? Was it money? Revenge? Jilted lover? Freddy thought he could rule that last one out. Might it be someone that Deputy Frederick Morgan had once arrested who was carrying a grudge? Was it personal? Was someone seeking some kind of revenge for who knew what? Might it be someone who'd spent more than they could afford gambling at the casino and wanted their money back? Could it just be someone, or several people, thought he'd be an easy ransom target?

It was a well-known fact Freddy was unquestionably the wealthiest man on the peninsula, but it was also well-known he continued to serve his community as a deputy sheriff. Who would be dumb enough to think they could actually get away with a crime like this?

And when Freddy wasn't busy contemplating all the known details of his kidnapping, or composing possible theories concerning his kidnappers, he allowed his mind to wander to thoughts of Sylvia.

Sylvia, Sylvia, Sylvia.

Just days before his abduction, Freddy had been thinking that six months was long enough for her to get her head together and come back home. He'd been thinking about forcing her hand by flying to Hawaii someday soon.

But Syl wasn't likely to take kindly to being ambushed and pressed again to make a decision. She'd clearly demonstrated that on New Year's Eve, on the dance floor, in front of the whole world, when she refused to be rushed into making any kind of life-altering decision.

The next edition of the *North Beach Tribune*, traditionally sporting a hearty Welcome to the New Year banner, had also displayed a photo of Kanji's and Freddy's humiliation, in full color, and above the fold!

At least now it looked like the passage of enough time had removed his competition, Freddy thought. But he didn't want to win by default. He wanted Syl to choose, and to choose him. Although… Freddy wanted to kick himself for thinking this… maybe Kanji was actually behind the kidnapping so Freddy would be the one who was permanently removed as a contender for Syl's affection!

No. That can't be right, thought Freddy. *Kanji and Lorraine were not faking it. They had become quite close, and for all appearances, they looked to be very happy.* Freddy nodded, as if punctuating the validity of his thoughts. *It just proves that I always loved her more than he ever did. Kanji's been able to regroup and move on, and I haven't.*

Freddy yawned. "Wilson, how can I be so tired when I haven't done anything all day?"

This time, his stomach didn't participate in the conversation.

"Wilson, how long has it been since I've had any food or water?"

Again, no reply.

"I think I might be dehydrated, Wilson." Freddy lay back on the mattress and closed his eyes. "Wilson? Are you there?" He felt the sadness close in around him. Even Wilson wasn't answering him. "Wilson?" he tried again. "Do you think it would be okay if I go to sleep now and just don't wake up again?"

The silence felt more deafening than any he had ever experienced. "Wilson? Please answer me, Wilson. I need you. Really. Don't leave me here alone." He took a deep, shaky breath, and tears stung his eyes. "I really need you, Sylvia. Sylvia? Where are you? Are you with Wilson?"

In the still-cognizant part of his brain, Freddy wondered if he should try to drink his own urine to save his life. The thought was disgusting, but he vaguely remembered seeing something about it on the PBS channel… No, wait! Survivalists had debunked that idea, saying how drinking urine actually caused dehydration at a faster rate. Whew! He was glad he'd remembered that little factoid in the nick of time, but oh, he was so, so sleepy… "Wilson, are you there?"

Sleepy? What had that television program said about sleepiness? What was the connection they'd made between sleepiness and dehydration? "Help me think, Wilson!"

No! I can't go to sleep right now! Freddy remembered the

show had mentioned that when dehydration sets in, your blood pressure drops and results in poor circulation and reduced blood flow to your brain, causing sleepiness.

"*WAKE UP YOU MORON!!*" Freddy shouted the words out loud. "You can't die now! You'll never get the girl if you die now!" And then he started giggling, uncontrollably, until he finally did collapse into a deep sleep, only to dream again of the woman in the short white dress. A woman whose face he couldn't see, but who wore flowers interwoven in her auburn hair.

What kind of flowers were they? Plumeria? Yes... The flowers smelled so sweet. They must be in Hawaii. He'd go there and claim her love, once and for all, just as soon as he could.

CHAPTER 6

True to the plan, Sheriff Carter Donaldson showed up on Brent's doorstep the next morning just a smidgen after the proverbial crack of dawn. If he'd given any thought to the fact that my body would still be functioning on Island Time, he might have waited a few hours, but everyone in the Willoopah house was already stirring, and Nautika's husband Cliff had left for the oyster beds some time ago.

I swung the door open wide with one hand and handed him a steaming mug of coffee with the other. "Come on in, Carter. What kept you?" I said dryly. I turned and led the way to the kitchen, where the big dining room table had a fabulous view out over the bay.

He took off his Stetson and placed it on the table before sitting down. "Couldn't sleep, huh?" he asked.

"Nobody's allowed to sleep past daybreak on an oyster farm," said Brent, as if the question had been addressed to him. He came into the kitchen and nodded to Sheriff D. "I see you've already got coffee."

"That I do," said Sheriff D, taking a sip. "And it's much appreciated."

You could cut the awkwardness around the table with an oyster shucking knife. "Carter, I...I just want to say that I'm sorry for your loss and—" I began.

"I know, Sylvia. I got your flowers," he replied. "They were beautiful. Thanks."

I nodded, not even bothering to pretend I hadn't sent them. "I'm sorry I missed the funeral, Carter."

"I know," he said again, and sighed. "It's not like she'd even recognized me the past few years. It got so stressful when I went to visit her that the staff at the memory care center thought it would be better for me not to come any more." He shrugged. "Her physical passing just brought the grief of losing her to a head all over again."

I stared at him. Who was this man? I'd never, ever, heard the sheriff talk of his personal life in such… such *personal* terms before. It must have been the result of Mercedes' good influence on him.

Mercedes and Sheriff D had begun a relationship just about a year ago, after Mary Ann had been in memory care for a long time already, and no one had ever found fault with their intimate connection, despite the fact the sheriff was technically still a married man. Nor should anyone have ever had a problem with it. It really wasn't anyone's business but theirs.

"So." said Brent, fumbling for a change of subject, "did anything new transpire while we were away?"

"We were only away for two days," said Nautika, emerging from her bedroom still in her bathrobe. "It was a whirlwind trip. One day over, and one day back." She yawned.

"Good morning, sweetie," said Brent, standing and kissing her on the top of her head. "No coffee for you, but how about some breakfast? You're feeding two now, you know."

"Yes, Dad, I know." Nautika looked a little embarrassed. "You say the exact same thing every single morning. And every morning I remind you that the smell of eggs will make me retch, and coffee isn't good for either one of us."

"Sorry, honey," Brent spoke softly to her as if the sheriff and I weren't even there. "Please be patient with me; I've never been either a dad or a grandad before."

Nautika smiled at him. "That makes us even, then. I've never had a dad before."

I had to blink back tears, and it looked to me like Carter was in pretty much the same frame of mind. "Please bring me up to speed," I said, abruptly bringing an end to all this early morning father and pregnant daughter mushy stuff.

"Sure thing," said Sheriff D, seemingly glad to get back to being all business. He pulled his little wire-bound notebook and stubby pencil from his shirt pocket and flipped the notebook open. "What have you been told so far?"

I trimmed it down to just one sentence. "I know Freddy is missing, his room was in great disarray, and his cell phone and the keys to both his Mazda and his Harley were left behind."

"Hhmm," said Sheriff D. "Great disarray. I suppose that's one way to put it."

"Then how would you describe the condition of his room?" I asked.

"Well..." The sheriff looked briefly at Brent and Nautika. "Now that you mention it, 'great disarray' is as good as any other choice of words."

My voice inadvertently turned a little shrill. "Apparently not, Carter, or you wouldn't have mentioned it. So how would *you* put it? What condition was his suite left in?"

Sheriff Donaldson consulted his notes. "All the drawers, in every room of the suite, were emptied out on the floor. Even in the bathroom and kitchen. The cupboards had all been emptied. The cushions on the chairs were sliced open, even the paper backing on the frames behind the wall art was torn off." He looked up from his notes. "I can honestly say I've never seen a room in such a condition."

I fought down my instant nausea. "So the room had been

thoroughly ransacked."

"It appeared someone was looking for something specific," said Sheriff D. "But didn't have any idea exactly where to look." He traced his mustache out from the center to the ends with his thumb and index finger, an endearing habit of his I'd almost forgotten about. "Are you okay?" he gently asked.

I nodded, but the nod was a lie. Taking a deep breath, I said, "So the intruder was looking for something flat... like documents, or photographs, or cash, or a key maybe. Something that could be concealed by taping it to the bottom of a drawer, or behind a wall picture."

Brent and Nautika spoke in unison: "Crime TV."

I shot them a dirty look. "I think we've long ago established that I enjoy learning how the minds of criminals as well as the functions of police departments work. And you know my penchant for cop shows has come in handy before, so just lay off," I snapped.

I immediately regretted my tone. "I'm sorry." I shook my head. "I don't need to be alienating my best friends. I'm just so..."

"Upset," Brent supplied, reaching over to squeeze my hand.

"It's totally understandable," added Nautika, patting my shoulder.

I looked at Sheriff D and asked a question I was afraid to know the answer to. "Was there... Was there any sign of foul play? Any blood or anything?"

"None," he said without consulting his notes. "Forensics went over the room with a fine-tooth comb. There was no indication that Freddy was even present when the perp, or perps, was or were, in the room."

I expelled the breath I'd been holding. "Any way to know if the room was ransacked before or after Freddy disappeared?"

"We're guessing after," said the sheriff. "Since there was no sign of forced entry, we think Freddy was kidnapped, his key card taken from his wallet, and the perps went back and looked for—whatever they were looking for."

"That makes sense." I nodded. "Although Freddy must have been taken from his room, or at least from somewhere inside the casino."

"How do you figure that?" asked Nautika.

"Crime TV." I winked at her, and almost mustered a smile. "His keys and cell phone were found in his room, but his wallet was not. His wallet is always in his back pocket, but when he's not planning on leaving right away, there's no reason to carry his keys around. Cell service is notoriously bad inside casinos, so Freddy could have also left his phone in his room on purpose."

Sheriff D nodded. "Good reasoning," he said. "The exact same deductions Deputies Bill and Bob and I came to down at the station."

I wasn't sure if he were making a point to tell me his cops weren't so dumb, or if he were just reinforcing my thought process, so I went with the latter.

"So…" I began. "What do we do now?"

"We wait," said the sheriff. He took another long sip of coffee.

"You know I'm not good at that, Carter," I said.

"That's a gross understatement," retorted Sheriff D.

Brent snorted coffee out his nose, grabbed a napkin, and wiped it off.

"I know it's not your strong suit, but you've got to give it your best effort," said Sheriff D. "I'm just glad you came back without putting up a fuss. You're needed here now. We have to be ready for whatever comes next, but we can't force the issue, so now we wait."

Nautika smirked. "There's nothing wrong with being women of action," she said. "We're known to get things done."

"And a few of you," the sheriff said pointedly, "are also known to take unnecessary risks."

"So let me repeat myself," I said. "What can we do now?"

"A trace has already been put on both of Wayne Korski's phones."

"He has two?" I asked rhetorically.

"Naturally we expect the ransom call to come in on his office phone, but the kidnapper will also know that, and might use his cell phone number to catch us off guard."

"And how would the kidnapper know his cell phone number?" I asked.

"Korski sells real estate part time," said the sheriff. He chuckled and shook his head. "Seems like you can't throw a stick around here anymore without hitting someone who sells real estate part time."

"That doesn't answer my question."

"He's passed out his business cards up and down the peninsula, taken out an ad in the *North Beach Tribune*, even had a professionally produced radio spot for awhile. So anyone with half a brain could easily get his cell number, which he uses for his real estate business, and wouldn't need to call the business line at the casino to reach him."

"It also means they could contact him in the middle of the night," I replied. "Is the tap 24/7, or does someone need to be there to start the recording?"

Sheriff D smiled. "We've got it covered, Sylvia. Rest assured."

The condescending way he said it, I almost expected him to tell me not to worry my pretty little head over it, and I scowled, deeply furrowing my forehead.

"What now?" asked Sheriff D.

"Korski lives just west of Unity, almost in the shadow of Sandstone Lighthouse. He's in a new housing development called

Pacific Bluff—the longtime locals refer to it as Poker Bluff because they're taking bets on when that whole hillside—now cleared of almost all the trees holding the soil in place—is going to slide right down into the ocean."

"And?" prompted the sheriff.

"And he was working the Open House events up there when Freddy's Uncle Harry was building luxury homes on spec. Korski drove one of the fleet of Town Cars with personalized license plates." I involuntarily shuddered at the memory of the thugs in "big, black cars" that had helped the notorious Harold Rodman the Third run drugs from the port in Unity up to the casino at Spartina Point.

"So Korski bought one of the spec houses," said Sheriff D. "There's no crime in that."

"So he owns one of those high-end homes—" I paused, trying to wrap my mind around what I was feeling and put it into words.

"He's the CFO of a major casino. I know Freddy pays him a good wage. And yet he works part-time in real estate? Something doesn't add up." I narrowed my eyes. "What do we really know about this guy?"

"Maybe he overextended himself when he bought the house," said Brent.

Nautika chimed in. "Maybe he has a dozen ex-wives and a bunch of kids in three different states and owes a ton of alimony and back child support and—"

"Whoa, Nautika! Slow down!" interrupted Sheriff D. "You're starting to sound just like Sylvia."

Nautika put her hands on her hips. Her eyes flashed. "I could do a heckuva lot worse," she said, stamping her foot for emphasis.

Brent reached over and patted her hand. "Maybe you should go lie down, honey. You've had a big week, what with flying to Hawaii and back and all. We wouldn't want you to get the baby all riled up," he said.

"Dad! I'm pregnant! Not sick, not frail, and definitely not a mindless ninny!"

My eyes filled with tears, but my heart was filled with love, and it told me that if I'd ever had a daughter, I would have wanted her to be just like Nautika.

Sheriff D cleared his throat. "Freddy vetted Korski himself, Sylvia."

"So I've been told." I shot a look at Brent and Nautika. "But that doesn't mean he didn't miss something."

Sheriff Donaldson sighed. "Wayne Korski came to the U.S. of A. as a Russian sailor who jumped ship in Portland when he was in his early 20s. He settled in with the large community of Russians in Woodburn and commuted to Portland State University. At PSU he studied business, and got his certification as an accountant. To date, he has a squeaky-clean record.

"Maybe too clean?" I asked, unwilling to give an inch.

"Always the suspicious one," said Brent. He gave my shoulder a squeeze as he got up to get three of the four of us more coffee. Nautika had already made herself a cup of herbal tea.

I chewed on my lower lip, mulling over what the sheriff had told us. Korksi was a little younger than me, and probably a little older than Freddy. I thought about the timeline and—*Good grief and gravy!*

"Sheriff?" I sat up a little straighter. "What year did Korski arrive? Must have been about 1990 or 91, right?" I didn't wait for confirmation. "That was right around the time of the collapse of the Soviet Union. Maybe Korski was able to pay his way through PSU because he was working for the Russian mafia. They had a whole underground system for stealing Ford and Chevy parts after the Soviet Union dissolved. Steel, particularly American made car parts, transmissions and such, were a hot commodity for the Russians back then.

"What ship did he arrive on? Did his captain willingly allow him to leave so he could be the guy with his feet on the ground who headed up that part of the operation?"

My sudden, and lengthy outburst received a collective sigh from Sheriff D, Brent, and even Nautika. It was like a wind tunnel blasting across the dining table.

"Number one," said Brent, checking it off on his index finger, "Russian organized crime at that time was more likely taking place in the major ports of New York or California. Number two," he added his middle finger to his list of points, "Russian ships very rarely docked in Portland, and Number three," he added his ring finger, "You really *DO* watch too much crime TV!"

"If I may," said Nautika, making eye contact with me, "aren't you the one who told me not all Germans were Nazis and not all Muslims were terrorists?"

I nodded, instinctively knowing exactly where she was headed.

"Well," she continued, "not everyone who worked for Freddy's Uncle Harry in the past were bad guys, either."

Sheriff D concurred. "As I said, Syl, Freddy cleared him personally."

Not one of them was on my side. Not even a little bit. Not one was as desperate as I was to find a quick and easy answer to our questions. "But you know Freddy always sees the good in people," I said, appealing to them from a different angle. "He believes in second chances. He even hired Jack and Tim to come work for him after school, despite the fact they tried to break into the slot machines in the casino during the hurricane last December, beaning Freddy in the process."

But my friends remained unmoved.

When the silence became overwhelming, I said, "Too bad

Kanji's not here."

Six eyebrows went up, but no one said a thing.

"Kanji understood about Occam's Razor," I explained.

"You mean how the easiest and most obvious solution is often the right one?" asked Nautika.

"Yes, that's right." I nodded. "Don't we need to at least dig around in Korski's background a little more?" I looked to Sheriff D, but he remained unmoved.

"Just my opinion," he said, "but I think it's a waste of time and resources."

I threw my hands into the air. "Okay! Okay! Fine! I give up! Consider me duly chastised! I'll never watch another crime show as long as ..." I looked at the expressions on their faces. "Oh, who am I kidding? I'll probably watch a rerun of NCIS this very evening."

The sheriff drained his coffee cup and declined the offer for another refill. "For the time being, I think it's best to keep your return to the beach a secret, Syl. Brent, Nautika, Cliff, and I will be the only ones who know you're back. No local calls, no local texts, no local emails, no showing your face outside this house. Got it?"

"No calls? Not even to my mother?"

"You haven't called your mother since you left her a message during her wedding on Valentine's Day," said Sheriff D. He turned his laser focus on me as if daring me to challenge him on this point.

"But I'm home now."

"And surely you can manage to wait another week." He sighed. "I can't even risk telling Mercedes."

"Telling Mercedes would be like taking out an ad in the *Tribune*," I said. "She's such a..."

"Blabbermouth?" offered the sheriff. "Gossip?"

"Yeah," I said. "Both of those, and maybe a few more."

The sheriff smiled. "Then we're agreed?"

"On the fact Mercedes can't keep a secret?" I said coyly.

"On the fact you're back in town, Syl. Don't pretend to be so obtuse. This is serious. We don't know who we can trust, and we need to play our cards close to our vest," said the sheriff. "This could mean life or death for Freddy."

Reluctantly, I nodded. "I hear you loud and clear, Sheriff, and believe me, we're on the same page. I won't do anything to jeopardize Freddy's safe return."

"What about Korski?" asked Brent.

"What about him?" asked the sheriff.

"He's going to have to know Sylvia's back because she going to have to get over there in the next couple days and sign for some of the more larger ticket items," Brent replied.

"That's true." Sheriff D sighed. "I guess I'll need to stop by and write him in on this. But if there's a ransom note, I'd prefer Korski'd be able to say in all honesty that large withdrawals take two signatures, and he only has checks without the second one. Korski is a very nervous guy, and we don't want him messing this up. The fewer deceits, the better.

"He knows, of course, you can co-sign the checks, Syl, but we heavily coached him to tell anyone who calls that Freddy is the only other signer on the casino accounts. He's to say he can't even get a bank loan for wind and water repairs without the boss's John Henry on the paperwork. Not even with the casino as collateral."

"And you're hoping to force the kidnapper's hand?" I asked.

"Something like that."

"So remind me again, why am I here?"

"Because, since Korski really is out of signed checks, he needs you to help keep the casino running as if nothing is out of the ordinary. Freddy went looking for you—that's the only story out there on the street—and we want to keep it that way."

"But what if…" I couldn't bring myself to finish the sentence.

"The 'what if' is also why you're here," said Sheriff D. "In an absolute emergency, we won't be able to waste any time, and you need to be close at hand so the money needed can be accessed almost immediately."

I nodded wordlessly, but I couldn't swallow the lump in my throat. These things never seem to play out the way you think they will. Something almost always goes haywire. And just for an instant, I wondered if Freddy were even still alive.

"You've watched the surveillance tapes, right?" I asked.

Sheriff Donaldson rolled his eyes and sighed. "Of course. But the cameras only cover the gaming rooms, not the hotel hallways or the elevators. It's a clientele privacy thing. So there's nothing to see there." He stood and put on his hat.

I walked him to the door, and he told me for the umpteenth time not to show my face outside. Then he put his hand on the doorknob, turned back to face me, and fired his parting shot.

"And by the way, Sylvia, on Valentine's Day your mother had forgotten to turn her phone off at the start of the ceremony. So when everyone in the church heard it ring, she just laughed and said, 'Gee, I wonder who's not here who might be calling to wish me good luck'?"

Oops. My bad. I'd have to find a way to make it up to Merri as soon as I was able to go see her. In the meantime, I had to figure out what I was going to do to entertain myself stuck out here on the mud flats of Shallowwater Bay.

CHAPTER 7

I watched as Sheriff D's Interceptor navigated the right turn at the end of the lane and disappeared from view. Then I turned and walked slowly back into the house, thinking of Freddy and awash with sadness. What if I never saw him again?

I plopped down in the window seat and stared out over the bay. For the most part, Brent and Nautika gave me my space, and let me feel each feeling as I roiled through the entire spectrum of emotions. When Nautika asked me if I was hungry, I just shrugged and didn't budge from the window seat, despite the fact I'd had nothing to eat all morning.

"The farm store is open 1 to 5 today," Nautika said, as she prepared to leave for the building next door. "Today's my day behind the counter." When I did not reply, she said, "I'll be back in a few hours." I grunted an acknowledgement, but again, I had nothing to say.

I don't know how much time passed while I sat there on the window seat. Another hour, maybe two. Everything in my body seemed to hurt—my head, my heart, my legs from being tucked under me while I stared out the window at nothing, even my eyeballs ached with a deep-seated pain.

Finally, I carefully considered exactly what language Sheriff D had used when he'd put communication limitations on me, along with the three-hour time difference between here and Maui. Then I texted Tom M: "Help. I hurt all over."

"Make your bed," he texted back.

My reply was just one punctuation mark: "?"

"Get your head out of that dark place. Get up and get moving. Do the next right indicated thing, even if it's just regaining some small sense of order by making your bed."

I got up off the window seat and went to the bathroom. I splashed some water on my face and ran a comb through my hair. My eyes appeared sunken and hollow. Even the healthy Hawaiian tan I'd brought back with me didn't help my ghoulish look. The ache was etched there across my face, and I quickly turned away from the mirror and walked into my bedroom.

My bed was unmade.

I stood there and stared at the disarray of rumpled bedding. I'd only been here one night. Did a person have to make their bed every day? I started to shrug it off. After all, I'd be getting back into bed in another 9 or 10 hours. Or I could just crawl in there right now, pull the covers up over my head, and spend the rest of my day howling.

For a moment, howling seemed like the best option. But then I suddenly found myself attacking the bed with a vengeance, jerking the covers up, smoothing the bedspread, fluffing the pillows. And Holy Criminitly—standing back and looking at the finished product, I felt a strange surge of satisfaction. I had accomplished something!

I took a photo of the bed with my cell phone and texted it to Tom M with "Ty" as the only other message. "Thank you."

Then I popped my head into Brent's cubbyhole closet turned office. "I need to get out of here for awhile."

"You know what the sheriff said," he replied without looking up from his paperwork. "No one can know you're around."

"And no one will. I'm sure there are plenty of oyster farmer duds around here, and I'll only walk south, along the bay. If I went north, I might run into Lorraine, or Kanji, I assume, but by going south and sticking to the trail through the marsh grass, I won't encounter anyone."

Brent looked up and met my eyes. "You've thought this through, haven't you?"

I nodded. "I just need to get out into the fresh air and take a walk. I need to clear my head."

Brent nodded. "Take whatever you want from the mud room. There are jackets on the hooks behind the door, and quite a few stocking caps piled on the shelf next to the laundry detergent." He leaned back and looked at my feet. "Nautika's boots might be a little too tight for you. Take a pair of heavy-duty socks and grab a pair of my boots."

"Thank you."

"Just don't get caught."

I suppose he had to say that, but it seemed unnecessary. I was dressed for the oyster flats in no time, and scooted on out the side door before he could change his mind.

I hadn't walked far before I came to the place where Brent had found the human skull right after the storm last December. The skull, which the hurricane-force storm had uncovered, turned out to be Nautika's mother's husband, who'd been missing for almost 25 years, but he was not Nautika's father after all. So much had happened since then!

"Life on life's terms," I said aloud, and my mind immediately returned to the friends I'd made at the Alano Club in Lahaina. Tom M had certainly been the right person to talk to just three days ago, and today, the right person to text. I was overcome with gratitude. Again I spoke aloud, sending a heartfelt prayer out into the Universe: "Thank you."

I was right about my body needing some fresh air and a walk. Getting up and getting moving put a lot of things into perspective. Must be those feel-good endorphins waking up inside me.

Wallowing had its place, I decided, but it's not somewhere for a person to stay for too long.

By the time I turned around to head back, a bit of my can-do attitude had replaced my feelings of hopelessness. But what could I do, stuck here, as if on house arrest? "Acceptance" a voice whispered in my ear. "Accept the things you cannot change."

I smiled, and almost laughed aloud. "Acceptance is great, but what about the courage to change the things I can?" I stubbornly replied to that first little voice. To be fair, the Serenity Prayer I now knew by heart actually concluded with, "and the wisdom to know the difference," which I also knew was advice I was pretty good at ignoring.

Brent had emerged from his office and was having a sandwich and coffee at the dining table when I came back into the house. "Feel better?" he asked.

I nodded. "Much." I took off my oyster worker disguise and put everything back in its place in the mud room. "Are there any sandwich fixings left for me?"

"As a matter of fact," said Brent. "I already made you a tuna sandwich. It's in the fridge. And the fresh pot of coffee is decaf."

I smiled again. "I know the decaf isn't just for me, Brent, but I appreciate you make enough for the two of us. I'm also glad you're following your doctor's orders."

Brent's mouth was full, but he nodded, then swallowed, and washed his last bite down with a swig of coffee. "I've got a lot to live for, Syl, so I want to stay as healthy as I can for as long as I can."

I put my late lunch on a plate, poured myself a cup of joe, and joined him at the table. "Good plan." I took a big bite of the sandwich, and didn't wait to swallow before I said, "And good sandwich."

"Nautika's still over in the store," said Brent. "Lorraine's over there, too. I hope Nautika remembers she's not to mention you're here to Lorraine."

"Well, if she does, she does," I said with a shrug. "But I bet she doesn't."

"They're making some executive decisions about which souvenir items to reorder to fill the shelves for the rest of the summer tourist season." He chuckled. "They may be awhile."

"My gratitude list just keeps getting longer and longer."

I realized my tone had been rather snarky when Brent tilted his head and looked at me with concern. "What's up, Buttercup?"

"I just don't think I can keep pretending to be perky around Nautika for one more minute today."

"Oh?" said Brent, his eyebrows arching and a smirk playing at the corners of his mouth. "I hadn't actually noticed you exuding an abundance of upbeat attitude around here before you went for your walk."

"Hrumpf," I grunted. "Inside I am feeling so much worse than what you're seeing on the outside. I just don't want to be responsible for stressing Nautika. Not while she's PG."

"Don't worry about Nautika," said Brent. "She's a strong young woman." He chuckled. "Kind of reminds me of you, back in high school."

"I'll take that as a compliment."

"You should." He nodded. "I had quite the crush on you back then."

"Really? Why didn't you say something?"

"Because your mother was a nurse, and my parents were oyster farmers."

"What's that got to do with anything?"

"You were headed to college," Brent continued, "and I was headed into the Navy to escape from the peninsula. We weren't functioning in the same social circle."

"You mean there's a *social circle* here on the North Beach Peninsula?" My laughter was genuine, for the first time in what seemed like months.

Brent wisely changed the subject as he got up to get us a coffee refill. "So now that your head is cleared from your walk, what's next on today's agenda?"

"I'm not good at just sitting here twiddling my thumbs, waiting for Korski to get a ransom phone call. I need something to do before I go batshit crazy."

"You mean batshit craz*ier*, right?" He paused, then repeated himself with more emphasis. "Batshit crazy-er."

I glowered at him. "Did I ask for a second opinion?"

"Sorry, Syl." He reached over and touched my lower arm. "I know it's nothing like Maui, but maybe you can try to pretend you're on vacation or something."

"Maui!" I leaped to my feet and went into my bedroom, retrieving my cell phone from the nightstand where it was charging.

"Didn't the sheriff stipulate your phone was for emergencies only?" asked Brent.

I glowered again. "First off, he said no local calls, and this isn't a local call. Secondly, and you'll have to trust me on this, this *is* an emergency." And I punched in one of the only three numbers I knew on Maui.

"Evie! How are you! It's me! It's Syl—I mean, it's Lee!" I stopped to listen, and Brent got up to quietly clear our dishes from the table.

"Yes, we got home just fine. I'm sorry I didn't call sooner. How's Rick doing?"

"He misses you. We both do. And we both hope things turn out well for your friend Freddy. Is he still missing?"

I smiled, and shook my head. "I've barely arrived here, Evie, but I'll be sure to keep you guys in the loop. And this time, I'll pinky swear."

Unfortunately, that's about as far as our conversation got before Evie had another call coming in. "Sorry, hon, business comes first."

"Yes, of course! Take care of yourself!" and I quickly hung up, surprised by the tears that sprang to my eyes.

"Everything okay?" Brent asked, coming into the living room.

"Sure. No problem." I swiped at my tears. "It's just a little unsettling that the Aloha State seems to be doing fine without me." I took a breath. "But hey—that's three minutes today I wasn't sitting here stewing about things I have absolutely no control over."

Brent cleared his throat "I'm not supposed to tell you this—I mean, it's not my business to tell you—but I happen to have it on good authority that Nautika has a little project for you when she gets home tonight."

"What is it?"

"Just wait and see. I've said too much already, so try to act surprised, okay?"

And suddenly I had a spark of purpose. Something to look forward to. And that little glimmer of hope was something I had desperately needed. In the meantime, though, I thought it best to conserve my jetlagged energy. I made myself a comfortable little nest of pillows in the window seat and snuggled down to take a short nap.

It turned out the "little project" Nautika had in mind was more of a huge, complicated, and multi-leveled undertaking.

"Without leaving the house, and without using my real identity to tap into my peninsula networking system, you want me to do *what*?" I asked.

"We," said Nautika, looking pointedly across the dinner table at Cliff, "would like you to take over the planning for the inaugural run of a little Blues and Oyster Festival coming up in a couple weeks."

"We," said Cliff, looking pointedly across the table at Nautika, "thought it might help distract you to give you something to do besides twiddling your thumbs."

I wondered if the three of them had conspired to create some busy work for me, until Nautika said, "Cliff is swamped out on the bay—no pun intended—and I am up to my ears in the operations of the farm store. Brent has his hands full with getting our shipments to market, so we're hoping you'll help us out."

"Okay," I said. "Sure. I'd love to help. Exactly when will this festival take place?"

All three of them responded at once: "July fourth."

"Holy Criminitly! That soon?"

"Cliff got the idea awhile back to put up a giant tent out there by the water. He already wired in that derelict oyster scow as a bandstand. He thought we'd have a few friends over to listen to some music and barbecue oysters after the Fourth of July Parade through Ocean Crest," said Nautika.

"But it kind of snowballed," said Cliff.

"That's putting it mildly," said Brent, under his breath.

"And now the whole town knows about it, and we need help because the planning got a whole lot more complicated than we first thought," said Nautika.

"I kind of thought this would be a small, private practice event for something we could do in the future on a larger scale. You know, just testing the water, but it suddenly took off," said Cliff, "and we've kind of accidentally opened it up to the public."

"You 'accidentally' invited the whole peninsula?" I echoed.

"It's just a word-of-mouth thing," said Cliff. "No flyers or ads in the paper or an event page on Facebook, or anything like that."

"You gotta hand it to them," said Brent, "it's a great way for more people to discover our tasty little oysters, and bring more people out to our neck of the North Beach Peninsula."

"Wow." The logistics of pulling this off were mammoth. "I'm not sure you know what you're asking," I began. "You need permits, and porta potties, and parking and—"

"Maybe we won't need so many permits," Brent interjected. "It's going to be a big party, but on private land, and we're not charging anyone for anything this year."

"So there's still the sanitation issue—we don't want another Woodstock on our hands, out here polluting up the cleanest bay in the USA."

Brent and I chuckled while Nautika and Cliff looked clueless, but I didn't stop to explain.

"And just one band isn't going to be enough, so we'll need to see what local musicians are available on short notice," I continued. "The sand will need to be raked free of sticks and shells for a dance floor. The oysters, of course, are right here, but we'll need to borrow several large barbecues, and buy gallons of tabasco sauce and we can grill up some garlic bread, too."

"You think maybe we could have fireworks out over the bay when it gets dark?" asked Cliff. "I know a lot of our friends would enjoy seeing a fireworks display on the Fourth of July."

"I'll leave that up to you," I replied. "Maybe tell them it's a 'bring your own sparkler' event."

"I'll notify the fire department," said Brent. "Just in case."

The event planning was progressing along a predictable snowball effect to a downright avalanche of people to call and things to do. "We need to make a list, then divide up responsibilities," I told them. "And at some point, sooner rather than later, we're going to need a lot more help divvying up the jobs to pull this off."

"See?" said Nautika, cheerily to the two men. "I told you Sylvia would know what to do!"

"And since there will be numerous unforeseen expenses incurred, I think I'd better get on the phone first thing tomorrow morning and start soliciting some donations from local businesses. We can put up a big banner with their names on it this first year, but in future years," I told them, "we'll need to get band sponsors so we can pay the musicians, and do some advertising, and charge the attendees. I imagine if this thing takes off, someday we'll have festival t-shirts and hand-painted wine glasses for sale, too."

Nautika was grinning ear to ear. "The right woman for the right job!" she crowed.

Cliff and Brent both mutely nodded.

"I guess I vastly underestimated the amount of work it would take to gather a few bands and barbecues together," said Cliff. He frowned and glanced over at Nautika. "Are you sure you're up to something like this—I mean—" he stopped, and looked a bit embarrassed.

"Do *not* go there!" said Nautika. "I'm pregnant, not incapacitated. In fact—" and we all could see a devilish twinkle in her eye— "in fact, I'd like to offer to sing *The Star-Spangled Banner* when we kick things off. That'll be right after you give the official welcome, and with your permission, of course…"

Cliff looked at her with so much love in his expression, it was hard not to get all teared up. "You promise not to go all Beyoncé on me, and the job is yours."

"And that's another thing," I said. "We need to get a band lineup figured out." I paused. "And will the musicians need to bring their own amplifiers and drum sets and things?"

"Only one drum set will be used, and that will be mine. The crowd wants to enjoy the music, not watch an entire space shuttle be taken apart and reconstructed between bands."

We all laughed.

"Each drummer will bring his—or her—own drumsticks, of course. Drumsticks are very personal. Some guys engrave their initials on them. Mine are going to have red, white, and blue LED-colored lights flashing in them for this event. Etiquette says even if you're at a jam and only going to play one song, you bring your own sticks."

Cliff smiled. "I think I'm going to put some of those LEDs inside the bass drum, too. That will look pretty cool. Almost like fireworks going off."

Wow! The inaugural run of a Blues and Oyster Festival right here in little old Willoopah, and everything must be ready in just a few weeks! No pressure there!

Funny thing, though, having something useful to do might be just the thing I needed to distract me from my constant obsessing over things I could not change. And it might be actually fun to impersonate Nautika via emails and on the phone if I was calling someone who didn't know either of our voices.

"So…" Nautika said, as she stood to clear the dinner dishes. "Cliff and I were thinking of heading down to Unity tonight to listen to a couple guys we know play a few tunes. We're hoping Fred and Bryan will agree to do a set out here on the fourth.

"I don't know where you find all your energy," said Brent. He kissed his daughter on the top of her head. "Just don't be too late. My grandchild needs to get plenty of his or her rest, you know."

"Don't worry," said Cliff. "We promise not to do any wild and crazy dancing."

Nautika shot him a look, then smiled, and winked. "I'm not promising any such thing!"

After they left, Brent and I finished up the dishes, and he invited me out on the back deck to watch the light fade out on Shallowwater Bay.

We scooted a pair of Adirondack deck chairs together and Brent went inside and grabbed the afghan from the couch.

"Good idea," I said as he settled it across both out laps. Even though June was rapidly coming to a close, it got a bit chilly after the sun went down. Of course it's still chilly out here in July, August, and September, too.

"You look so serious," he said. "What's on your mind?"

I tilted my head out toward Elk Island. "Your life could have ended right out there just six short months ago."

"It clearly wasn't my time," Brent replied.

"But if Freddy and the county's search and rescue dog hadn't tracked you down and gotten you to medical help—"

"But they did," Brent interjected. "And I'm still here to tell the story."

I nodded. "I just hope that Freddy…"

Brent reached under the blanket and squeezed my hand. "Everything's going to turn out fine," he said. "We've all got a good long life left ahead of us."

Oh how I wanted to believe him.

"Trust me," he said, as if reading my mind.

Our eyes met, and we looked at each other for a long time, without saying a word. I even surprised myself by not pulling my hand away. He was so confident things would be okay that I felt totally safe, and amazingly calm, for the first time since I'd learned Freddy was missing.

We chatted amicably for several hours, and then somehow we both fell asleep, snuggled together out there under the moon and the stars. And that's exactly where the kids found us, sneaking in like teenagers, shortly after midnight.

CHAPTER 8

Sunrise was mere minutes away, and the sky was flaming with the entire hot end of the color spectrum. Reds, oranges, pinks, even variations of lavenders painted the sky palette with glorious vibrancy. I had my coffee—the good stuff—and was sitting once again in the bay window taking in the amazing morning light show.

"Isn't it beautiful?" asked Nautika, coming up behind me. "This is my absolute favorite time of day; I never get tired of watching the sun come up over the hills on Elk Island."

I nodded, but said nothing. I took tiny sips from my coffee mug, not taking my eyes off the impending start of a brand-new day, a fresh start, a clean slate of nothing but opportunity to do better than the day before. I hugged the mug against my chest with both hands, feeling the warmth penetrate my bathrobe.

Nautika picked up on my silence and quietly sat down on the other end of the window seat just as the sun peeped over the top of the wooded old-growth forest. The cedar grove out on that 6-mile-long island is estimated to be over 4,000 years old, and the oldest living trees there now have seen roughly one thousand years.

I could barely wrap my mind around a thousand-year-old tree, and certainly it would take several people to wrap their arms clear around one. In awe, I thought about those towering 150-foot trees, what storms they'd weathered during the past 10 centuries, and it gave me the shivers along with some small sense of comfort.

The world keeps turning, come what may.

We watched the day dawn, and with the spreading light, my growing anxiety welled up in my throat no matter how hard I tried to push it down. "Red at night, sailors' delight. Red sky in morning, sailors take warning," I whispered, then involuntarily shuddered again, this time with a sense of despair. I wondered whose fate was being foretold by the cosmos this day.

"Freddy will be fine," Nautika said softly. "Strong trees and strong people always survive."

It was like she'd been reading my mind about the trees, and I deeply appreciated the way she'd said what she'd said. I turned and smiled at her. "I certainly hope you're right."

"My dad's just one example," she replied. "Freddy will be fine, too. You just wait. Freddy and my father are like the old-growth cedars. They will survive."

We watched as the blaring colors melded into the early morning light of a pale blue dawn. Today's show was over, but the day was just beginning, fresh with unspoken promises, as well as a myriad of unanswered questions.

Nautika refrained from mentioning finding her father and I cuddled up under the stars just hours before. She knew Freddy and I had a long and intimate history, and she respected that bond. It wasn't time to be poking fun at me, and I was grateful for her discretion.

Breakfast was a little awkward, though. Whereas a day earlier, when my hand accidentally brushed against Brent's, it wouldn't have meant a thing, today it felt just too... too... too what? Comfortable? Lustful? Weird? Yes, weird was probably the best word for it at the moment, and I decidedly avoided any further physical contact.

The conversation over waffles bounced between the band the kids had heard the night before and Cliff's ongoing work trying to contain the burrowing ghost shrimp out on the oyster beds.

"I never thought my college degree would lead me to 12-hour days of slopping through the muck of an estuary fighting for its existence," he said, shaking his head. "But then, a year ago I never thought I'd be married with a child on the way, either."

The smile that passed between Cliff and Nautika put a hard lump in my throat. They were obviously so in love, and so young! I turned away and my eyes met Brent's. Being a proud father, about to be an even prouder grandfather, suited him well, and we shared a knowing nod of acknowledgement that comes with age. We were both happy he'd lived to see this day.

The moment passed, and Cliff went on telling us about the progress the farm had made on developing local oyster seed, and new methods of ensuring the spat was able to fatten up in the pristine waters of Shallowwater Bay.

I thought we'd kept the chatter light and away from anything too personal until Nautika announced she and Cliff were going out again that night—all the way to Fort George—to listen to another band, this one from Portland. "And we've decided to spend the night over·there with my friends Lori and Ned," she concluded.

Cliff nodded. "It's not that Fort George is that far, but driving home would make it another late night for the three of us, and we thought you two might also enjoy having a little more privacy as well."

Nautika obviously kicked him under the table—hard enough that he jerked his leg back, connected with the table leg, and everything on the top of the table was jostled. She glared at him.

It was clearly a set-up, but Brent took it good-naturedly, and just told them to be safe, drive carefully, and have fun.

Cliff's Saturday crew was already pulling into the parking area, and he made a timely retreat for the scow. Nautika excused herself to go take a shower. That left Brent and me alone to clear the table and do the dishes from breakfast.

"Is this starting to feel too familiar?" Brent joked as he filled the sink with soapy water.

"I assume you're talking about us always getting stuck with doing the dishes."

Brent smiled and rolled up his sleeves. "That, too."

I couldn't bring myself to look directly at him, so I got busy putting the butter and syrup and leftover orange juice back into the fridge. When I turned around, he was just standing there, looking at me, and I racked my brain trying to recall if he had asked me a question I hadn't heard, and therefore hadn't answered.

"You're right," he said. "I kind of like how familiar having you here is feeling."

"It's just temporary," I said, unnecessarily. "And I mean no offense when I say this, Brent, but I can't wait to get back to my own house."

Brent nodded. "I know." He turned and plunged his hands into the hot dishwater. "But that doesn't keep me from hoping that tonight we might pick up where we left off last night."

I was glad he had turned his back to me before he said that. I was afraid maybe if he looked into my eyes he might see I was thinking along those very same lines.

"Let's wait and see how many donations I collect for the Blues and Oyster Festival today," I said coyly. "No promises, but maybe we'll have something to celebrate tonight."

I didn't need to see his face to know Brent's smile mirrored my own.

My morning passed quickly. Once I got the hang of it, and stopped thinking of myself as a glorified panhandler, or a solicitor begging for money, or a telemarketer trying to lure someone into their scam, it was relatively easy to use Nautika's Messenger app to query peninsula businesses about supporting a new festival start up.

I was maintaining a spreadsheet to show which businesses had immediately responded favorably, and which had asked me to call back at a time when the person who could make such decisions would be available. There was also a space for those who turned me down flat, but that group was definitely in the minority.

The hardest part were the callbacks. I'd already pitched to that business, but then I had to start from the beginning, as if it were another cold call. Though more time consuming than anything, at least it was still yielding some strong supporters.

Most who replied positively readily offered donations of food or money or other volunteer help for a spot on our advertising banners. It was a win-win kind of thing, and I was feeling on top of the world by early afternoon. When I decided it was time for a well-deserved break, I made myself a sandwich and took it out on the back deck.

I carried Nautika's laptop out there too, and enjoyed scrolling through Facebook through her eyes and checking out a few pages I hadn't been able to access as Lee Gardner on Maui.

Just the thought of my time in Maui made me feel a little homesick, if that was the right word in this situation. I'd been there only six months, but they'd been pretty darn good months, and I'd made some pretty darn good friends there, too. Not a lot of friends, but they were definitely quality over quantity.

I wasn't sure if I were merely procrastinating the return to my festival work, but I suddenly got a very strong urge to connect again with Tom M. After all, I'd left the island in such a rush I hadn't said a proper good-bye, and I felt he deserved to hear "the rest of the story."

Well aware my afternoon was slipping right through my fingers, I went in and collected my cell phone, pulled on a sweatshirt, poured myself some herbal iced tea, and went back out on the deck. I stopped for a moment to appreciate my natural surroundings once again. *Where else would you want to live? I* thought, almost overcome with emotion. Then I settled back into my Adirondack chair and placed my call.

Tom M and I chatted for over an hour, as I brought him up to speed. I was just telling him about the big plans my young friends had for a new festival on the Fourth of July, when an enormous black lab bounded around the side of the house and up the steps to the deck.

"Roof! Roof! Roof! Roof!" he barked, wiggling his entire body, from the end of his nose to the tip of his tail, expressing obvious delight at discovering me there on the deck.

"ELVIS!" I exclaimed, attempting to fend off the big, excited dog with one hand and trying not to fall out of my chair in the process.

"Elvis?" asked Tom M.

"I'm sorry Tom, I'll have to fill you in some other time. It's all okay, I'm fine, but right now I have to go!" And I quickly hung up.

I knew Elvis would never be allowed to run around outside on his own, so I knew I didn't have a moment to spare. Unfortunately, I was unable to stand up to run for the house with such a large, wriggly dog now sprawled across my lap, pinning me down and joyously licking my face all over like I was an ice cream cone someone might try to take away from him.

Closing my eyes, I willed myself to just disappear. Maybe if I held really still, Elvis would get bored and go away on his own before anyone came around the back of the house looking for him. Maybe he had simply accompanied Lorraine to her shift at the farm store, and had somehow gotten loose, but surely he would return to where he belonged as soon as someone noticed him missing and loudly called his name. Maybe.

I kept my eyes closed while I listened attentively for Lorraine to holler for the dog's return. Elvis wasn't the kind of dog you wouldn't miss right away. Any second now, I was sure the dog would take off like a bolt of lightning back around the house and over to the farm store. Maybe.

But that's not what happened.

"My dearest Sylvia," said a deep, melodic voice that instantly ignited all kinds of strong memories in all kinds of places in my body. "Is it really you?"

I opened my eyes and looked up at Kanjirappally Kumera, standing at the top of the deck steps, looking as tall and handsome as ever. He held an empty leash in one hand, and a travel mug, with what I assumed was Chai, clasped in the other.

"I am sorry to see my ill-mannered canine has intruded upon you," he began. "But I am most certainly not sorry he has led me to see you once again."

"Hello, Kanji. It's good to see you, too." All my thoughts of a later rendezvous with Brent evaporated like the morning mist on the bay. I swallowed hard, forcing myself to do the next right indicated thing. "If you have time, Kanji, please pull up a chair."

"For you, my dear Sylvia, I will always be able to make the time."

I didn't want to start crying, so I did what I've been accused of being best at—I deflected my feelings with humor. "That's great, Kanji. Thank you. And would you mind first removing Elvis from my lap before you sit down? I'm afraid he's gotten so big he'll squeeze all the air out of me and I won't be able to catch my breath in order to talk." I wheezed for emphasis.

"I am sure your request would not be beyond my immediate considerations," he said. His eyes twinkled in mirth, but his voice was so smooth and inviting, I just wanted to close my eyes again and let him do all the talking for like maybe the next week.

I waited until Kanji got Elvis back on his leash and settled into a chair before I began making my blundering amends. For someone who'd had six months to predict how this conversation would play out, I certainly felt unprepared.

"Kanji," I began. "I never meant to hurt you."

Kanji held up his hand to stop me. "There is no need for you to elaborate on the past, dear Sylvia. I accept your apology, and for the record, I hold no ill will against you."

"Thank you for that." The tears were threatening, but I was determined to hold them at bay, so I bit hard on my lower lip and waited for Kanji to say something more.

Now it was his turn to take a deep breath. Apparently, he'd also had time to rehearse his end of this conversation. "Some might call me old school, or old fashioned," he began. "I was raised to believe when a man is on his knees, diamond engagement ring in his hand, proposing to a woman he loves in front of her friends and family in a most romantic way, the answer is either a very happy and resounding yes, or their relationship is ultimately over. There isn't much in between." His deep brown eyes met mine and held them for just a moment. "Is that not true?"

I looked down at my hands. "Yes, it's true."

"Then the woman should not want nor expect that man to wait for her to change her mind and decide to marry him. Is that not also true?"

"Yes, that is also true." I swiped at some unmanageable runaway tears. "And I'm glad—I'm really glad, Kanji—to know you're happy with Lorraine."

Kanji nodded. "Lorraine is quite an amazing woman. Last December, when she organized the quilt show at the casino, as well as when she helped in the kitchen during both the hurricane aftermath and again on Christmas, I could not help but notice the strength of her charitable character and the depth of her commitment."

There it was—the "C" word. Commitment. Something I knew very little about, but something that maybe not everyone on the planet needed to have to be happy.

"Lorraine's a great gal," I admitted. "And she and Nautika have turned the farm store into a very attractive and profitable business. She's got a good head on her shoulders."

"She is not afraid of hard work," said Kanji, nodding, "whether it be in business or in relationships."

Ouch. That kind of stung. A lot. And I wasn't sure how I should respond to a statement that was nothing but the truth, and in no way intentionally mean. Fortunately, while I debated how best to reply, Kanji continued.

"Lorraine thinks we should take it slowly," he said. "She wants to be sure I'm not… what do you call it?" His eyebrows knit together in thought. "On the rebound."

"What do you think?" I asked, not sure which answer I wanted to hear.

"Upon unexpectedly seeing you here sitting on the deck today, I must admit, my heart was somewhat troubled. But since you did not call, even once, in all the time you were away, and you did not let me know now you had returned, I am finally able to embrace acceptance and know our lives are truly playing out as they were destined to do."

I wiped another tear away and nodded.

"Sweet Sylvia, may I ask…" Kanji began, "was it Freddy who was able to convince you to return… to him?"

"Freddy?" Oh dear. Apparently, Kanji hadn't been included among those who knew Freddy's absence at the casino had not been of his own choosing. The sheriff had said he was playing this very close to his vest, but this was much closer than I'd thought he'd meant. Kanji was basically second in command at *Spartina Point*. Why had the sheriff not told me Kanji did not know his boss had been kidnapped?

"Uh… No. I have not seen Freddy since I returned." It wasn't a lie, but it was certainly a sin of omission. I wanted to tell him everything I knew, and not hold a thing back. I wanted his comfort, and concern, his compassion, and his caring, but I knew the sheriff would have my hide if I said a word on this subject.

So it wouldn't be me who dropped this bombshell on Kanji. *For all any of us knew, Kanji might even be in on the kidnapping, and…* I literally shook my head to clear such thoughts. The idea Kanji could be involved in any way was simply ridiculous. Wasn't it?

"Sylvia? Are you feeling ill?" Kanji leaned closer and studied my face. "You have become very pale and uncharacteristically quiet. When I asked you if it was Freddy you returned for, I did not mean to upset you. I just assumed, since it was not the thought of reuniting with me that helped you find your way home, it must have been him who holds your heart." He frowned. "So he did not come to Maui to find you?"

Good grief and gravy! Had everyone on God's green earth known exactly where I'd been all this time?

"No, he did not," I said. "It was simply time for me to come back, and—I'm sorry, Kanji, but I'm really not ready to talk any more about this."

"I'd like to say I now understand, but I am afraid I still do not," said Kanji. "I will have to trust you will share more when you are comfortable doing so."

"Thank you."

Kanji stood to leave, and I stood up too. He hesitated, then opened his arms and I willingly walked into them. It was a warm, inviting, and memory-filled hug, and for a moment, when he pulled back, I thought he might kiss me, but was glad he did not. No sense muddying the waters again after we'd just gotten things right between us.

"I cannot wait to share with Lorraine that you have returned, dearest Sylvia. She, too, will be most happy to see and speak with you again."

I didn't bother to tell Kanji to keep the announcement of my homecoming to himself. I knew Nautika had been having a tough time keeping the news from Lorraine over at the farm store, so I felt somewhat relieved it would not be Nautika's fault that two more people knew I was home. If I told Kanji my return was supposed to be a secret, he would undoubtedly press me to tell him why, and it was not my place to tell.

In other words, the sheriff would want me to keep my lip zipped. He was going to be pissed enough as it was that I'd been outed by Elvis.

CHAPTER 9

The jig was up, and after only two full days at home. Three long, worry-filled, anxious days in which no ransom call had come in, and we were no closer to finding Freddy than if I'd stayed on Maui, oblivious to what was going on back on the peninsula.

I went inside, plopped down on the couch, and called Sheriff Donaldson on his private cell phone line. I didn't want my call to be routed through the dispatch when I confessed that I'd been discovered out on the deck by Kanji's dog.

"It had to happen sooner or later," said Sheriff D, much more pragmatically than I had dared to hope for. "And don't think I don't appreciate you letting me know right away. We've been hitting dead end after dead end, and I've been thinking it's time to call the Brain Trust together."

The Brain Trust. That's what the sheriff called our little eclectic group of people who have been able to collectively think outside the box and have somehow managed to help solve several—okay, make that five—major crimes in the past 15 months.

"When?"

"First thing tomorrow morning," Sheriff D replied. "I'll pick up Jimmy and some donuts from the Buoy 10 Bakery, and see you at 8 am, if that works for you."

"Yes," I agreed. "That will work. Cliff and Nautika are staying over in Fort George tonight, but is it okay if Brent sits in with us?"

"Absolutely," said the sheriff. "And I'll call Kanji and have him meet us there too."

"But… But… Kanji doesn't know Freddy's been abducted—does he?"

The sheriff had the audacity to chuckle. "I'm sorry about this, Sylvia. I should have told you. Kanji knows Freddy did not leave the casino of his own free will, but he did not know that you knew that, nor did he know you were back on the peninsula."

"*SAY WHAT?*" I held the phone away from my ear and glared at it. "You mean to tell me—" I got my angry accusation halfway out of my mouth before I realized I was being overly sensitive and abruptly stopped my tirade. "Oh."

"I'm sorry," Sheriff D said again. "Kanji was aware that if there was a ransom note, and a large amount of money was needed, your signature would be required, of course, but I didn't tell him Nautika and Brent were going to go get you, and you'd be staying with them for awhile because, well…" He sighed. "It's not easy for a man to keep something from the woman he spends all his free time with. I know I've had a helluva time keeping quiet around Mercedes, and I didn't want Kanji to have to keep the news from Lorraine."

Silently, I nodded. "I'm actually relieved," I said. "I was afraid Kanji might be on your suspect list."

"He's got a solid alibi," said the sheriff. "His face is all over the casino security tapes—in the bar, in the restaurant, in the gaming rooms. He's always been a hard worker, but he's putting in double time over there since Freddy disappeared."

"So Kanji *was* a suspect?!"

"Not really, but we couldn't leave any stone unturned."

I supposed I should appreciate his thoroughness, and not take issue with him just doing his job. "I understand. See you in the morning, Sheriff."

We ended our call, and I looked up to see Brent standing in

the doorway to the mud room.

"I didn't mean to eavesdrop," he said. "I was just coming in from the gear shed. But did I hear enough of that conversation to assume we're having company early tomorrow morning?"

"The Brain Trust." I nodded. "Sheriff D is picking up donuts and Jimmy, and then you, me, and Kanji will see what we can piece together to move this investigation along."

"And you've talked to Kanji?" Brent asked. "How did that go? Are you okay?"

Tears suddenly welled up in my eyes. "Yes, I'm okay. It was good to see him, and I'm glad we had a chance to privately clear the air between us, but—"

"But?" Brent prompted.

"But—" I repeated, getting to my feet, "I could sure use a hug."

Brent immediately crossed the room and put his arms around me. Holding me tight, but not too tight, he said into my hair, "That must have been really hard."

I sniffled and nodded with my head against his shoulder. "Yes. It was."

We stood there for several more minutes. Brent just letting me cry without interruption. Once I thought I had gotten it all out—at least for the moment—I stepped back and wiped my sweatshirt sleeve across my eyes. "Thank you."

"Anytime," he said. "You know how much I care about you."

"Yes," I nodded, and mustered up a small smile. "I am very fortunate to have you in my corner."

Brent smiled back. "But I suppose this turn of events puts a damper on any possibly intimate rendezvous I might have been hoping for tonight."

"Yes," I agreed. "I'm afraid it does. I'm feeling pretty emotionally drained. But—"

"Another but?" Brent teased.

"But I wouldn't mind having a rain check."

"Sylvia! Sylvia! Sylvia! Sylvia!" Jimmy bounced into the room carrying a bright pink Buoy 10 Bakery box. "I called dibs on the bear claw!"

"Is that any way to greet me?" I laughed.

Jimmy set the box on the dining table and gave me a quick hug. "So what did you bring me from Hawaii?"

I rolled my eyes, and didn't even address the fact he, too, had known where I'd been. "There wasn't a whole lot of time for souvenir shopping between finding out I was coming home and getting on the plane, Jim."

"Right." Jimmy nodded and took a big bite out of the only bear claw in the box. Then with his mouth still full of the pastry, he asked, "How long have you been back?"

"You mean you don't already know that too?'

"Sheriff D didn't tell me anything until he picked me up and we were on our way."

I looked over at the sheriff, who had removed his Stetson and was busy setting up the portable white board he'd carried in from the Interceptor. "Is that true, Carter?"

"I knew he'd be busting his buttons to tell Julio, and then Julio would share it with the guys he works with, and then their wives would make sure the whole peninsula would know within hours," Sheriff D replied. "This way, maybe we can keep a little bit of a lid on it."

"Oh, yeah! Julio moved in with me, Syl!" exclaimed Jimmy.

He was literally bubbling with enthusiasm, pastry bits flying out of his mouth, and I handed him a paper napkin. I chose not to steal his thunder by telling him I was already aware of his new roommate situation. "That's wonderful, Jimmy. Just wonderful.

I'm very happy for you."

Brent set five cups of coffee on the table just as Kanji rapped twice on the front door and came on in. "Lorraine sends her most sincere regards," he said, bowing his head in separate greeting toward each of us. "And she further insisted I bring this most delicious sausage and egg breakfast casserole with me, in case there is anyone who wants something a little more substantial, or perhaps a tad more healthy, than donuts."

Brent got out some plates and forks, and as we helped ourselves to the casserole, I sidled over to Kanji. "Remind me never to play poker with you," I said.

"I am most sorry for the deception, dear Sylvia," said Kanji. "Please forgive me for not talking with you yesterday about Freddy's disappearance. It was a most uncomfortable situation for me as well, not knowing how much you knew or did not know, about his whereabouts."

I nodded. "We're good," I said, taking a big bite of Lorraine's breakfast offering. "And so is this casserole!"

"So," said Sheriff D, as we settled around the table, "Freddy was last seen on the security camera in the casino restaurant 11 days ago."

My eyebrows shot up. "Nobody's seen him in 11 days?"

"That is correct." The sheriff nodded. "Two days after that, the motel maid called and reported the appearance of his room looked 'suspicious.' After investigation, and considering many possible scenarios, Brent and Nautika came to retrieve you on Day 6 and you returned Day 7 and that was four days ago, counting today."

"Eleven days," I echoed softly.

"The research tells us the longer someone is missing," said Jimmy, "the less likely it is the victim is still alive."

My stomach clenched, and I wanted to throw up, right then

and there, but I didn't want Kanji to think I didn't like Lorraine's casserole. "Jimmy! You're not helping!"

"We shall assume the victim is still alive," said the sheriff. "Although not receiving a ransom call or note in this length of time is rather worrisome."

"Perhaps Freddy made a break for it and got away." said Brent, trying in his own way to reassure me. "He may be hundreds of miles from here, working his way back home."

"Deputy Morgan is a well-trained police officer," said Sheriff D. "He would not have attempted escape, due to the fact that he might have been shot or killed in the process." He looked at me. "I know this is hard for you to hear, Sylvia, but we need to get everything out on the table."

I nodded. "Go on."

"Deputy Morgan would have tried to befriend his captor, tried to sympathize with him, worked to find a way to make him feel understood."

"Excuse me," said Kanji, "but would not such behavior create the possibility of Freddy succumbing to what I believe is called 'The Stockholm Syndrome'?"

"The Stockholm Syndrome occurs when hostages or abuse victims bond with their captors or abusers," Jimmy quickly inserted. "It's a psychological connection that develops over the course of days, weeks, months, or even years."

I glared at Jimmy. "Freddy might let his captor *think* that was happening, but he'd never actually fall for it."

"I know," said Jimmy. "According to data from the FBI, only about five percent of victims display any evidence of the syndrome upon their release."

"Only five percent?" I was sure people in the next county could hear my eyes roll, and wanted to be angry with him for even bringing it up. But Jiminy Cricket, with his encyclopedic brain, had often stumbled upon a vital clue that was needed to unravel one mystery or another, so I refrained from chastising him. At least in public.

Sheriff Donaldson sighed. "It is very unlikely Freddy would develop Stockholm Syndrome, but he might still employ the tactics of empathy."

That, I could wholeheartedly agree with. "So let's go back to the condition of his room," I said. "I know we talked about this when you were here before, Carter, but I think it's important we all know what everyone else knows."

I couldn't help it—I shot a look at Kanji, who pressed his palms together and bowed his head as if praying, which I decided to interpret as a further apology.

"Yes," said Jimmy, nodding enthusiastically. "Good idea. Let's all get on the same page."

The sheriff cleared his throat and smoothed his mustache out from the center to the ends. It was the first time I'd ever considered this habit of his might roughly correspond to my frequent eye rolling. He summarized the condition of the room in just two sentences: "Freddy's room was ransacked. Cushions were slashed, pictures taken off walls, drawers dumped out, but his cell phone and his vehicle keys were still there."

"Wow," said Jimmy. It was brand new information for only him, but it still sickened my stomach to hear the sheriff repeat it.

"Any sign of foul play?" Jimmy asked.

'I'd say every sign," said Brent.

"Not really," said Sheriff Donaldson. "There were no fingerprints that shouldn't have been in the room, no blood spatter, and nothing to draw a chalk outline around. So when you look at it that way, it could have been much worse."

As the realization of just how much worse it could have been dawned on me, I felt a little lightheaded. Thinking I might have low blood sugar, I wondered if another donut might help.

"You know," said Jimmy, matter-of-factly, "a lot of people think it's blood splatter instead of spatter, but they're just showing their ignorance when they say things like that."

Brent cleared his throat. "Before Jimmy says anything about chalk outlines," he said, "I'd like to put my two cents in. Chalk outlines were used in the 1930s through 1960s, but they stopped doing that because it contaminated the crime scene. So that's when they began using photographs."

"And may I also share something I happen to know on this particular subject?" asked Kanji. When no one said anything to stop him, he continued. "*The Case of the Perjured Parrot,* on the television drama *Perry Mason,* was the first time a chalk outline was used on television, in—"

"1958!" Jimmy and Brent both tried to out shout Kanji.

"Ah-ha!" I surprised both Sheriff D and myself when I punched him gently in his upper arm. "Perhaps I'm not the only one around here who watches too much crime TV!"

"And none of this is getting us any closer to figuring out what happened to Freddy." Sheriff D sighed. "There were no fingerprints, not a trace of anyone else's DNA—really nothing for the forensics team. No fibers, no bullet casings, nothing at all to collect, preserve, and analyze."

"Okay, then let's go back to the casino restaurant." I looked at Kanji. "Were you working in the lounge or the dining room that night?"

"As I have related to Sheriff Donaldson, it was a rather slow night," said Kanji. "I had sent some of the staff home early and had been working both rooms myself."

"And did you see Freddy?" I asked.

"Yes. Of course. Freddy and his guest were dining together that night. Since I was filling the roles of both bartender and server, after I turned in their food order to the kitchen, I went behind the bar to prepare them each a Spartini."

Whoa! I looked from Brent to Sheriff D. No one had told me anything about Freddy having dinner there with someone the night of his abduction. Were they hiding this specific tidbit of information from me because his dinner companion was a female? I felt my face begin to flush, starting at the neck and moving upwards, and hoped no one would notice.

"Syl?" asked Sheriff D. "Are you alright?"

I glared at him, and racked my brain for a quick, believable lie. I certainly didn't want everyone here to know I was suddenly jealous about Freddy's choice of dinner dates, so I fell back on playing the girl card. "I'm in my 50s, Carter. It's just a hot flash."

"Sorry," he said, turning a bit pink himself.

"So who was Freddy with?" asked Jimmy, saving me the embarrassment of being the one to ask the question myself.

"Wayne Korski," said Kanji. "It was a regular occurrence for the two of them. They had a business dinner together about once a week. Sometimes they ate in the dining room, but this time they were in the bar. There were people at only one other table, having cocktails, so I decided to close the dining room because it was easier for me to serve everyone in the lounge."

"Who paid?" asked Jimmy.'

"Nobody," said Kanji. "I believe you would call it one of the perks of being the business owner."

"And after dinner?" I asked. "Did they leave together?"

Kanji shook his head. "No. Mr. Korski was leaving for the day, so he went out through the casino to the parking lot, and Freddy went upstairs to his suite, via the back elevator."

"We verified Korski getting into his white Honda Civic and exiting the parking lot on the security tape," said Sheriff D. "But since Freddy took the private elevator to his room, he was not seen coming or going again on any tape, anywhere."

And after that discouraging news, we shifted our focus to possible suspects, and the sheriff got busy at the whiteboard. Our list included people who'd lost money at the casino, and people who had once been arrested by Deputy Morgan. It included environmentalists who didn't like the fact that the casino was built on wetlands after a land trade deal was made with the county commissioners, and Native Americans who felt Freddy didn't have enough Native blood in him to have inherited a casino built on formerly Native lands.

"Boy," said Jimmy, "there are sure a lot of different suspect pools on that board."

"Perhaps it would be easier," said Brent, "to make a list of people who might not be a suspect."

"Flip the board over," I instructed Sheriff D. And as he did so, I said, "Let's make a list of facts we know for certain about the circumstances of the abduction."

The four men nodded.

"We know it was after dinner," said Brent.

We all nodded, and Sheriff D wrote it on the white board.

"We know it was likely after dark," said Jimmy.

Again, our heads bobbed in unison, and "after dark" was added to the board.

"I think it is likely," Kanji tentatively said, "that someone knew where to park along the far side of the building in order to escape camera surveillance."

Instant agreement!

"And he must drive a big car or van or something large enough so that Freddy could be hidden in the back or the trunk," said Brent.

That was a tough one, and we set it aside for the time being.

"What about the private elevator?" I asked, and turned to

Kanji. "Does it still take a security code to operate it?"

"That is correct, Miss Sylvia," said Kanji.

"So would it have to be somebody who works at the casino?" I asked.

"Not necessarily," said Brent. I could tell he was thinking out loud when he said, "Perhaps it was a crime of convenience. Wrong place, wrong time."

I shook my head. "No, I definitely think this was well planned—at least to a point."

"I was thinking the same thing," said Jimmy. "We don't know if Freddy was carried out, or if he was conscious when he left the building. It could be he left willingly, put in the elevator code himself, was bopped on the head after he got outside, and his key card was stolen for the abductor to return through the main door at another time and ransack his room."

Wow. The number of "what ifs" piling up was really starting to make me dizzy.

"So we don't know if it had to be someone strong enough to carry Freddy," I said. "Or two people, working together."

"It is quite obvious," said Kanji, "we have many more questions than answers."

"It is also quite obvious," said Sheriff D, plopping back down on his kitchen chair, "that I've made a huge mess of my white board, and we have very few absolutes to go on." He took another swig of coffee and stood back up. "Let me see if I can pull this a little closer together.

"We can agree that the abduction took place after dark, by someone or some two that parked around the far end of the hotel. He or she either took Freddy from his room unconscious or Freddy walked out under his own power." He looked to us for confirmation.

"Yes," I said. "The lack of blood spatter or other DNA in his suite indicates there was no fight. So—" The thought hit several of us at once. "He might have been drugged!"

Sheriff D nodded, added that idea to his board, and continued. "It's likely the perp took Freddy's key card and went back later that night, or maybe even the next day, just walking right in through the front door without a care in the world, and in broad daylight."

"We have saved the security footage for the entire week after Freddy disappeared on a DVD locked in the office vault," Kanji said. "It will remain there for further review until his return."

"But wait," I said. "When, how, and who would have had the opportunity to drug Freddy?"

"That," said the sheriff, "would depend on what kind of drug it was. It could have been placed in his food or drink, not only at dinner, but in his food inside his suite. It could have been sprayed in his face when he opened his door for the motel maid or some other visitor. It could have been injected by needle after he stepped outside under his own power."

"We've been at this for hours," I said, standing up and twisting my back this way and that. "Nautika and Cliff will be back soon. So can somebody point to any real leads we've found to follow up on?" I asked.

Silence.

"I think there is one thing we do know for sure," said Sheriff D after a few moments. "Either the perp, or perps, were extremely well-prepared, and were able to pull this off without detection, or they were very, very lucky."

"So why haven't we heard about a ransom?" asked Brent.

"It may be that he, or they, already found what they were looking for when they ransacked the suite," said the sheriff. He sighed, shifted in his chair and spoke directly to me. "I'm sorry, Syl, but if that's the case, then it's likely Freddy is already dead.

CHAPTER 10

Freddy was not dead—yet—but he was not conscious when his captor finally came and banged on the door that day, so he could not answer.

"You know the drill," the kidnapper called out, still using the falsetto. "Tie your blindfold over your eyes and turn away from the door." But there was no answer from inside. He waited a few minutes, and pounded louder, and harder, with his fist. "Did you hear me?" Still nothing.

The kidnapper considered what no answer could mean. Had Freddy escaped? He examined the door frame. Not likely. Had Freddy fashioned a weapon and was lying in wait to jump him when he opened the door? Maybe. Was he desperate enough to have found a way to take his own life? He didn't seem like the type, but who really knew?

He pounded on the door a third time. "Hey! You in there! Last chance! Are you hungry? I've got pizza!"

If Freddy had been conscious, he would have been surprised that the kidnapper was so desperate for some type of response he hadn't even bothered to use his squeaky fake voice as he pleaded for an answer. "Did you hear me, Freddy? Aren't you hungry? Are you okay? Answer me, dammit!" The kidnapper hadn't dropped his falsetto intentionally, and now as he spoke, his voice rose higher and higher in sheer panic.

The kidnapper set the pizza and a bottle of water down on the steps behind him. What should he do? Although he had threatened to shoot Freddy, he didn't actually own a gun; he hadn't wanted the state to fingerprint him for the concealed pistol license. Now he kind of wished he'd gotten one illegally. He almost chuckled at the irony.

He held the flashlight in his dominant right hand, hoping, if he had to, he could either blind Freddy with the light, or use it as a club. Or maybe both. Silently, he turned the dead bolt back and leaned his head against the door. He held his breath and listened carefully. No sound came from within.

The kidnapper suddenly made up his mind and swung the door open with all his might, which was considerable, and it slammed into the wall with a resounding *BANG!*

The LED lantern was not on. Maybe the batteries were dead. He shined his light on the mattress where Freddy lay, face down. The kidnapper's heart started slamming against his ribcage. Maybe it was Freddy who was dead and not the batteries.

Muttering an oath under his breath, the kidnapper rushed to the chair next to the mattress, unmindful that Freddy could be faking it. He pressed the button on the lantern, and discovered it still had plenty of power, illuminating the whole room. It was so bright, the kidnapper had to squint his eyes tight and turn away. Had Freddy been conscious, this was when he would have made his move. But Freddy lay deathly still.

The kidnapper grabbed Freddy's wrist and checked for a pulse. He couldn't find one, but he wasn't a nurse, and he could be doing it wrong. At least the body was warm, so he hoped that was a good sign—a sign that perhaps Freddy still had a pulse, but a very weak one.

"Damn it, Freddy, you better not be dead." He put his hand in front of Freddy's mouth and felt the slightest breath. Okay. Good. Time to calm down and do what needed to be done. Nobody was dead, and he better make sure it stayed that way.

He found Freddy's blindfold lying next to the mattress and tied it securely back over his victim's eyes. Now was not a good time to get careless. As if there was ever a good time!

He retrieved the pizza and water from the stairwell, came in, and closed the door. Taking a slice from the box, he waved it under Freddy's nose, hoping the spices in the pepperoni would have the same effect as smelling salts.

No reaction. How long since he'd been here? A day? Maybe two? He opened the bottle of water, put an arm around Freddy's shoulders and pulled him to a semi-upright position on the edge of the mattress. He held the bottle to Freddy's lips, and poured just enough to moisten them. Freddy moaned, and managed to run his tongue across his lips.

The kidnapper poured a small sip into Freddy's mouth and was rewarded by a series of gasping, rasping coughs.

"Try not to drown me," said Freddy between coughs. He blindly reached out and the kidnapper put the water bottle into his hand. Freddy managed to take a small sip.

"You sure know how to scare a gal!" said the kidnapper. His voice came out in his usual high-pitched squeak. "I thought for sure I'd have to bury you in the backyard this afternoon."

Freddy drank another small sip or two, trying to refrain from downing the entire bottle without stopping and perhaps choking on it. He'd heard somewhere as little as a half cup of water could drown a person if the water entered the lungs, and he didn't want to be the one proving that theory today, so he forced himself to take it easy and slow his sips down.

"Leave your blindfold on, but hold out your hand," said his captor. "I'll give you a slice of this pizza while it's still warm. You need to eat."

Freddy shook his head. "No. Can't eat pizza I can't see. I have allergies. I'm allergic to mushrooms."

"Then it's your lucky day," said his captor. "No mushrooms. Just pepperoni and cheese. You're not allergic to pepperoni or cheese, are you?"

Freddy was on his second slice when something wriggling in the back of his brain came to the forefront. The food had helped him come somewhat out of his fog and he suddenly remembered it was Sylvia who was allergic to mushrooms, and not him. That's why they never ordered pizza with mushrooms. It was her allergy, not his, but— He struggled to think this thought through. There was some clue tucked in here somewhere, but he wasn't quite able to wrap his mind around it. Yet.

"Just sit here and eat your pizza," said the kidnapper. "Leave your blindfold on and don't move off the mattress. Can I trust you to do this?"

Freddy nodded, but said nothing.

"Because it would be a shame to have to shoot you now, Señor, after bringing you back from the almost dead." His kidnapper had moved to the corner of the room and was fiddling with the bucket beneath the porta-potty. "Please, Señor," and to Freddy it sounded like a heartfelt plea, "don't make me shoot you because you decide to do something dumb."

Freddy wasn't dumb. He had no intention of doing anything that would make his kidnapper angry at this time. He was too weak to fight, and he knew it. The kidnapper also knew it and had decided now was a good time to take the honey bucket upstairs and empty it.

Freddy heard the door open and close, and the lock slide back into place. He lifted his blindfold and did a quick visual reconnaissance. Other than the addition of the pizza box, nothing had changed while he'd been out of it. Nothing else had been brought into the room. He drank the last of the water and barely managed to crumple up the plastic bottle in his fist. No, he wasn't in any shape to take on his captor today. Maybe tomorrow.

He heard the footfalls on the stairs and quickly put his blindfold back into place. His captor knocked on the door, then opened it slowly. "I see you have followed my directions. That is good. I will not have to shoot you today."

"I need more water," said Freddy. "A case of water. Could you do that for me... please? Could you bring me a case of water? I've behaved myself. I haven't tried to escape. I've followed your directions to the letter. Please? I need more water. I got dehydrated. I could have died."

Freddy knew there was a reason he wasn't dead yet, but he'd not figured out what it was. Nevertheless, it was clear to him his kidnapper wanted him alive.

"I suppose I could bring you more water," said his squeaky-voiced captor. "I don't see how that would hurt anything."

"Thank you. And thanks for the pizza. It was a nice change."

"No problem," said his kidnapper, standing up and heading for the door. "It was a nice change for me, too." A pause, then, "Do you need anything else—within reason?"

"Well, since you asked," said Freddy. "Would you mind sticking around a little while? Just stay and talk for a bit? I've been pretty starved for conversation, just sitting here twiddling my thumbs day after day, and night after night, although I cannot tell which is which."

"I am not here to be your friend."

"Didn't ask you to be my friend," said Freddy. "I just thought, like the pizza, maybe we could mix it up a bit. I'm just starved for the sound of another human voice." He paused. "Or maybe you could bring me a TV set?"

Freddy heard his kidnapper move the folding chair a little farther away from the mattress and he sat back down with a heavy thud. "No TV," he said. "What would you like to talk about?"

"For starters, what should I call you?" asked Freddy. "You already know my name, but I can't just say, 'Hey you, kidnapper abductor person, I need more water.'"

"You can call me by any name you wish. It will not matter to me what name you choose."

"Okay," said Freddy. "I'd considered calling you Mickey, because the voice you use sounds like a southern or Spanish Mickey Mouse. But I didn't think you'd particularly like or appreciate that name."

"You would have been correct," said the kidnapper. "That name would not have shown me the respect I deserve. It would have made me angry, and I might have shot you."

"Right," said Freddy, "and you do deserve respect. So I think I'll call you Mr. Falsetto." He stopped talking and waited for some reaction from his kidnapper. When no discernable reaction was apparent, Freddy pressed the issue. "You can use that phony high-pitched voice as long as you want, but I'd bet my life you're a man trying to sound like a woman."

"An unfortunate choice of words," said his kidnapper. "You should not be so careless as to bet your life on anything in your situation. But calling me Mister does show me you have some respect for me, so for today, I will not shoot you."

"And speaking of 'today'," said Freddy, quickly changing the subject, "it would be nice to know how long I've been here. I can't even tell if it's day or night out there, so I have no idea."

"Does it make a difference?" asked his kidnapper.

"Well… I just wondered what has taken them so long to get the money together. How much did you ask for?"

"I haven't asked for any money yet."

Freddy had not expected that answer, and he felt his stomach lurch. "Why not?"

"It's complicated," said the squeaky voice. "Now change the

subject or I'm out of here."

"You know," said Freddy, "I'm a strong believer in second chances. If you're temporarily down on your luck, I might be able to hire you at the casino or hotel. Have you ever been a waitress? Or perhaps a motel maid?"

The kidnapper said nothing.

"Or maybe those jobs are too girly for you," said Freddy. "How about a maintenance or custodial position? Or maybe a groundskeeper at the golf course, if you prefer working in the outdoors."

Still nothing.

"Well I know you must be big and strong because you somehow got me here. You got me into your car, then out of your car, and then you got me down the stairs to this basement. I'm not exactly sure how all that happened, but I'm absolutely certain I didn't get here by myself."

"I might have had help, you know."

"Did you?"

"Next subject," said the kidnapper.

"No, seriously," said Freddy. "not many men can carry another man's weight up or down stairs by themselves." He paused. "Maybe a fireman. A fireman's carry could do it, but you don't strike me as the kind of guy who's a member of the volunteer fire department."

Mr. Falsetto grunted. "It is not so hard to carry another man's weight if you carry him like a rucksack."

"Nevertheless, if you got me in here by yourself, you must be very strong," said Freddy. "Do you go to the gym or lift weights to stay in shape?"

"Next subject."

"Do you have any pets?" asked Freddy. It had not escaped his notice that the kidnapper had used the word rucksack. Not backpack, or knapsack, or kit. Freddy wondered if that might mean the guy have served in the military. Or maybe he had traveled in Europe as a youth.

"Pets are too much trouble." The kidnapper's sigh seemed to come from clear down in his toes.

Freddy interpreted the deep sigh as the kidnapper was getting bored and would soon be leaving if he couldn't hurry up and find a way to connect on some topic.

"I have to agree with you, there, Mr. Falsetto. Dogs have to be walked every day, and let in and out to go to the bathroom every few minutes, and cats... Well, I do know some cats are okay, but then there's the issue of someone having to clean the litter box."

"Yes, we have that in common," said the kidnapper, still in falsetto. "But don't think we're going to bond over our mutual dislike for cats and dogs."

"Got any hobbies, then, Mr. Falsetto? Do you like to go fishing?"

"I do enjoy fishing," said the kidnapper.

"Out on the ocean or in the river?" Freddy asked.

"I am partial to surf fishing. I appreciate being able to wade out in the shallow waves a short distance to see if I can cast far enough to catch a few perch."

"I've never done that," said Freddy. "Tell me more about it."

"What I don't like is that I recently encountered thousands of those little blue jellyfish washing in on the beach. About the size of a fifty-cent piece. They stuck to my car tires, and on my boots. It was hell and high water to get rid of them. Not even a commercial boot scraper could get them all off. And they stink to high heaven when they're dead."

"*Velella velella*," said Freddy.

"Who?"

Freddy tried again. "Those little blue jellyfish you mentioned are called 'By-the-wind sailors,' or *Velella velella.*"

"Oh," said the kidnapper. "I didn't know that."

"Lots of things get washed up on the beach," said Freddy. "One year, back in the early 1970s, we had a Green Banana Tide. A load of incoming tropical produce got washed off a freighter, and there were bananas all over the beach. As it turns out, saltwater doesn't penetrate banana peels, so everyone with a pickup truck was down there gathering them up. The local restaurants put Banana Pancakes, Banana Cream Pie, and Bananas Foster on their Specials boards, and housewives filled their freezers with banana bread."

"Well, I'll be damned," said the squeaky voice.

"And in 1990," Freddy continued, well aware he was starting to sound a lot like Encyclopedia Jimmy, "a container ship called the *Hansa Carrier* filled with brand new Nikes lost its load off the northern coast of Oregon. That's referred to as *The Great Sneaker Spill.* There were over 61,000 tennis shoes washing up from south of Seaside clear up to Vancouver Island.

"The Seaside Convention Center was one of the places where people went to see if they could match up the shoes they found so they could have a complete pair."

The kidnapper chuckled. "I would have liked tracking down those tennis shoes. It would have been a lot more fun than finding those... what did you call them?... 'By-the-wind sailors'? all over the beach. Those things are quite nasty."

"I agree," Freddy said, "but they might have brought fish with them. Did you catch any perch that day?"

"As a matter of fact, I did," said the kidnapper. "And they were mighty fine eating."

"You know," said Freddy, "if you let me go without hurting me, Mr. Falsetto, I don't have to press charges. You haven't done me any permanent harm, so it's kind of at my discretion. Maybe you could show me how to catch some of those perch sometime."

"Nice try," said the kidnapper, "but I'm looking for a lot bigger score than finding a fishing buddy." He stood up a second time. "I'll be back tomorrow—with your water."

The door closed behind him and Freddy pulled off his blindfold. He'd made several important discoveries during their brief conversation, and now he reviewed them. For one, the kidnapper never dropped his voice from falsetto, at least not when he was conscious, so it was likely he had a voice Freddy might have recognized. In other words, the guy might be someone he'd spoken to before.

For two, the guy hadn't been around the peninsula very long—he hadn't known about either the green banana tide or the tennis shoe tide.

For three, after a couple years, any local fishermen worth their salt could tell you when the *Velella velella* would appear. They were normally quite seasonal, showing up in the spring and early summer when the wind was just right, hence their more common name of By-the-wind sailors. Any *Velella velella* coming in during the late fall would be quite a bit smaller, and in much fewer numbers.

And for four, at some point, this guy had had access to a commercial boot scraper, so he might have been staying at one of the larger local hotels during the last *Velella velella* infestation. Or he might even be working at one of the big time-share resorts even now.

Not a bad day's work, thought Freddy. In his police training, he'd learned about Stockholm Syndrome, of course, and he didn't really have much sympathy for this guy, but maybe if he could pretend to make a real connection with Mr. Falsetto he could manage to survive this ordeal.

But why hadn't his kidnapper made a ransom request? Something was definitely wonky about that, and maybe Freddy could work their next conversation around to exploring that subject in detail.

Before he'd become so dehydrated, Freddy had been trying to recall the plot points of a short story he'd read in high school. "The Ransom of Red Chief" by O. Henry. In that story, the kidnapped boy drove his captors crazy with his game playing and demands and they ended up paying the father of the boy a ransom to take him off their hands.

Freddy was pretty sure he was much too old for his father, Captain Rich Morgan, to be paid to come get him, but thinking about stories like that kept his mind occupied with times which turned out well for the victims of abduction. Perhaps his story still had a chance of turning out well, too, if he'd pretend to show the guy a little kindness and compassion.

As the saying goes, thought Freddy, you can catch more flies with honey than you can with vinegar. But as he'd always joked, "so who wants flies?"

Suddenly Freddy, who'd been sitting on his mattress, slumped there with no back support, sat up a lot straighter. His mind flitted back to what had been bothering him earlier about mushrooms and allergies and pepperoni and connected it now to honey and vinegar. *Vinegar!*

In a flash of insight, Freddy realized that although the mini-tsunami burgers the kidnapper had been bringing him always came loaded with condiments, none of them had ever had pickles on them.

And the people who knew how much he hated pickles was a very short list.

CHAPTER 11

The "healthy eating habits" I'd been following while living in the islands went right out the window during our Brain Trust meeting. I'd been stress eating donuts and Lorraine's breakfast casserole all morning, trying to quell the fear inside me. So after the sheriff left, I decided to skip any thought of lunch and get back to gathering donations for the upcoming festival.

Things were going pretty well in that regard. Many people volunteered their services doing everything from grill master to garbage patrol. One business even offered several 36-packs of toilet paper! My heart was overflowing for the goodness of the community, and my list of those who said they'd help out with whatever was needed when they got here that afternoon was growing longer with each contact I initiated.

Nautika and Cliff called to say what a great band they'd heard the night before. Nautika put the call on speaker phone on their end and I did the same on mine so Brent wouldn't have to ask me to repeat everything later.

Cliff said since one band was coming all the way from Portland, they'd need a place to stay if they were going to come perform on the Fourth of July. Then Brent suggested maybe they'd be happy if we just offered them a campsite.

"Maybe more people than just the bands would like to camp out here along the bay," said Nautika. "In the future, we could offer that option, too."

I laughed like crazy when she said that. "I'm going to need a full-time assistant to track down all these little extras you guys are finding for me to take care of!"

"Sorry," said Nautika.

She giggled, and I knew she wasn't really sorry, but I instantly forgave her.

"We're just so excited," said Cliff.

Combining business with pleasure, Nautika and Cliff decided to do some heavy-duty bulk buying for the festival while over in Fort George, but promised they'd be home by dinner.

"Sounds good," Brent told them. "Just get home safely."

It warmed my heart to hear him being so protective. He was a good guy, right down to his toes, always there to give someone the shirt off his back and to help them out if they got in a pinch. As the thought crossed my mind, I felt a twinge of guilt for what I'd decided to do—taking advantage of that generous spirit of his—but for the life of me, I couldn't reel myself in.

"Excuse me, Brent," I said, as he headed back to his office cubbyhole, formerly known as the hall closet. "But would you mind doing me a small favor?"

Brent gazed at me over the top of his cheaters. "Is this going to get me into trouble with the sheriff?" he asked.

I gave my best shot at smiling coyly and narrowly resisted batting my eyes at him. "Only if he finds out."

Brent shook his head, as if to reprimand me, but his smile widened. "What can I do for you, Sylleegirl?"

I took a deep breath and plunged in, hoping at least one of my "reasons" would strike a sympathetic chord with him. "I want to go home, Brent. To my house. I need clothes. I want to water my plants. I need to see if there's anything needs attending to after six months away."

"The sheriff hasn't given you permission to leave the house, much less go home yet, Sylvia."

"I know." I sighed, and then, so help me, I did resort to batting my eyes. "But couldn't you just drop me off at home for a few hours? I could text you when I was ready to come home." I felt like a kid in junior high planning to break curfew as I crossed my fingers behind my back.

Brent looked deep into my eyes. "It's definitely against my better judgement," he said.

I brightened. "But you'll do it?"

"Yes, I'll give you a lift over there. But don't insult my intelligence by pretending you're going to text me when you're ready to come back."

"Am I that transparent?"

"On a scale of transparent to opaque, you'd definitely fit in with the cleanest window group."

I laughed. "That's a funny way to say you can see clear through me."

"But you got my point," said Brent. He stood up and stretched his back. "I needed a break anyway, and I might as well go now to pick up a few groceries in Ocean Crest."

Clearly, he was trying to rationalize giving in to my request so easily. Gotta love a guy like that. One who breaks the rules for you, then tries to reason his way out of putting the blame where it belongs. Yes, there were a lot of things to like about this guy.

Less than 15 minutes later we pulled into my driveway, and I let out a little gasp. It was obvious my lawn had been mowed, probably a week or two earlier. Oh, it definitely could use another trim, but I was actually expecting to see at least a knee-high goat pasture when we'd navigated the long driveway and pulled up to the house.

I wondered if Freddy might have been the one who mowed my lawn, just before he disappeared. A lump caught in my throat, but I held it down. Then I told Brent there was no need for him to come inside with me. He could just drop me off and go on about his business, and I'd either text him or find a way on my own to be back in Willoopah in time for dinner.

He smiled. "What you mean by that is if you can't get your motorcycle started, you'll break down and call for assistance." He clicked his tongue. "So all I am to you is your back-up plan."

As soon as he'd said it, the air dropped a few degrees inside the car. I reached over and put my hand on his forearm. "Don't think like that." Tears stung my eyes. "You're so much more than that, and you know it."

"But…" said Brent.

"But we need to take things just one day at a time." I knew I was tap dancing around the real issue, but I just couldn't get into this right now. I leaned over and gave him a quick kiss on the cheek. "Thanks for the lift, Brent."

Everything looked just as I'd left it inside my house, except the two plants I had which were not silk had been watered not too long ago and shock of all shocks, they were still alive.

I opened my fridge and was pleasantly surprised there were no "science projects" growing in there. In fact, the entire refrigerator had been purged of anything that would have turned quite nasty by now, including my complete stock of take-out food containers. In their place was a new foil-wrapped package of cream cheese and some of those fruit cups that apparently have no expiration date. The only thing down on the lower shelf was an unopened 12-pack of diet Pepsi.

In the freezer I found a neat stack of assorted TV dinners, and a bag of my favorite "Everything" bagels. Of course! Why else had the cream cheese appeared in the fridge?!

Freddy. It must have been Freddy who had prepared for my eventual return. So he hadn't given up on me. I sat down on my couch and bawled for a good 10 minutes. Then I wiped my eyes and set my jaw, determined not to give up on him either, despite what the sheriff had said. There was no way Freddy could be dead. No way. I could feel it in my heart. Freddy was alive, somewhere here on the peninsula, and it was up to me to find him.

I changed into my biker leathers and cranked up the hot metallic cranberry red Harley-Davidson Sportster 883 out in my garage. Good thing I'd kept the battery charger plugged in. Or had I? I'd been in such a rush to leave six months ago, I couldn't remember. Was that yet another thing Freddy had done for me?

"Hang on Freddy," I whispered as I pulled on my matching red helmet. "I'm on my way."

But first, I was off to see my mother in Ocean Crest. Meredith was going to be rather ticked off I hadn't called her the moment I'd returned. I thought maybe I could sidestep her anger by telling her she could take it up with the sheriff, but then I remembered she didn't know anything about Freddy's current MIA status, and it wouldn't be me who would tell her.

I'm not sure if the gods were smiling on me, or teaching me a lesson, but when I got to Mom and Lester's place there was no one home. Undaunted, I used the key hidden under one of the two or three dozen flowerpots on the porch and let myself in.

There was clear evidence Merri and Lester were away on a little trip: A stack of unopened cat food cans lined the kitchen counter on one side of the sink, and a pile of empty cans took up the other side. There was also a pouch of their special treats, which are usually kept locked in a cupboard, sitting next to the unopened food.

I was disappointed, but in a strange way, relieved. Now when she learned I'd been by, she might think I'd come here first, directly upon returning home, and she wouldn't rag too hard on me for all my slights and transgressions the past six months.

There was a note on the table for someone who must be

coming in daily to feed Harlan, Chuckie, and Bob, the cats named after Merri's deceased husbands I'd told Evie about. I smiled when I thought about Evie and her seven cats. And I was bound and determined to go back to Maui to spend more time with both Evie and the cats after Freddy was found. Heck, I might even take him with me if he played his cards right.

I pushed the thought away that Freddy might not ever be found. I just refused to let it take up residence in my head. Freddy not surviving, whatever his current situation, was not an option.

Mistaking me for their cat bowl filler, Merri's cats were clamoring at my feet for attention. It was still early afternoon, and way too soon for their dinner, so I gave each of them a good belly scratching and went on my way.

It was a beautiful day for a bike ride, and I decided to burn a little carbon out of the carburetor and roar down the highway into Tinkerstown to Goodie and Patrick's place. It felt wonderful to be riding my Harley again; the bike Freddy had given me so I could go riding with him as an equal, and not as a passenger on the back. I'd forgotten how much I enjoyed it. "We'll ride together again soon," I whispered to the Universe.

Just out of general principle, I waved when I passed the *Clamshell Motel.* I knew Jimmy couldn't see the highway as I flew by, but maybe when he heard the unmistakable rumble of the Harley, he might think of me. If he and Julio weren't otherwise occupied, of course.

My mouth watered as I rode by Buoy 10 Bakery, despite the fact I'd nearly gone into a sugar coma eating their donuts just a couple hours ago. After all, Jimmy had denied me the bear claw, and I hadn't had one of those in over six months!

When I passed the Sandy Bottom Coffee Cup, I was sorry it was too late in the day for me to stop for a cup of the good stuff and catch up with Bim and Geri on the latest peninsula gossip.

Soon, I silently promised myself, I'd do just that, but not today. The sheriff was unlikely to take kindly to the fact that I'd gone tootling down the peninsula, so it was best I kept a low profile, at least on this first trip through town.

The fact Goodie and Patrick had ended up as perfect—and platonic—roommates after Nadine's passing was one of the happy surprises which occur during life's strange twists and turns.

I pulled into their driveway, took off my helmet, and was clipping it to the side of my bike when I was almost knocked off my feet by Hans, Stella, Goodie, and Patrick, arriving in the driveway in that precise order.

"Sylvia! It's so good to see you!" exclaimed Goodie, nearly hugging the stuffing out of me.

"You're just in time for tea and a little toke," said Patrick, stretching his arms wide enough to wrap them around both of us.

The dogs, for their part in this homecoming greeting, continued to bounce up and down, barking and wriggling their tails like I was their long lost best friend. I reached down and scratched behind their ears, thinking back on how in their own way, Hans and Stella, both rescue dogs Goodie had brought home from the Humane Society, had been instrumental in the solving the rash of home burglaries last fall.

"When I heard the sound of a Harley pull into the driveway, I hoped against hope it was you," said Goodie.

"Yeah," said Patrick, "There's no mistakin' the racket those engines make, and it was harshing my mellow something fierce."

"Sorry, Patrick."

"No worries," he replied. "We don't have too many friends with Harleys, and none of them have visited in the last six months, so my mellow is hanging in there." He backed away enough to take a good look at me. "I was hoping it was you, too, but I didn't think you'd be so tanned."

I smiled. I was probably their only friend with a Harley, unless Freddy came to call, and— NO! I reeled my negative thoughts back in. Not. Going. There.

"So what's new?" I asked, as I finished extracting myself from the group hug.

"Come around back," said Goodie, leading the way around the outside of the house in a pair of her signature strappy sandals. "I can't wait for you to see my new greenhouse. I always wanted one, and Patrick had it built for me a few months ago."

"Yeah, come see," said Patrick. "It's pretty gnarly. And Goodie even lets me grow a few of my special plants in there."

"It's legal to smoke it now," Goodie said. Then she whispered, "But it's not yet completely legal to grow your own plants, so we have to keep it real quiet."

"It was also legal to smoke it when I left, Goodie." I chuckled. "And don't worry, your secret is safe with me." I gave her shoulder a gentle squeeze. "You know I haven't been gone all that long."

"It sure seems like a long time," Goodie replied softly. "We've missed you."

Goodie didn't have to add she missed Nadine most of all. Those two members of *The Veiled Rainbow*—Goodie wearing sunshine yellow, and Nadine in Greenpeace green—had been inseparable friends for decades. I gave her shoulder a sympathetic squeeze and said, "Show me that greenhouse of yours, Goodie. I bet it's a beaut."

After duly admiring Goodie's gardening prowess, Patrick pointed to something up on the roof of their garage. "That's new, too," he said with obvious pride.

"Um, yeah," I said, not knowing exactly what to make of it. "I don't know too many people with an inflated yellow rubber raft on top of their homes." I looked at Goodie; she was all smiles.

When it became uncomfortably clear neither of them was

about to give me an explanation, I had to prompt them. "Okay, fine. I'll bite. What's that raft doing up there on the roof?"

Goodie spoke first. "After I got the greenhouse, Patrick wanted a new hobby, too. So he put the raft up there where he has a better vantage point to watch for tsunamis."

"Tsunamis?"

"I wanted to do something important," said Patrick. "Something for the good of the community."

I bit my lip to keep from smiling.

"When I'm on duty, I sit up there with my spyglass and scan the ocean, looking for bigger than average waves," he continued. "Of course, I can only watch for tsunamis during the day. If it's nighttime when I go up there, I just look at all the pretty stars."

"Of course." I nodded. "That makes perfect sense."

"I've got the raft outfitted with two floatation jackets, a pair of oars, a couple bottles of wine, a corkscrew, and some snack crackers," said Patrick, using his fingers to count off his necessary survival items.

"No pot?" I couldn't keep myself from asking.

Patrick patted the special chest pocket Nadine had once sewn into his bib overalls. "I keep my toking supplies right here, close to my heart."

This time I went ahead and smiled. "So your raft is kind of like a tree house. Do you have a secret password for visitors?"

"Yeah," said Patrick. "I had one, but Goodie said not to bother, cause she won't be joining me up there, come hell or high water." He paused. "Get it? *Come hell or high water?*"

"Yes, Patrick, I get it."

"I think mostly he's just up there getting stoned and spying on the neighbors," said Goodie.

Patrick heard only the good in what Goodie had said. "I was thinking I might want to organize a Neighborhood Watch."

"A Neighborhood Watch?" I echoed.

"I told him not to bother," said Goodie. "Everyone already knows Mrs. Kravitz walks her dog at 3:05 every day, right after she watches *The Young and the Restless*, and Mr. Stephens is having a terrible time keeping the deer from eating everything in his wife Samantha's garden."

"Yeah," said Patrick, "but it's still a lot better than what's on daytime TV."

"So Mr. Stephens is having trouble with the deer and not the bears?" I asked.

"Oh, once in a while the bears still come around," said Goodie, smiling softly.

"I think they're still hoping that Nadine will return and start putting dog food out on the back porch for them again," said Patrick. "I'm sure they miss her as much as we do." He sniffled and wiped a sleeve across his nose.

"But on another subject," Patrick continued, "I've also been watching to see if anyone's going to move into the empty house on the other side of the Stephenses' house. There was a realtor who was showing it quite regularly for awhile, but about a month ago he took down the For Sale sign. I thought for sure it was sold, but I haven't seen any moving vans."

"Maybe it's in escrow," I suggested. "Have there been any inspectors or contractors over there?"

"Nah," said Patrick. "Not so far as I know, but I'm not up on the roof 24/7, either."

Goodie giggled. "He has to come down every once in a while to use the bathroom."

"Hey! It's a human function! Nothing to be ashamed of! Sometimes a man's just got to go."

It was a joy to hear Patrick and Goodie squabbling like an old married couple. I was glad Nadine had left the house to Patrick when she'd passed, on the condition he continue to let Goodie live there. She must have known how much they needed each other.

Before my thoughts got me too teary-eyed, Patrick returned us to the topic at hand. "The realtor guy is over there every couple days to check on the place."

"Oh?"

"If it's morning, he drives a little white car, and if it's getting toward nighttime, he's driving a big black sedan, but I know it's the same guy."

"Oh yeah?" I looked over toward the house, but without the advantage of the height of Patrick's yellow rubber spy station, I couldn't even see it. "How can you tell?"

"Before he goes in, he sits on the porch and has a cigarette. He even has his own little ashtray tucked under the porch steps."

"A funny cigarette, like yours?"

"No, but it smells different. Stronger."

Goodie nodded in agreement. "Sometimes even I can smell it, when I'm out in my greenhouse and the wind is right. It smells more like a cigar than a cigarette."

"And when he finishes his cigarette, he takes a fast food bag inside. Never eats out on the porch. And he's always carrying a flashlight."

"Even in the daytime?" I asked.

"Maybe the electricity bill hasn't been paid," said Patrick, shrugging.

"I'd guess the bank actually owns that house," added Goodie. "I think the mortgage went into default."

"Maybe the bank wants to avoid any more debt by keeping the electricity on," said Patrick.

"That's probably okay in the summer," I said. "But when winter comes, they're going to have to turn some heat on to keep the mold out."

I pulled my cell phone out of my pocket and peeked at the time. "Sorry, kids, I've got to get going."

"It's been great to see you," said Goodie.

"Would you like to take some brownies with you?" asked Patrick. "I made them myself."

I squinted my eyes at him. "Are they the kind with leaves and stems in them?"

"Do you have to ask?" Goodie laughed.

I passed on the brownies and headed north, straight up Sandspit Road, toward Willoopah. As it was getting late in the afternoon, I buzzed right on by my own house without stopping.

I noticed a few additional "roadside memorials" as I rode. I wondered how many of those markers indicated a biker who'd lost their life along this stretch of asphalt. A lot of people just don't see motorcycles, even though the headlights are always turned on. My reverie soon had me trying to remember the words to Robert Frost's poem "The Road Not Taken."

I was so lost inside my head inside my helmet, that when I saw a vehicle I recognized coming south, I automatically raised my hand and waved—to Sheriff Donaldson!

CHAPTER 12

In less time than it takes to say, "*Holy Criminitly, I've been caught with my hand in the proverbial cookie jar,*" Sheriff D had engaged the Interceptor's flashing lights and whipped a U-turn in the middle of Sandspit Road, coming up fast behind me with siren wailing.

I pulled the bike over, climbed off, and removed my helmet. "Were the lights and siren really necessary, Carter?" I asked as he approached on foot.

"What part of 'stay put and keep your head down' did you not understand?" And without waiting for a response, he asked, "Where all have you been?"

"Mom and Lester weren't home, so I took a ride down to Goodie and Patrick's."

The sheriff pushed the front of his Stetson up an inch or two on his forehead, put his hands on his hips, rocked back and forth on his heels, then blew out a lot of hot air when he exhaled.

"You really think it matters that much who knows I'm back on the peninsula?" I asked.

"Listen, Sylvia. I know there's a criminal, or criminals, who abducted Freddy, and that there must be some reason they haven't sent a ransom request. He—or they—may or may not know that it takes two signatures to access the casino's major accounts. He, or they, will count on Korski for one, but if Freddy is refusing, or unable for some reason to be the second signature, then all bets are off." Sheriff D continued to glare at me. "At this point, we can't be too careful. I wouldn't want anything to happen to you, too, Syl."

The sheriff's words, while meant as a reprimand, were actually rather endearing, so I knew he wasn't really that mad about me connecting with a couple of my friends.

"And to that end," Sheriff D continued, "you need to turn that bike around and take it right back to your own garage. I'll follow you and give you a lift up to Willoopah."

"Nope, nope, nope, and nope," I said. "I'm taking the bike up to Brent's. I'll keep it in his garage, if you want me to, but I can't remain stranded there without my own wheels. What if the ransom call comes in, and I have to wait for someone to come all the way out there to get me? We'd be unnecessarily wasting a whole lot of time."

Sheriff D shook his head. "That argument doesn't float. I'm quite sure in that situation you'd just commandeer the farm truck," he said, rather resignedly. He turned and looked at the Sportster, then back at me.

"I don't see you wearing a backpack," he said, "and there aren't any saddlebags on your bike. Don't you need to take a few more personal items of clothing up to Willoopah by now? Let me take you back home so you can leave the bike and gather some more clothes together."

"Here's a newsflash for you, Carter. Willoopah is quite civilized. Brent even has a washer and dryer, along with the electricity needed to run them both, so the two suitcases filled with the clothes I brought back from Hawaii are plenty. If you thought you were going to entice me to return home so I can retrieve a larger wardrobe, you've got another thought coming."

The sheriff rolled his thumb and index finger along his mustache. Then he sighed. "You've got quite the mouth on you, Sylvia." He took a breath, and continued, "Here I am, just trying to do my job and keep you safe, and you're fighting me every step of the way."

"I want my car, dammit!"

At the mention of my car, his mood lightened considerably. "You never did get those bullet holes in the trunk lid repaired, did you?"

His question took away a lot of my outrage. I shrugged. "Those flower-power decals you put over the holes kept my trunk waterproof," I said. "And they kind of grew on me."

The sheriff sighed again. "Hard to believe that was only 15 months ago."

"How time flies."

Our eyes met, and held. And I didn't have to ask what he was thinking. I was happy he was with Mercedes now, and not wasting his time trying to woo me. Things have a way of turning out exactly as they should, and this was a prime example.

"I suppose you might as well go bring your Mustang home from Portland," he said, catching me off guard. "Just promise you'll drive sparingly. Your car has the only chameleon paint job on the North Beach Peninsula, if not the whole Pacific Northwest. It's one of a kind, and stands out like a sore thumb, even without the decals on the trunk, so park it inside the farm gear shed, along with your bike. The fewer people who know where you're staying, the better. Agreed?"

I flew into his arms for a big, friendly hug. "Agreed!"

As it turned out, only Brent was available to drive me in to Portland to pick up my Mustang on Monday, and since we weren't able to leave Willoopah until after lunch, we decided to stay overnight in the big city. I thought that was probably a good thing, since I didn't want to push Brent's behind the wheel endurance level by driving the five plus hours round trip in a single day.

But when I started putting my overnight bag together, I encountered a bit of a conundrum. Should I pack a sexy nightgown, or go with my standard extra-large and extra-comfy t-shirt to sleep in? I stood a long time, staring at my suitcase, and knew I was definitely overthinking the whole "sharing a motel room" situation. But in the end, I threw in both the t-shirt and the negligee, because, well, better to have it and not need it than not have it and wish I did.

We drove down Sandspit in Brent's pickup, chatting like the old friends we were. I was excited to get my own set of wheels back, but felt very comfortable being in the passenger seat sitting next to Brent. It felt—my brain struggled for the right word—was it safe? Is that what I wanted most in my life now? To feel comfortable and safe with someone?

And niggling in the back of my mind was another pressing thought. Brent and I were, what you might call, "age appropriate." Freddy and I were not, although he swore, every time I pointed out our nearly 15-year age difference, that the years between us didn't matter one whit to him, and never would. I sighed. If I could only believe that.

"Why the big sigh?" asked Brent.

"Just thinking."

"Care to share?"

I smiled, and bought myself some time to make up an answer for him. "You've been pretty quiet too, Brent. Why don't you go first?"

"I was actually thinking about Kanji," he said.

"Kanji?" Of all the things I'd thought Brent might say, Kanji was not even on the list.

Brent nodded. "He's a great guy."

"I totally agree."

"So what happened between you two, if you don't mind my asking."

I kind of did mind him asking, but chose to answer his question anyway. "Kanji arrived here last summer under false pretenses. He was investigating possible insurance fraud, and used me to gather information about my mother and her friends."

"But after that," said Brent, "you two got close enough for him to propose to you."

"That's true," I admitted. "We became very good friends. And yes, before you ask, we were 'friends with benefits' on one occasion. I don't know if I was attracted by his accent, or the fact he's so darn well-mannered, or simply because there's a definite dearth of single, age-appropriate men on the North Beach Peninsula."

"Are you still in love with him?"

Wow. Blunt, and to the point. "I don't think I was ever 'in love' with him," I replied, surprising myself when I said the words out loud, and realized they were true. "But I shall always care deeply for him. Lorraine is a much better match for him than I would have ever been, and I'm sincerely happy for them."

Brent nodded, keeping his eyes on the road. By this time we had crossed the Columbia River, driven through Fort George, and navigated the twists and turns of Tongue Point.

At last he said, "So if any romantic feelings are behind you for Kanji, might an ex-Navy seal and semi-retired oysterman now stand a chance?"

It was a fair question; it deserved a straight answer.

"I am very fond of you, Brent," I began.

"But?" he prompted.

"But... Well, I'm just not ready to answer that right now."

"Because of Freddy?"

"Yes, of course. Freddy and I have over a year's worth of

history. We've faced a lot of challenges together. I don't know how or what he's feeling after I left him on his knees on New Year's Eve, and..." I took a breath. "And I don't know exactly how or what I'm feeling either."

"Fair enough," said Brent, nodding but not looking directly at me. "At least you didn't give me a definite 'no'."

The rest of the way to Portland was pretty quiet, as both of us were lost in our own thoughts. As we got closer to town, I pulled out my cell phone and helped him find our way by reading the navigational directions, one by one, to the long-term storage garage. The late afternoon traffic was brutal, but the facility's website said they were open till 9, so I wasn't worried about getting there before they closed.

"I'm sorry," said the man sitting at the computer behind the caged-in counter when we finally arrived. "We tried to reach you, but you didn't reply to any of our letters or phone calls."

"You're sorry about what?" I asked. "Why were you trying to reach me?"

"My wife and I bought this storage complex several months ago," he said. "We requested you to come in to renegotiate your contract with us or surrender your unit. So when you didn't respond to certified mail, we assumed you might have passed on."

"Passed on?"

"Died," supplied Brent.

"Well I'm here now, and as you can see, I'm very much alive!" I could feel the veins in my neck starting to bulge and my face was in full flush.

"I'm sorry," the man said again. "If you changed your contact information, you should have let us know."

"But I paid for six months, and my six months isn't over until the end of June."

"You didn't read the fine print," the man said.

"Screw the fine print!" My voice had gone up to that ugly octave where it cracks and screeches and sounds like I'm deranged. "I want my car, and I want it now!'

"You had until the end of June with the old owner," he continued, "but you only had 30 days from the time we took over to update your information before you forfeited the contents of your unit." His meager explanation sounded well-practiced.

A bright light suddenly dawned on me, and my question came out both shrill and very loud. "Where's my Mustang?!"

The man consulted his computer screen. "We ran a check on the Washington state license plate, S-Y-L-L-E-E, and contacted the sheriff in Tinkerstown, where the registration said you resided. The sheriff told us to notify him immediately if anyone came to claim it, but since no one did, the Mustang went up for auction and was sold about six weeks ago."

"Auction?!" I looked from the man to Brent and back again. "You sold my car?! You can't do that, it's not legal. That's *MY* car! You stole my car and sold it! I'll sue you for this!" I looked back at Brent, who was busy studying the storage contract.

"I'm afraid they are within their contractual rights," said Brent.

I took a deep breath. "Well, where is it?" I asked the man. "And how do I get it back?"

He consulted his computer screen again. "You're in luck," he said. "The party who bought it still stores it here with us. He took it out once, ran it through a car wash, had it detailed, and arranged for automatic monthly payments taken directly from his bank." He squinted at the screen, scrolling down to the next page. "But he hasn't signed in with us since then." He shrugged. "Maybe he bought it for a graduation present or something. It's that time of year again, you know."

I wanted to climb right through those window bars and

strangle this guy, which is why the window had bars on it, I suppose. "I want my car." I dangled my key chain with my car keys on it in front of him. "I want my car, and I want it *NOW!*"

"Let me make a phone call," he said. "Come back in an hour." And he abruptly slid the window shut.

I turned and looked at Brent, my vision clouded by unshed tears. "Come back in an hour? Seriously?" I swiped at my eyes. "Why do I get the distinct impression he has gone to consult with the Wizard of Oz?"

"I'm glad to see you're maintaining at least a tiny bit of your sense of humor," said Brent. "Come on, let's go get some Stumptown Brew."

"Some what?"

"Coffee."

"Good idea," I said, and I allowed him to take my hand and lead the way.

We returned to the office in exactly an hour. "I have some news," said the man behind the desk as he slid the window open.

I noted he didn't say he had "good" news, but I held my tongue and let him finish.

"The man who bought the car didn't answer his cell phone, but I left a message. Turns out he lives in your neck of the woods. I suggest you contact him directly and handle this between the two of you." He slid a computer printout under the window bars.

I glanced at the name at the top of the page and my knees started to buckle. Brent put a supporting arm around my back to steady me and I handed him the paper.

Brent read the name aloud: "Frederick Harold Morgan."

In the brief silence after that, the man behind the window said, "Now what's wrong? I did what I could. You'll have to follow up on your own. I can't give you the car; my hands are tied.

My eyes met Brent's and I sent him an unspoken prayer. He

nodded.

"Thank you," said Brent. "You're right, we'll take it from here." With his arm still around my back, he led me away from the storage office. Neither of us said a word until we were around the corner where the little man inside the window wouldn't be able to overhear.

"What are we going to do?" I asked him. "It's not like I can just call Freddy and get this straightened out."

"No," Brent agreed, "but you can do the next best thing."

"Which is?" I asked. I felt like there was something I should know, but I couldn't quite access the part of my brain that was able to function at the moment.

"It's time to call in the big guns."

My brow furrowed—one of the bad wrinkle-forming habits I've been trying to break—and then my face broke into a big, wide grin. "I just love a guy who knows the proper time and place to use an appropriate idiom."

I pulled out my phone and pressed the call button for the biggest, most powerful, and most important person of influence I knew.

Sheriff Carter Donaldson picked up on the fourth ring. "It's dinnertime, Sylvia," he said. "Mercedes and I certainly hope this call is important."

"It is," I assured him, and in the fewest words possible, I quickly filled him in.

"Okay," he said. "Here's what you do. Go get some dinner, then get some sleep. In the morning, but not too early, you can go back to the storage unit and get your car."

"But—" It was all I could choke out before my emotions got the best of me, and I handed the phone to Brent.

Brent said hello, then all I heard was his end of the conversation, which amounted to "Uh-huh. Yes. Okay. Right.

Thank you." And he hung up.

"Well?" I asked him.

"According to the sheriff, we're to go get some dinner, get some sleep, and pick up your car not too early in the morning."

I barely managed to keep from kicking him in the shins. "Did he say anything else?"

"He said to tell you not to worry, not to overthink it, and to trust him."

"But worrying, overthinking, and distrusting are my some of my greatest skills," I said.

Brent nodded and smiled. "I'm pretty sure the sheriff already knew that."

We ate at a cute little bistro not far from our hotel, and climbed into bed less than an hour later. It probably wasn't how either one of us had imagined this night would end. Brent got into his bed, and I got into mine, after discretely changing into my comfy t-shirt in the bathroom.

Brent waited until I was settled in before turning out the light. And then, under the cover of darkness, when neither one of us had to look the other in the eye, Brent began a most intimate conversation. "Syl? Can we talk for a minute?"

"Of course."

"I just want you to know," he began. "That I really respect you. And I really care about you. And I really want to come over there and hold you in my arms tonight."

He paused, and I held my breath, waiting for him to go on.

And when I was almost sure he'd fallen asleep before finishing telling me what he was thinking, he said, "And I know you and Freddy have had something very special, but I'm hoping you and I can have that same kind of connection someday."

I didn't know how to answer that, so I didn't say a word. I didn't even murmur a non-committal "uh-huh" because I was afraid he would misinterpret that as a consent that I wanted the same thing.

"Syl? Are you still awake?"

"Yes, of course."

"I just want you to know that I really want you in my life, but I don't think tonight's a good night for us to start something new. I know you well enough to know you'd think that was a betrayal, and when—or if—we get together, I want it to be a fresh start with no regrets. Now please say something."

I almost giggled when he said that, but instead, I said, "I like and respect you too, Brent. And I won't rule anything out, but I also can't make any promises."

"That's all I need to hear," he said. "Thank you, Syl. Sweet dreams."

I wouldn't have believed I'd get a wink of sleep, but I surprised myself and slept fairly well. And when I awakened, I could hear Brent's rhythmic breathing coming from the bed next to mine, and felt the same rush of comfort and safety I'd felt driving into town the afternoon before. Brent Booi was a good man. A gal would have to be nuts not to accept his advances.

And there it is, I thought. *I'm nuts.*

While I was in the shower, Brent went out and got us two steaming cups of "the good stuff," two breakfast burritos, and a copy of *The Oregonian* to read while a little time passed.

Finally, as the clock was nearing 10, he folded up his section of the newspaper and stood up. "Ready?" he asked.

I'd been "ready" to collect my car for nearly a week, but merely nodded without saying anything. It was time to go find out if Sheriff Donaldson had any pull in Portland.

The sheriff, bless his heart, had faxed a warrant directly to the Multnomah County Sheriff, which allowed his "deputized agent," meaning me, to retrieve a specific car from the specifically named storage facility needed as "evidence" in an ongoing Pacific County investigation.

"Remind me when we get home," I said to Brent, as I slid behind the wheel of my car, "that I owe Sheriff D big time for doing me this favor."

"Oh, I don't think he'll let you forget about it anytime soon," said Brent. He leaned in the window and gave me a kiss on the cheek. "Now promise me you won't drive so fast that you get a ticket on the way home."

I looked up at him with a big smile and a full heart. "I promise."

CHAPTER 13

Driving home, my heart ached every time I looked in the rearview mirror and saw Brent's pickup truck rumbling along behind me. It hadn't been that long since Freddy had followed me home from Vancouver in his Mazda RX-8 after he'd bought himself a Harley, but didn't have the proper endorsement to ride it home himself. Yes, Freddy and I had plenty of history, and I was hoping we'd have an opportunity to create a lot more.

Now I knew, with 100% certainty, that Freddy had not simply gotten over me and moved on, but was still waiting for me to come home, to him. That knowledge made me more determined than ever to shake things up when we got back on the peninsula. It was time to quit passively sitting on my hands, waiting for something to happen, and take positive action!

Somewhere along the way, I came up with a half-baked idea about using myself as bait to lure the kidnapper into tipping his hand, but it needed a little more work before I'd risk sharing it with the sheriff. Okay, maybe the idea needed a lot more work, and I was sure Sheriff D would try to shoot it down even before hearing me out, but he knew me well enough to know I wouldn't rest until we'd come at this from every possible angle.

While driving, I'd let my mind wander to how the good guys on TV always caught their prey. I could picture myself wearing a tight skirt and a low-cut blouse, and concealing a wire, or some other kind of listening device. I might even learn how to use my cell phone's recorder if I had to. I'd utilize ear buds, of course, carefully combing my hair over my ears to avoid detection, so the people in the nearby van could communicate with me. I could even strap a small revolver to the inside of my thigh—if my skirt wasn't too short!

Allowing my fantasy heroism full rein to run amuck, the trip home seemed a lot shorter and more pleasant than the trip into town. I wasn't eaten up with anxiety, as I had been on the trip in, wondering about my car, plus I didn't have to dodge Brent's relationship questions while driving alone. And besides, driving the Mustang again was just plain fun!

When we got to Fort George, we both pulled into the Safeway gas station to fill up, and I got out to stretch my legs. There was a large group of freighters out on the water, strung along from the Washington-Oregon bridge clear up to Tongue Point. Most of them were sitting low in the water, undoubtedly loaded with grain or lumber, waiting for a Columbia River Bar Pilot to come aboard and navigate the treacherous water ahead.

I thought about the rough and tumble history of Fort George, and of the hundreds, maybe even thousands, of men who were shanghaied from this port in the late 1800s. Many of them drank a whiskey that had been laced with laudanum, which rendered them unconscious, and eventually came to aboard an oceangoing vessel, never to be heard from again.

They called it shanghaied back then because it was thought many of the ships needing crew members were headed to exotic far eastern places like Hong Kong or Shanghai. But no matter what you called it, it was kidnapping, plain and simple.

"Earth to Sylvia," Brent said, coming up behind me.

I hadn't heard him approach, and I jumped when he spoke.

"I'm sorry," he said. "I didn't mean to startle you, but we need to move our vehicles."

"Of course." I turned to walk back to my car, and shot him a quick look. "What if the reason there hasn't been a ransom note is because Freddy has been shanghaied and shipped out as a crewman on one of these ocean-going vessels against his will?"

"You know that's highly unlikely, right?" he said, as he climbed back into his pickup.

I nodded, and slipped into my Mustang. But my door window was still open, and I heard Brent continue his thought, which he probably hadn't meant to say aloud. "But that would mean less competition for me."

My overly-active mystery mind suddenly wondered if Brent had something to do with Freddy's disappearance. Wouldn't *that* be a strange twist of events? He had motive, opportunity, and who knew what else might have come into play? That would make it a crime of passion, one of the most common of the motives—at least on television.

But that's ridiculous, I told myself. And by the time I got to the highest part of "the longest continuous steel cantilever through truss bridge in North America," I realized there was no way on heaven or earth Brent would be involved in any plot against Freddy. I looked back at him in my rearview mirror, lifted my hand, and wiggled my fingers at him. I knew without reservation this was a man I could trust—and maybe even love.

Then I glanced to the right, where the line of freighters was making their slow turn with the changing tide. Anchored off the bow, the bulk of the ship swung around every six hours, a delicate dance performed out on the surface of the river, just like clockwork. Changing tides. Perhaps changing hearts? But what it didn't change was my resolve.

"Hang on, Freddy," I said aloud. "I'll find you. Just hang on."

Back in Willoopah, I parked the Mustang inside the gear shed/machinery garage as I had promised Sheriff D. He was right. There was no point in advertising the fact I was home, and certainly no one needed to know I was staying here at the oyster farm for the time being.

In fact, if someone did come after me, I wouldn't want anyone in Willoopah becoming accidently involved. The last thing Brent, or Nautika, or any of them needed was to be caught in the crossfire if I became a target. That, alone, is what finally had convinced me to listen to what the sheriff had said and keep the car out of sight.

But now there was also no point in hiding from friends like Mercedes, either. Sheriff D had been at her place when I called for his help getting my car back, so I knew he was no longer keeping the secret of my return from her.

I changed into my leathers and fired up the Harley, which was a lot less recognizable while traversing the north end backroads of the peninsula, and headed her way. Mercedes lived in her motorhome in the overflow parking lot of the *Spartina Point Casino and Resort*, so while I was there, I could also check to see if the grand ballroom was available as a back-up location for the festival if the weather turned crappy on the Fourth of July. I knew I could have done that by phone, but this way I could catch up with Merc, too, so I considered it a good example of multi-tasking.

"About time you came to see me," Mercedes huffed. She stood inside her motorhome, all 5'4" of her bottled-blonde, slightly overweight self, and glared at me, sticking her lower lip out in a little pouty-face to complete the effect. "And I'm more than a little miffed that I'm the last one to know you're back."

"Magdelina Mary Johnson! You are *not* the last," I said. I'd used her full legal name just to prove a point, as I am one of about three people in the world who is close enough to her to know her true given name. "My mother doesn't even know I'm back yet."

"Only because your mother's out of town," Merc countered,

ignoring my attempt to deactivate her pout. She was dressed head to toe in sequins, and I briefly wondered, not for the first time, if Liberace was the dominant influence behind her wardrobe. She held her dog Brutus under one arm and swung the screen door open with the other. "Come on in."

I stepped inside, and closed the door behind me. Merc set Brutus, her long-haired dachshund, down on the floor and he scooted to his usual hiding place back behind the couch. Although Merc had insisted she got him "for protection," I knew he was more of a dust mop than a guard dog. But since Mercedes isn't known as the world's greatest housekeeper, I knew she needed one of those, too.

"So where's Freddy?" she asked before I'd even had a chance to sit down.

"Why do you ask? I replied.

"*AH-HA!*" she exclaimed, her blue eyes flashing as bright as her tattooed eyeliner. "Every time you answer a question with a question, I know I'm on to something big."

"So tell me what you know so far," I countered.

She continued glaring at me. "Even though that's technically not a question, you're still trying to wrangle information out of me before you tell me what's up with Freddy."

"Is it going to work?" I asked, smiling hopefully. Mercedes sighed in resignation, passed on pointing out that I just issued another question, and began to talk.

"Well, I know he's been gone from the casino well over a week, because he hasn't stopped in to say hello when I'm playing in the lounge. I figured he'd finally left to go bring you home from Hawaii, but if that were the case, Carter wouldn't have kept your return a secret from me." She put her hands on her hips. "So if he didn't come to get you, where is he?"

It was my turn to sigh. "I wish I knew."

Merc frowned. "You mean he finally got some sense into that hard head of his and decided to get over you and now he's off chasing some other skirt?"

"Mercedes!" I nearly shouted. "How could you say such a thing as that?"

"I've been right here the past six months," she replied. "I've watched him mourn for you. He's lost weight, and he's sad all the time. That man wanted to marry you, Syl, and you just hightailed it out of here and headed for the tropics without giving him—or Kanji—another thought."

"That's not true!" I declared. "There hasn't been more than a minute in any day I haven't thought about the way I left here. I couldn't think of what else to do but leave. And then I couldn't find the courage to come back to face either one of them." I shook my head. "And I wouldn't be here even yet if Nautika and Brent hadn't come to get me."

Mercedes' frown deepened. "Then…" she paused. "I'll ask you again. Where's Freddy?"

"You can ask your boyfriend about that later. It's not my place to say anything."

"So it's an ongoing investigation?" asked Merc. "That's what Carter always says when he can't tell me something."

"I guess you could call it that."

Mercedes drummed her fingernails along the arm of her chair. "I knew something bad was going on when the new sound system Freddy promised me arrived, and then abruptly left, last week. The truck drivers refused to unload their delivery before they got paid, and took all my new toys back to Portland with them. I asked Wayne Korski about it, and he said Freddy hadn't left enough signed checks with him when he went on vacation."

Our eyes met, and we just looked at each other for several minutes. "You don't have to say another word," Merc said. "I'll take it up with Carter later."

"Well, there's one thing I can do," I said. "I can fix your new equipment delivery problems."

"How?" asked Mercedes.

"I'm an authorized signature on the casino accounts." I stood to leave. "I'll go see Korski about getting your new equipment back here right away."

Mercedes also stood, and reached out to squeeze my hand. "He'll be okay, Syl. Try not to worry."

Trying not to worry was not my strong suit. Freddy'd been missing for close to two weeks now, and every day that went by filled me with added fear I'd never see him again. I left my bike parked at Mercedes' and walked across the parking lot to the east entrance of the casino. This side door opened into a hallway to the main casino, a stairwell, and two elevators.

One of the elevators was for public access to the hotel rooms, and the other was a private elevator straight up to the fifth floor where there were a few VIP rooms, most of them reserved for high rollers and/or friends of Freddy's, the CFO's office, and Freddy's personal suite.

I stood in front of the private elevator and stared at the keypad. Had Freddy changed the security code since I'd left? Or was he still willing to give me a second chance?

There was only one way to find out, and I quickly tapped in my own birthdate. When the elevator door swung open, I had my answer. Oh, Freddy... Freddy, Freddy, Freddy.

I got myself semi-composed by the time I stepped out of the elevator on the fifth floor. I rapped twice on Korski's office door and went on in. He looked up from his desk and leapt to his feet, grabbing the stapler and brandishing it out in front of him as if to defend himself.

"Wayne! It's me! It's Sylvia!"

"Uh, yes. Yes, of course." He set the stapler back down and the color started returning to his face. "It is just that when you came in, dressed like that, I did not recognize you."

"Oh." I hadn't thought about the effect of barging into his office wearing my black leather jacket and chaps at a time when he was anxiously awaiting to hear from Freddy's kidnappers.

"I'm sorry, Wayne." I gave him a weak smile and attempted to deflect the discomfort between us with humor. "I musta looked like a gangsta comin' in plannin' to rob the joint."

"Uh, yes, at first glance, you do look rather threatening." Korski attempted to chuckle. "I... um... It is such a surprise to see you, Sylvia. I was not expecting you." He fumbled to choose his words. "Did, uh... Did Freddy find you?"

Now it was me who was caught off guard. "No. I, uh..." Then I rushed in with a bunch of words to keep him from asking me anything I wasn't quite sure how to answer. "Well, Mercedes said you needed someone to co-sign a few checks while Freddy's on vacation, and I was coming over anyway to find out if it would be okay to book the grand ballroom as a back-up venue in case of inclement weather on the Fourth of July for a new Blues and Oyster Festival Cliff and Nautika are hosting and I thought I could take care of both by coming over to say hello."

At first, Korski just stared at me, trying to process what in the world I was babbling about. Finally he nodded and said, "Yes, it is true I need a few checks signed to continue business running smoothly in Freddy's absence. Thank you for coming in to take care of that necessity."

I was suddenly struck by Korski's careful diction and enunciation. I don't believe I'd ever noticed that before, but then again, I don't believe we'd actually had a private conversation before either. In some ways he sounded exactly like Kanji, carefully choosing his words and hardly ever using contractions, but as to the accent, they were miles apart.

Korski now sat down at his desk and went to work on his computer, bringing up the schedule for the ballroom. "And I do not see a problem with the reservation of the ballroom for that particular day either," he said, nodding. "No one else has it booked."

An awkward silence fell between us, and Korski blinked first. "Sylvia, you do know that Freddy is not on vacation do you not? That in fact, he is missing?"

"Oh, whew!" I let out a big breath of air I hadn't been aware I'd been holding, grateful that Korski had brought it up first. I really hadn't thought this through, and couldn't remember if Sheriff D had told me when he would tell Korski I was back in town, which apparently he hadn't done yet. But now the elephant on the table, we could address it directly.

"Yes, Wayne. Nautika and Brent came to bring me home a couple days ago, and they and the sheriff have brought me up to speed."

Korski nodded.

"And there's still been no ransom request?"

"Not a word," said Korski, changing his nod to a shake indicating no. "No calls, no notes, no emails, not any attempt at communication."

"Why do think that is?" I asked.

Korski shrugged. "He, or she, probably knows the call will be recorded. And a note might have some DNA on it, or be written on paper that can be identified in some way. As for emails, it is very difficult for the ISP to be untraceable, if you believe what you see on television."

"That's true," I replied, nodding. "But they've got to do something pretty soon. I mean, unless Freddy's..." My voice trailed off as the lump in my throat grew too large to talk around.

"Do not allow yourself to think such thoughts," Korski said. "You must remain steadfast in your belief that things will turn out for the best and Freddy will soon be returning home." He picked up the tissue box from his desk and held it out to me, but I waved his offer off.

"Thank you for your kind words," I said, taking a deep breath. "So what can we do?"

"We can carry on," said Korski. "You came here today to co-sign some checks so I can keep things running smoothly in the absence of my boss. We can at least do that much."

"Of course." I nodded. I pulled a visitor's chair over to the front edge of his desk and sat down. "I know Mercedes is anxious for her new sound equipment."

"Then let us start with that bill of lading," said Korski. He cleared off a space on his desk by removing the ashtray filled with stubby, smelly cigarette remnants and several stacks of papers. Then he handed me the original bill for the sound system upgrades, a check already made out, but with his signature only, and a pen.

"When did Freddy start allowing you to smoke in here?" I asked, motioning to the ashtray.

"It is a time of great desperation," said Korski, shrugging. "I will stop again once he returns; I am under a great deal of stress. Every time the phone rings—or someone knocks on the office door—I jump." He shook his head again. "So I'll apologize later, but for now, I need those cigarettes to calm me."

"Oh." I didn't know what more to say. Here was this big, burly guy, built like a cross between a buddha and a sumo wrestler, and he was admitting he jumped every time the phone rang. Geez, I never would have expected that.

But I had expected to see most of the checks he handed me, one at a time, and signed them without question. But then came a check made out to North Beach Peninsula Mentorships for an even $10,000. "Tell me about this one."

"Oh that," he said, waving his hand dismissively. "That is a charitable organization Freddy set up. It provides resources for businesses on the peninsula to hire, and pay, high school interns."

"You mean like a work/study program?" I asked.

"Exactly," said Korksi, nodding. "Freddy hired Tim and Jack to work here at the casino, doing everything from setting up and maintaining our computer systems to sweeping the casino floors. He realized not only how much the students learned, but that a lot of peninsula businesses could benefit from hiring and training high school apprentices."

I smiled. "That sounds just like him. But—" I frowned. "This check is dated July 1st and I'm pretty sure school's already out for the summer."

Korski smiled. "But the businesses need the help throughout the year, particularly during tourist season."

"How often does he make this donation?"

"It is a monthly donation," said Korski, with another shrug to punctuate its insignificance. "I do not know why he even bothers to insist on two signatures for this one. It is what you call a rubber stamp approval."

I hesitated, and Korski used two fingers to push the check a little closer to me across the desktop. I hesitated, but then shrugged and signed it anyway.

Then Korski handed me a half dozen checks in one group.

I took a look at them and shook my head. "Nope, nope, nope, and nope. These checks are blank. I'm not signing anything that isn't already made out to a company. Freddy might feel comfortable doing this, but I'm not."

"Why not?" asked Korski. He abruptly stood up and drew himself up to his full height, towering over me in an attempt to intimidate me. "It will save you a trip up here next month, or next week, or even tomorrow, whenever we have a large, unexpected bill. Do you really want to be running in here to sign a check every couple days just because we have a leaky toilet and the plumber needs his money?"

It bothered me that Korski wasn't entertaining any thought of Freddy being back to sign these checks himself anytime soon, but I let that thought go and answered his immediate question.

"If the plumber demands to be paid on the spot," I replied, "then we definitely need to find a different plumber."

CHAPTER 14

I retrieved my bike from in front of Mercedes motorhome, and waved good-bye when I noticed her standing in the window holding Brutus. I gave her a thumbs up, indicating she'd be getting her sound equipment soon, and hoped she understood. I wheeled out of the casino lot and motored on south into Ocean Crest.

This time Meredith's red Saturn was parked in its usual spot under her carport, and I pulled in for what I hoped wasn't going to be a long and time-consuming lecture from her.

A good offense is often the best defense, especially when my mother is concerned, so as soon as she opened the door and stepped aside to let me in, I set my hot metallic cranberry motorcycle helmet on her couch, then turned and pulled her into a tight bear hug, taking the wind out of her and me both. Afterwards, I hit her with a barrage of questions about her recent trip away.

"So where have you two been?" I asked. "What social issues were you and Lester involved in bringing awareness to this time? Human trafficking? Global warming? Racial injustice? Immigration reform? Disbanding the Electoral College? Gun violence? Ending Daylight Savings Time? World peace?

"I came by as soon as I got back, but you were nowhere to be found." It was an itsy-bitsy, teeny-weeny, whopper of a lie, but I was pretty sure Merri hadn't known how long I'd been staying out at Brent's, or even that I was at Brent's and not at my own home.

"Tariffs," said Lester. "It's a revolving problem that keeps perpetuating itself. One country charges you more on import duties, then you have to raise your prices to cover the increases on the things you need to stay in business.

"For example, when I export my iron ore to be processed overseas, then I can't afford the steel I need from you to make my car parts. Bottom line is that workers will have to be laid off to make the balance sheet balance, and then— Well, you get the idea."

"Yes, I've heard all it does is make everyone poorer. It's sad the way so many people end up losing their jobs because their bosses use layoffs to continue making a profit. In theory, it's supposed to encourage companies to keeping their manufacturing base inside the United States, but in reality, it's a nightmare.

"It's wiped out a lot of Mom and Pop farmers in the Midwest, too," said Lester. "It's going to set us up for shortages in soybeans, corn, wheat, you name it."

"And the shortages will make the price of food go up at the grocery stores because that's the way supply and demand works," I said, agreeing with him.

"A rather complicated issue," said Meredith, running her hand up through her now shorter-than-I'd-ever-seen-it bright red hair. "But I think we made some headway helping American workers, including farmers, understand how it works, and why they end up being the ones affected the most by it." She smiled at Lester. "Peaceful picketing and speaking out. It's a grassroots tradition." She reached over and gave Lester's hand a squeeze. "If you're not part of the solution, you're part of the problem." She looked up at him adoringly.

He leaned down and kissed her. "Just like the good old days."

I ignored their blatant public displays of affection, coming to the realization in the nick of time they weren't exactly public in their own home, and asked, "Just out of curiosity, are there tariffs on Wayne Korski's Russian cigarettes?"

"Yes, of course," said Lester. "And he pays a pretty penny for them, too. Belomorkanal is a cigarette of a specific design called apairosa in Russian. It's different from the usual cigarettes in that it's generally produced without a filter."

I nodded, thinking about the overflowing ashtray in Korski's office, and those remnants of strong-smelling cigarettes without butts. "And that special vodka Freddy imports just for him because it's got his name on it and a photo of the Kremlin?"

"Korski Vodka," said Lester, unable to contain a small chuckle. "It's not subject to tariffs because it's not imported."

"You mean that stuff he drinks is not authentic Russian vodka?"

"No, it's not. It's actually made in Iowa."

We had a good laugh at that, then Meredith brought the conversation back around full circle. "We missed you at the wedding, honey, but I'm glad you're home safely now." She tilted her head and studied my face. "That tan looks good on you... But have you been able to make up your mind about anything... uh... important?"

"I'm not getting married again, Mom. To anyone. Ever." And until I heard myself say it aloud, I hadn't realized it was true. "I've been married, and I've been single, and I like single a heckuva lot better."

Lester nodded. "We thought that might be the case."

"I like having my own space, and doing things my own way, and..." I felt a blush heating my face when I realized I might be oversharing in front of my mother and father, and gently reined myself in. "And when I want a guy's company, to, you know, do things together, I like to have choices about where and when and with whom."

Lester nodded. "We understand, Syl, and we'd be the last ones to judge you for that."

I smiled my thanks at him, not even a little upset they'd been talking about me and my lifestyle choices behind my back, but in gratitude that I wasn't going to get a big lecture about my so-called commitment issues.

"I'm sure you've heard Kanji and Lorraine are a couple now," said Meredith, making quick eye contact with Lester and then me. "But where do you stand with Freddy?"

"Freddy…" My voice cracked, my lips trembled, and I couldn't finish the sentence.

"Oh, honey. What's the matter?" asked Meredith.

"Do you need a glass of water?" asked Lester.

I couldn't bring myself to lie to either of them. I had planned to say I hadn't yet seen him, since I'd been home such a short time. At least the first part was quasi-true—I hadn't seen him, but the reason was breaking my heart.

"This is totally off the record. I'm serious. Not a word of what I'm going to tell you can leave this room." I looked from face to face. "Promise?"

Meredith held out her little finger, and solemnly said, "Pinky swear."

Lester just looked at me and nodded, bracing himself for whatever news I had.

Satisfied I had their assurance it would go no farther, I told them while everyone had assumed Freddy had finally come after me, he'd actually been kidnapped.

Meredith's eyes grew wide and her hand flew to cover her mouth. "Oh no! Not Freddy!"

Lester put his hand on my shoulder and squeezed. "Is that why you chose now to come home?"

"Yes." I nodded. "Sheriff D thought maybe I could help them solve Freddy's disappearance, and he sent Nautika and Brent over to Maui to retrieve me. Right now I'm on my way to the *Clamshell* to see if Jimmy can help me shed some light on a few things that just don't seem to add up about Freddy's MIA status. I'm thinking Jimmy might be able to access some information on the dark web that the sheriff's staff might have difficulty finding, if they follow the strict rules of legality."

"You and your obsession with crime TV," said Merri, shaking her head. "Someday, I'm afraid that's going to backfire on you, young lady."

Lester surprised me by taking my side. "Our daughter's got a good head on her shoulders, Merri," he said. "My money's on her for bringing Freddy safely home."

"Just be careful," said Meredith, her eyes meeting mine. "Please."

I hugged them both and pulled my helmet back on, calling out over my shoulder, "Don't worry. I'll keep the shiny side up and dirty side down." It was an old motorcyclist's classic farewell, and I wasn't sure either one of them understood it, but I couldn't think of anything else to say. "See ya later alligator" didn't seem appropriate at the moment.

The ride on down the highway was uneventful, if you don't count the shivers that ran up and down my spine and throughout my entire body when I passed the place I still refer to as the scene of "my Charlie's Angels' look-alike shoot out."

Fifteen months ago, as we closed in on Uncle Harry and his henchmen in those big, black, Lincoln Town Cars, my Mustang had been forced off the road, and then I was shot at. Fortunately, the only thing they'd hit was the trunk lid I'd ducked behind to load my Glock. That was how the bullet holes got there that Sheriff D had put flower decals over.

I shook my head as I passed that wide spot in the road, remembering it in great vivid detail. What had confused us was the fact Harold Rodman the Third had a fleet of matching vehicles, and we'd had trouble figuring out who was where driving which car at what time. It didn't really matter, but I wondered if Korski was still driving the one he'd had when he sold those houses on spec up on Pacific Bluff. Probably. Those were good, solid, reliable cars.

When I pulled into the *Clamshell Motel*, a wave of nostalgia overtook me. It was here that Sheriff D's "Brain Trust" had gathered to solve crimes in the past 15 months, and this would be the first time we were trying to put the clues together without Freddy's help.

Out of respect for the fact Julio was now living there, too, I stopped inside the motel lobby door and waited for someone to come answer my knock on their private living quarters' door rather than charging right on in.

"Sylvia!" exclaimed Julio. Bouncing up and down and clapping his hands. "You're home!"

I stepped up into the kitchen from the motel registration lobby and caught Jimmy's eye. He was in the main living area of this large room, and he took his cat Priscilla off his lap and set her on the floor before joining us on the kitchen side. He gave me a lopsided grin. "And you and the sheriff thought I couldn't keep a secret."

Julio's head snapped in Jimmy's direction. "You knew she had returned?" he asked. "And you did not tell me?"

"Sorry," said Jimmy. "It was on a strictly need-to-know basis."

I swung open the refrigerator door to retrieve one of the diet sodas he always kept in there and was struck by a sudden thought. "Jimmy?" I asked. 'It wasn't you who stocked my fridge with a new

12-pack of pop, was it?"

Jimmy shook his head. "No, of course not. I had no idea when you'd get your head out of your butt and come home."

I rolled my eyes. "That's a fine thing for a man to say to me who willingly aided and abetted my escape from the casino ballroom on New Year's Eve."

He nodded. "You're right. I'm out of line. And although you haven't asked, I'm not the one who mowed your lawn a couple weeks ago, either."

"But you know who did." It was a statement, not a question, and I looked him in the eye, daring him to lie to me.

"Yes, I know. And you know who did, too, Syl."

It was momentarily very difficult for me to speak around the lump in my throat. "Moving on," I finally said, "I was wondering if we could kick a few things around that just don't seem to add up right. I need a fresh pair of eyes to take a look at a couple of so-called facts."

"Would you mind, Miss Sylvia, if I also put my fresh eyes on your questions?" asked Julio.

"Of course not!" I answered him immediately. "The more the merrier."

We moved over to the living room, and took more comfortable seats. I noticed that Jimmy had added another "Commander's Recliner" in front of the 85" television screen, and he and Julio assumed those two spots. That left me to sit on the couch, which I happily shared with Priscilla, who barely waited until I was seated before jumping into my lap and curling up contentedly.

"So what's on your mind?" asked Jimmy as we all settled in.

"Remember the trouble we had with Uncle Harry's henchmen and their big, black cars?"

While Jimmy nodded and exaggeratedly shivered, Julio

scowled. "I'm afraid that was before my time," he said.

"Not really," I replied. "You were working in the kitchen at The Cinco Amigos Chinese Cuisine the night Jimmy picked up take-out when it started. Driving home, he was threatened by a guy waving a gun at him out the window of a big, black car, and when he got home, there was a threatening message on the motel's answering machine.

"I don't think we need to bring all of this up right now," said Jimmy, squirming in his leather seat. "Unless it's totally relevant to the fact Freddy is missing."

"Freddy is missing?" asked Julio. His eyes were about to pop out of his head when he turned to Jimmy and said, "You live a very dangerous life, Jimmy. It has a lot of drama in it."

"I concur," I said. "Jimmy's a first-class drama queen."

Neither one of them thought I was being all that funny, so I brought us back to the point of my visit, bringing Julio up to speed with just three words. "Freddy's been kidnapped."

"Kidnapped?" echoed Julio. Then his brow furrowed. "But Freddy is not a kid."

"A kidnapping does not have to include a kid," said Encyclopedia Jimmy. "To kidnap is to take someone illegally by force, whether they be an adult or child. Some synonyms for kidnap are to abduct, or to take hostage. There is no such thing as adultnapping."

"I believe you are mistaken," said Julio, with just a hint of a twinkle in his dark brown eyes. "Is that not what you do every Sunday afternoon on the couch? Are you not adultnapping?"

Jimmy looked fondly at Julio and smiled. Then he turned to me. "You see why I love this guy? He's absolutely adorbs."

I couldn't argue with him, but I didn't want us to get sidetracked. "What statistics do you have in that Jiminy Cricket head of yours pertaining to kidnapping?"

"Washington state ranks number five for missing persons," said Jimmy. "Right after California, Florida, Texas, and Arizona."

"California has lots of people to abduct," said Julio. "But in Florida, I bet a lot of those missing people are just senior citizens who wander off."

"According to NamUs," continued Jimmy, "which is the National Missing and Unidentified Persons System, more than 600,000 persons go missing in the United States every year. And somewhere between 89 to 92 percent of those missing people are eventually recovered, either alive or deceased."

"That particular bit of information is not what I'd call being altogether helpful, Jimmy." I glowered at him.

"You asked for stats, I give you stats," Jimmy declared. "Not my job to sort them out into happy stats and sad stats for you." He pushed his glasses up with his middle finger, a habit he knows annoys me, and purposefully pushed my intolerance button in the process.

There it was again—another eye roll. I swear, hanging out with Jimmy totally destroys my ability to be annoyed without showing any outward signs of it. "Love and tolerance is our code," I muttered under my breath. "Love and tolerance is our code."

"What is that you say?" asked Julio.

"Okay, Jimmy. Point taken." I sighed, choosing to ignore Julio's question and move on. "So, I'm not convinced Wayne Korski isn't somehow in on Freddy's disappearance, and I came here to ask if you could look a little more closely at him than what would show up on a standard background check."

"Why don't you trust him?" asked Julio. "Is it because he is Russian?"

Julio and Jimmy looked at each other and suddenly busted up laughing at some inside joke I was not privy to.

"Actually, that is quite refreshing," said Julio, wiping away his tears of mirth. "For once, someone around here is being profiled for wrongdoing who is not Mexican."

I looked at Julio with new eyes. He had just shown he had a wicked sense of humor, but at this particular moment, I felt more defeated than amused.

"It's funny you should bring up the Russian mob," said Jimmy.

All three of us knew I hadn't done that, but I kept quiet to see where Jim was headed.

"I didn't wait for you to ask," said Jimmy. "I already did a deep dive on the internet. It's not that I don't think Sheriff D's staff can handle it. But even though Freddy is one of their own, they've got a whole county full of problems to deal with on a daily basis. I, on the other hand, have a great deal more time to spend skulking around and sleuthing on the dark web."

I was holding my breath, wondering what he'd already found, but I didn't dare interrupt him to ask he cut straight to the chase. I had to be content to let him tell the story his way.

Jimmy continued talking about how the police departments were overworked and underpaid, particularly in a small county such as ours, and we couldn't expect them to give Freddy's case 100% of their attention, particularly since it had been several weeks, and...

And I just folded my hands on top of the pleasantly purring Priscilla and stayed perfectly still until Jimmy was ready to come to the point.

"So I found this one article from a few years back—" Jimmy got up and retrieved his laptop, then sat down next to me on the couch. "Here it is. June 7, 2017. The headline reads: Russian Gang Hacked Slot Machines and Plotted Over Stolen Sweets."

"Stolen sweets?" asked Julio. "Sweets? You mean like candy?"

"Yep," Jimmy nodded enthusiastically. "A large shipment of

chocolate confections. Ten thousand pounds of the decadent stuff, to be exact."

"Wow," said Julio. "Did it say if that was dark or milk chocolate?"

"Hold on you two! I'm salivating just as much as anybody over the thought of that much chocolate, but we've got to keep our focus here."

Jimmy ignored me for the moment, turned, and whispered to Julio, "This article doesn't say. I can isolate the incident and look deeper into it after Syl leaves."

"Can we please get back to those hacked slot machines?" I glowered at Jimmy. "That's what's really got my attention, and it should have yours right now, too."

Jimmy nodded. "This is an overview article referencing indictments against 31 people, most of whom had ties to the former Soviet Union."

"Got it." I nodded. "So far, so good."

"I'm paraphrasing here," Jimmy continued, "but it says there was a scheme to defraud casinos with a hacking device that predicted the behavior of particular models of electronic slot machines."

"Are there any of these electronic slot machines at *Spartina Point*?" asked Julio.

I nodded once again. "Pretty much everything is electronic in casinos these days." Turning to Jimmy, I asked, "Does it say which models? Or where these machines were located that were being hacked?"

Jimmy consulted the article. "Those indicted were based in New York City, Florida, New Jersey, Nevada, and Pennsylvania."

"New Jersey and Nevada make sense," said Julio. "There are lots of casinos there."

"So nothing mentioned about the west coast?" I know I

sounded a tad disappointed.

Jimmy shook his head. "Sorry, Syl. Nothing west of Nevada."

"But this is an article from 2017," said Julio. "That is already several years ago."

I brightened considerably. "You're right, Julio! And if the heat was on against the Russian mob along the east coast, wouldn't it make sense for them to continue their research in an area off the beaten path, where they could fine tune their hacking of slot machines?"

Both men readily agreed, and we excitedly toasted our discovery with raised diet sodas.

"Can you please print me a copy of that article?" I asked Jimmy. "Maybe it will motivate Sheriff Donaldson to dig a little deeper into Korski's personal background."

While Jimmy was getting me a printout, I sat and absentmindedly stroked under Miss Priss's chin and was rewarded by an even stronger purr. Perhaps, I thought, I should get my own cat. Cats were a lot smarter than dog people gave them credit for. It was Priscilla who had helped us solve our first mystery here, outside in the big cat box of the beach dunes.

At the thought of solving that first crime, unbidden tears sprang to my eyes. It was then, and right here at the *Clamshell Motel*, that I'd first met Freddy.

CHAPTER 15

Freddy heard the heavy footfalls on the stairs and knew his captor had returned. In whatever time he'd been held there, which he assumed with a large degree of confidence was in a basement somewhere on the peninsula, only one person had ever come to check on him, and he'd grown accustomed to the sound of Mr. Falsetto's approach.

He had wondered if that meant there was only one person behind his kidnapping, or if a team of two or more had decided only one of them would deal directly with their captive, thereby eliminating any chance of more than one of them ever being identified. It made a lot of sense for them to do it that way, if indeed there was a "them."

Freddy smiled ruefully when he mulled things over late at night. He considered what Syl would think of his deductions. He imagined she'd say the person who dealt with him had drawn the short straw. She'd say the kidnapper could kiss his sorry butt good-bye if Freddy ever saw his face. The others in on the kidnapping would surely eliminate him before he could be caught so he'd have no opportunity to roll over on his co-conspirators. The first one to give the others up always got better deal. Everyone knew that. That's what crime TV had taught her.

However, in reality, it was just as likely it would be Freddy who would be killed if the kidnapper's identity were exposed. In real life, the good guys don't always prevail and end up living happily ever after, but he'd never share that little true crime factoid with Sylvia. It would only frighten her.

"You got your blindfold on?" asked the high, squeaky voice after a few not-so-subtle pounds on the basement door.

"Yeah, yeah, I know the drill," Freddy called out. "And I assure you, the blindfold is firmly in place, and I'm sitting on the mattress with my back to the door."

Freddy heard the deadbolt slide in the latch and the door slowly open. This time Freddy had turned on the lantern as soon as he'd heard the car in the driveway, so the kidnapper could quickly see all was as it should be inside the room. Now Mr. Falsetto came in and set something substantial down on the floor, uttering an "uumph" as he did so.

"You stay put now," the kidnapper said. "Don't move a muscle." He came up behind Freddy and used zip ties to quickly fasten Freddy's wrists together. "I'm going to go out and empty your toilet and I don't want you getting any ideas about trying to pull some funny stuff when I come back in."

"Did you bring me a television set?" asked Freddy. "I sure have missed the news."

"Ha! You're quite the comedian today," said Mr. Falsetto. "You've missed the news, but apparently not too many people on the peninsula have missed you. Your disappearance hasn't even made the *North Beach Tribune*." The man harrumphed. "Not even on an inside page."

"Is that what you're waiting for?" asked Freddy. "Public acclaim? Notoriety? Maybe a book deal in the making? If you're waiting to read about your crime in the newspaper, I can make that happen a lot quicker if you just let me go."

Mr. Falsetto harrumphed again, but ignored Freddy's questions. "Now you just stay put," he said. He went out, taking the makeshift honey bucket with him, closed the door, and turned the deadbolt behind him.

While he was gone, Freddy thought over what he'd just learned. He knew it was standard operating procedure his disappearance was being kept quiet by the sheriff's office, but maybe the kidnapper didn't know that. Maybe the guy really was looking for publicity, recognition, and fame. Maybe that was his major motive. Maybe. But what about the money?

Well, it was certainly something else to add to the criminal profile Freddy had been building in his head for the past few days. When—not if—he was released, he wanted to have as much information as possible for Sheriff Donaldson so it would quickly lead to his abductor's capture.

The kidnapper returned and replaced the bucket beneath Freddy's commode chair. "One more trip," he said, then he took a deep breath and left the room again.

This time Freddy didn't hear the deadbolt slide back into place, and if his hands hadn't been bound, he would certainly have considered doing whatever that "something funny" thing was his kidnapper had warned him about. He filed another mental note that perhaps Mr. Falsetto was getting sloppy, and to stay on the lookout for opportunities to use the apparent sloppiness to his best advantage.

The kidnapper returned, and this time the smell of freshly baked donuts accompanied him. The smell immediately set Freddy's mouth to watering, but he was hoping he could get the man to stay and chat for awhile so he could learn as much as he could about him. His growling stomach could wait a few minutes more.

"Will you be joining me for lunch today?" asked Freddy.

"More jokes," said the kidnapper. "Why don't you just ask the maitre d' what the specials are so we can order what's fresh?" Mr. Falsetto laughed almost maniacally. "But we already know what the catch of the day is, Freddy—it's you!"

This side of the kidnapper's personality worried Freddy. Perhaps Mr. Falsetto was getting as weary of this game as Freddy was. He quickly decided to steer the conversation on to something a little less ridiculous than what they'd order when having their lunch together.

The guy sounded a bit winded, and Freddy wondered if he might be overweight or just out of shape. Climbing up and down those stairs a few times seemed to have taken a toll on him. That, too, was useful information and needed to be filed away for future consideration.

"Uh, Mr. Falsetto?"

"What is it now?" the kidnapper's impatience was clear as he spit out his words.

"Do you think you could maybe check the fuse box upstairs? I think a couple fuses might be blown. Maybe the power surge after the outage during the last storm messed with them. It gets real cold in here sometimes. The thermostat doesn't work, and I don't have a blanket."

"Next you'll be telling me you want daily maid service and for her to come and put clean 3,000 count satin sheets on your mattress every afternoon and a hand-dipped Belgium chocolate on your pillow each night."

"If the heater is too much trouble," Freddy said quickly, "then just a blanket, please."

Mr. Falsetto didn't answer.

Freddy wondered why such an angry and resentful reaction after he'd simply asked for a blanket. Did this guy have issues with the perceived rich and famous? Freddy clearly imagined the veins bulging out on his neck as he'd sounded off about the satin sheets and chocolates.

No doubt about it, the kidnapper had a bone to pick with those who lived a luxury lifestyle. Did that mean he was poor? Or maybe he'd just gone through a divorce. Or lost money in the stock market. Or… What if he'd lost a lot of money gambling at *Spartina Point*? That was a motive Freddy needed to check into as soon as he got out of here. He was certain the man carried a sizeable chip on his shoulder, and money could very well be at the root. One more thing to consider later, when he was alone in the cold and the dark.

"I'm sorry if I upset you, Mr. Falsetto," said Freddy. "I truly appreciate you brought me the little lantern so I have a bit of light now and then, but wouldn't it be easier to just replace a couple fuses so that the overhead light will work? Or do you think it's a lightbulb that's out?"

"It's not a light bulb," said Mr. Falsetto. Then he abruptly redirected the topic. "You don't need to worry about the heat or the lights. I don't think you're going to be here much longer."

"How do you know it's not a light bulb?" asked Freddy.

But as soon as the words were out of his mouth, he wished he could pull them back. If both the electric heat and lights were out, then it was probable that for some reason the electricity in the house had been turned off. Or perhaps Mr. Falsetto was afraid someone from the PUD coming by to read the meter would see there was power usage in a home where nobody lived.

And that theory instantly triggered another one. Was the water turned on in this house, or did Mr. Falsetto have to dump his toilet outside somewhere so that no water usage appeared on a meter, either?

Fortunately, the kidnapper chose to ignore Freddy's question about the lightbulb. Instead he said, "I brought you that case of water you asked for and a gallon of orange juice, too. So don't press your luck. This ain't *The Ritz* you know."

"You brought me orange juice?" Freddy's voice had a quiver of disbelief to it.

"Got to make sure you keep your blood sugar steady."

Freddy wondered if Mr. Falsetto was a diabetic, but he kept the question to himself. It was just one more thing he could add to the potential clues list. Instead, he said, "I thought the orange juice must mean it's a special occasion. Like there was something to celebrate. Like maybe you got your ransom money."

"No such luck," said Mr. Falsetto. "But in a way it *is* a special occasion." He chuckled slightly, and Freddy realized the chuckle was in a lower, rather sinister-sounding register.

But when the kidnapper offered no other details, Freddy was forced to ask. "Okay, Mr. Falsetto, I'll bite," he said. "So what's the occasion?

Freddy sat and tried to be patient while the man considered his reply. Why the hesitation in giving him an answer? What clues might the wrong answer give away? The silence dragged on, and after a few minutes, Freddy was afraid he wasn't going to get any kind of answer to his question, so he asked, "Are you going to make me guess about this so-called special occasion?"

The voice was back up in the squeaky register when the man said, "You could guess all day and not get the answer right."

"Then unless you've got all day—and I certainly wouldn't mind the company—I guess you'd just better tell me," said Freddy.

"Sure. Why not? As it turns out, Mr. Morgan, your girlfriend's back in town."

Freddy's throat was suddenly blocked by a huge lump and his chest felt tight and constricted as he fought to draw a deep breath. When he could finally swallow his emotions down, he asked, "Have you seen her?"

After a short pause, his abductor said, "No. I've never even had the pleasure of meeting her. I just heard she'd returned through the peninsula grapevine."

The reference to a peninsula grapevine was another piece of the puzzle, as was the fact the kidnapper had called Freddy "Mr." and not "Deputy" Morgan, and Freddy dutifully filed both those tidbits away. He was already pretty sure this guy had been a local for a couple years, and it was likely now he worked in a place with many employees who apparently liked to gossip around the watercooler, so to speak.

The fact the kidnapper knew who his girlfriend was didn't come as much of a surprise, as photos of the two of them together had been in the newspaper several times in the months preceding her rapid departure on New Year's Eve.

"So you don't know how she looks, or if she came back looking for me, or if she just came back on her own and doesn't even know I'm missing?"

"You ask too many questions."

"You brought her up," said Freddy. "And I'm supposed to just sit here and take that kind of news in silence?"

"You hush up now," said Mr. Falsetto, "or I'll have to crack your skull with the butt of my gun." Another chuckle, also deeper in tone, and definitely more sinister. "Cracking your skull would definitely save me a whole lot of trouble right about now."

"Look," said Freddy, "how much ransom have you asked for? This *is* about money, isn't it? Maybe we can work this out amongst ourselves. I'm a pretty reasonable man. I'm sure we can come to some agreement. Or... do you have something against me personally?"

The silence stretched out until it became more than uncomfortable, and Freddy was afraid he might be feeling the butt of that gun against his head sooner rather than later.

"Look, you don't need to go any farther than me," Freddy continued in a last-ditch effort to get some kind of handle on the situation. "My CFO can't access the accounts without both our signatures, so you need to keep me healthy. I can get you all the money you want—well, within reason, that is—"

More silence, then, "It's not personal, Mr. Morgan, I assure you. I had no intention of using your girlfriend in this, but now that she is back, there has been a slight change of plan."

"This doesn't have to involve Sylvia," Freddy begged. "She has nothing to do with this. If you've got a beef, it's with me, and there's no reason for you to hurt her."

"Hurting your girlfriend will depend on how well she knows how to play ball."

Freddy's brain flitted for a moment to the first time he'd met Sylvia, and how they'd sat together on the couch at the *Clamshell Motel* and shared popcorn while watching a Mariners' ballgame on Jimmy's television. "Play ball?" he said weakly. "What does that mean?"

"She needs to know how to follow directions without asking a lot of questions."

"You really don't know her," said Freddy with a kind of half-snort and half-choked up emotional response escaping him. "She always asks a lot of questions; she can't help herself."

"This time she better make an exception," said Mr. Falsetto. "She doesn't know it yet, but when this goes down, she is going to be the one I will use as bank courier for the money transfer."

Freddy was suddenly glad a blindfold covered his eyes and his back was to the kidnapper. Did what the man said mean he knew Sylvia could co-sign for the money, or was Freddy not totally understanding what he'd said? To his knowledge, not many people were privy to his financial set up at the casino.

"Okay," said Freddy. "I suppose Syl could do that. But first you'll have to get Wayne Korski, my CFO, to sign a check and bring it to me so I can also sign it."

A noncommittal grunt, and the kidnapper fell quiet.

"I guess you didn't know," said Mr. Falsetto, after a period of silence had elapsed.

"Know what?" Freddy asked, almost afraid of the answer.

"A lot more people than you'd imagine know about Sylvia's ability to co-sign casino checks. It's practically public knowledge. You shouldn't have had a girl try to keep a secret like that."

Freddy's first thought was that if Sylvia heard this guy insinuating that "a girl" couldn't keep secrets, he'd soon be having to protect his groin from her liberated wrath.

But Freddy's second thought made his heart sink. Who might Sylvia have told? Her mother? Mercedes? Jimmy? And then it begged the question as to who each of her confidants had told. Had Meredith told Lester? Had Mercedes told Sheriff D? Had Jimmy told Julio? And so it went, on and on and on, and his faith in Sylvia keeping his confidential business to herself was falling like dominoes inside his head.

Mr. Falsetto was right. Freddy might as well have posted his private information on Facebook. Information he had considered tightly guarded might actually be very close to public knowledge. And that indiscretion could cost both he and Sylvia their lives.

"There's some donuts in the bag over here," said the kidnapper. "I'm going to cut you loose now, but don't move until I'm outside the door. I got a bullet that still has your name on it, but I don't want to have to use it—yet."

Freddy didn't reply. For the first time during his captivity, he considered he was not going to get out of this situation alive, and it grieved him no end that it might be because Sylvia had betrayed him at some point by sharing a confidence.

He waited until the door closed, then took his blindfold off. He sat for a long time before he got up and retrieved the donut bag sitting on the floor by the door. He played every word of his conversation with the kidnapper over and over in his head. There had been a lot of pauses—as if the kidnapper had to weigh and perhaps edit what he was about to say. And there had been several chuckles, sinister but in someway optimistic and hopeful, as if Sylvia's return had been the answer to the kidnapper's prayers.

Sylvia. *Sylvia!* Freddy's heart ached. She was so close, and yet so far away. Would he ever see her again? Would he even want to?

At last, Freddy opened the bag and devoured a couple pastries, washing them down with orange juice. It was kind of like a train wreck in his mouth, what with the sweetness of glazed donuts and the acidity of the juice, but beggars couldn't be choosers, and he knew he had to keep his strength up.

He picked up a bear claw and bit into it. He thought back to the time, not so long ago, that Sylvia had thrown a bear claw at an actual bear in order to make a dash for the safety of her car.

The story made him smile, and everything he knew about her came rushing back. There was no way in hell Sylvia had betrayed his trust. She wouldn't have told anyone about being his co-signer. Freddy had let Mr. Falsetto's insinuations and lies get way too far inside his head.

The sugar rush from the pastries was undoubtedly affecting his cognition, but Freddy suddenly saw no reason to doubt Sylvia's integrity. "She'd never tell anyone," he said aloud. But inside his head he wondered what her price would be. Everyone had a price, and if her family or friends were threatened… well, who knew?

But having his faith in Sylvia tentatively reinstated didn't change the facts of the matter. The bottom line: the kidnapper knew she could sign checks. Maybe the kidnapper worked at the bank and had seen the signature cards. Maybe one of the maids had seen the paperwork on the desk in his suite. And to be honest, there really could be dozens of people who were privy to the information, and Freddy realized he hadn't been as careful as he could have been.

Kanji knew Sylvia was a back-up signer, but Freddy doubted Kanji would have offered that up in a casual conversation with Lorraine or anyone else. Wayne Korski knew, and by now had shared that information with Sheriff Donaldson, which was probably why Sylvia had suddenly returned. Yes. Sylvia was back because Sheriff D had sent for her. That made perfect sense.

But what if Sylvia now steadfastly refused to co-sign a check, or be the courier for the kidnapper? What if she arched her back and refused to negotiate with terrorists, as surely she would view his kidnappers? What if, what if, what if?

Freddy shook his head to clear it. No. Sheriff D would talk some sense into Syl, and she'd do exactly what she was told to obtain his safe release. Nevertheless, the kidnapper had found out she could sign in Freddy's stead, and Sylvia was now in as much danger as he was.

And there was nothing Freddy could do to save her.

CHAPTER 16

"So what do you think of this article, Sheriff?" I asked, after giving Sheriff D a few minutes to read over the internet piece I'd had Jimmy print off.

Although I could have just gone by the Sheriff's Office after I left the *Clamshell* the night before, I'd gone back up to Willoopah so the sheriff wouldn't be so ticked off about me running all over the peninsula on my bike.

I had Brent call him the next morning to ask him to stop by, and as luck would have it, Sheriff D had been "visiting" at Mercedes' motorhome parked behind the casino and he was able to come right over.

"What do I think?" said the sheriff. "I think you're grasping at straws, Sylvia."

Sheriff D was sitting at the dining table with Brent and me. He had an untouched cup of coffee sitting before him, cooling as he scrutinized the paper. When I asked him the question, I think he realized he was going to be here for awhile and finally took his Stetson off. He reached for the coffee and took a few sips while he organized his thoughts.

Next he clasped his hands behind his head, leaned back and stretched his back while still seated, gazing at the ceiling as if to find the right words printed up there among the spackling.

By this time, I think we were all surprised how well I was managing to wait patiently while the sheriff worked his way through his thought process. But it wasn't easy, and inside I wanted to scream at him to just say something! Anything!

"You know how statistics work?" Sheriff D had asked the question of no one in particular, and didn't bother to pause for an answer. "You can say 30% of all people are opposed to beach driving, or you can say 70% are rabidly in support of it." He chuckled. "You can make statistics—even 100% factual ones—say whatever you want just by putting a particular spin on them. So you have to be sure you're not watching any Faux News or you only get their already-biased slant on whatever issue it is that day."

"Carter, what does that have to do with—"

He held his hand up to stop me. "Statistics work about the same way as internet research," he said. "You just keep going until you find something that supports your particular point of view, then you print it off, pass it around, and call it the gospel."

"Still not quite sure I'm following you."

"This is one article, Sylvia. There are plenty of others that say the Russian mafia has cleaned up its act and are not in any way involved with anything illegal." He looked at me pointedly. "Just depends on who you ask—or what television station you're tuned in to."

I went into pout mode and put my hands on my hips. "Well, at least I'm trying to do something that could lead us straight to Freddy! At least I'm not just wringing my hands and saying 'oh woe is me' and 'fiddledee' while Rome is burning."

Brent shot me a puzzled look. "For a moment there, I thought you were going for a scene from '*Gone with the Wind*,' but then you morphed right into Nero fiddling while his city was in flames." He shook his head. "You going for the title of Queen of Mixed Metaphors?"

The sheriff wisely ignored both my implied professional insult, and Brent's valiant attempt to derail my pointed frustration, and continued to peruse the article, unconsciously stroking his mustache as he did so.

"Don't you find it high coincidental the Russian mafia was attaching things to slot machines in order to control or manipulate their payouts, and here at *Spartina Point* we have a Russian CFO, who previously worked for a high-end drug runner, whose boss has suddenly been kidnapped?"

"You're baiting me." Sheriff D looked up from the article. "You know as well as I do these events are probably just two isolated incidents. But you also know I don't believe in coincidences."

"Neither does Leroy Jethro Gibbs," said Brent. He puffed out his chest and assumed a funny pseudo-Gibbs voice as he said it.

I bit my lip and looked away to keep from laughing.

"And you think because Freddy owns a casino, the mob would come clear across the country to mess with an obscure little place like *Spartina Point*? That's quite a stretch, even for you," said Sheriff D.

"But is it really a stretch?" said Brent, now thankfully speaking in his normal voice. "I don't mean to be politically, or ethnically, or any other possible kind of incorrect, but don't you think the Russian mafia knows exactly where there are other Russians working in casinos, no matter how small?"

I nodded enthusiastically, grateful for the back-up. "Korski lived in the Russian community in Woodburn just south of Portland for many years. I'm sure he still keeps in touch with his friends there."

"And you think it got too hot for the mob back east, so they decided to chill out in the Pacific Northwest while they fine tune their hacker skills?" asked the sheriff.

"Exactly!" I exclaimed. "They already had a guy on the inside, and—"

"Whoa there!" said Sheriff D. "You can't just jump to the

conclusion that Korski, simply because he's from Russia, is an undercover operative working for the mafia."

"Oh, yes, I believe she can—and did," Brent said dryly.

"This is exactly where Kanji would bring up the notion of Occam's Razor," I mumbled pointedly. "The easiest and most obvious answer is often the correct one."

"Conspiracy theories will always abound," said Sheriff D, just as pointedly ignoring my mumbling. "That doesn't mean there's any credence to them. Next thing you'll be telling me is the Russians have been tampering with our country's voting machines."

"Haven't they?" I asked, my voice going up several notches. "You'll never convince me the 2016 election wasn't off-the-charts bogus. Anybody in their right mind could see there was massive international interference when the person with three million more votes isn't proclaimed the winner. We should have had our first female president way back then!"

"Focus," said Brent, putting a hand on my shoulder. "Focus, Sylvia. You need to rein that anger in and just focus. Focus on finding Freddy."

It seemed strange, but rather endearing for Brent to say that, and I became immediately contrite. "Sorry."

"Look, Sylvia," said the sheriff, taking a deep breath, "based on this one article, several years old, there isn't enough reason to bring Korski in for questioning of any kind. That's not how we do things here. And as much as I know you want to believe he had something to do with Freddy's disappearance, the fact that he's Russian doesn't mean he's not a valued and trusted employee."

"Carter!" The little voice in my head said I didn't have to get louder to make my point, but I raised my voice again anyway. "These slot machines are all alike. It doesn't matter how big or small the casino is, they work the same way, no matter where they are. If their hacking devices work here, they will work anywhere. It only makes sense the Russian networking system knew about Korski from the first day he got the job here. They might have even been installing their equipment for years already. And maybe Freddy discovered what was going on and they had to remove him in order to continue their research."

At this point I stopped talking simply because I'd run out of air, but neither man took the opportunity to say anything. I looked from face to face. "So you both agree with me?"

Brent reached over and put his hand on mine. "If this theory of yours is true," he said softly, "it would mean there will never be a ransom note."

"*OH!*" My hand flew to my mouth as I realized the horrible truth behind his observation. "That's not at all what I meant!"

"But it still might be the reality we have to consider," said Sheriff D.

I swallowed hard. "So maybe we're way off base," I said, backpedaling like crazy. "Maybe Freddy's disappearance has nothing to do with the Russians, or slot machines, or the casino. Maybe it was just…" I stopped and thought for a second, wanting to choose my words more carefully than during my last outburst. "… just a crime of opportunity by someone totally unconnected to the casino, or to gambling. Just a couple thugs looking for an easy mark. It's no secret Freddy is a very wealthy man."

Sheriff D nodded, then totally surprised me. "Freddy's the one who vetted Korski," he said, "and maybe that has colored my thinking. I guess it won't hurt to take another hard look at him."

"At this point," I said, "I don't know if that's good news or bad news."

Brent squeezed my hand. "Isn't that what you've been asking him to do?"

"Yes, but right now, what we might learn is starting to scare the wits right out of me."

"I'm going to come at this from a different angle than the way Freddy approached it," said Sheriff D. "Freddy was looking at Wayne Korski as a man who wanted to keep his job as a casino accountant after it was discovered his boss was the major drug runner in this county, if not in the entire Pacific Northwest. Freddy was willing to give him a chance, and in over a year, I haven't heard him question his decision to keep the guy on. Not even once."

"But maybe Korski was on best behavior, just waiting for a full year to pass," I interjected.

"That's not as far-fetched as you may think," said Brent.

"I'll get my staff to go back and look at solved and unsolved crimes in the Portland area with possible Russian ties back in the 1990s," said Sheriff D. "I'll have them do a search for criminals with Russian names who suddenly disappeared. I'll ask them to see if they can find any potential aliases or previous names Korski might have used back then." The sheriff stood to leave.

"I still think you're grasping at straws, Syl," said the sheriff, putting his hat back on. "But you've raised some interesting questions."

"And it couldn't hurt to look," said Brent as he walked the sheriff to the door. "Thanks for coming over, Sheriff." He handed him a couple cans of smoked oysters. "I heard you enjoy these. They're the ones made with jalapeños."

"Nice touch," I said, as soon as the door closed behind the sheriff.

"Oh, you saw right through that, huh?" asked Brent. He chuckled. "It's no secret that to get on the sheriff's good side you have to go straight through his stomach. I didn't have any donuts handy, so I had to grab the closest thing I had and improvise."

"Too bad we didn't have access to some of that stolen

chocolate," I said. "I could use a large quantity of that myself right about now."

"Was that milk or dark chocolate?" asked Brent.

I threw a couch pillow at him, and we got back to work on the festival planning, figuring out who'd be the go-to person responsible for each major area of concern.

It was a big job, and I was glad this year it was only a small trial run, because we'd need about six more months, rather than just a few days, to successfully pull off a large-scale event. It seemed like every time I crossed something off the list, we were adding two more things to attend to, and the phrase "treading water" kept popping into my head.

"Man, oh, man," I finally said, standing up and stretching my back this way and that. "If this festival takes off, and there's no reason it won't, it will quickly become an annual Fourth of July event leading up to a huge fireworks display."

"Yes," said Brent, nodding. "Next year we'll probably be setting off fireworks from one of the scows out on the bay. Can you imagine?"

"Next year?" I said, consulting my notes. "I don't know how to tell you this, but I believe Cliff has already arranged for that very thing to take place this year!"

Brent laughed. "More oyster-loving tourists!" he said happily.

"More tourists," I echoed, but without any hint of enthusiasm.

I remained standing and started stacking my papers a little neater. "My eyes are glazing over. I think I'm done for the day."

"Me too," Brent agreed.

I walked over to the window seat and sat down, patting the cushion next to me. "Will you join me? There's something I'd like to talk to you about."

"Uh-oh," Brent replied. "When a woman says 'we have to talk,' it's not usually good news."

"Well, we'll have to wait and see if it turns out to be good news or not," I said, giving him a small smile.

"I'm intrigued." He plopped down beside me. "So what's on your mind, Syl?"

"Whether we find Freddy anytime soon or not, I think it's about time I moved back into my own house."

"When?"

"July 5th. The day after Independence Day. Kind of symbolic, don't you think?"

"Ironic is more like it," said Brent.

"I need my independence, Brent. I need to go home."

"And here I was hoping you'd want to turn your presence here into a little more permanent arrangement."

Brent's face looked so sad, I just wanted to hug him, but I didn't want to complicate things any further. "I've come to realize I never want to get married again, and I can't imagine being in a totally exclusive relationship either."

"Oh?!" said Brent, his eyebrows shot skyward. "So you're just content to become a hermit, or a crone, or whatever you call it, and isolate there in your house alone for the rest of your life?"

I shook my head. "No. It's not like that. I never said anything about being alone." I smiled. "Just because I'm too old to have kids doesn't mean I've stopped enjoying intimacy. My house is already paid for, and it suits me just fine. It suits me, Brent, not me and anybody else. I'm not likely to be going the co-habitation route with any of my relationships.

"That doesn't mean I don't like having you around, because I'm really quite fond of you. But I won't be doing the 'till death do us part' legal bonds again. I think two people should be together because their bond is love, not law."

I watched Brent's face go through a series of emotions, waiting while he started to process what I'd just said, and I felt genuinely sorry for hurting him.

"So," I said after a decent amount of time had passed, "would you like to share what you're thinking?"

"I think..." said Brent, his voice clearly choked with feeling, "I think that now I know exactly how Kanji must have felt."

Ouch! That stung. "Hey look," I said, not letting him finish but immediately jumping in to defend myself, "I'm not some kind of a floosy or anything. I just believe there's more than enough love in the Universe to go around, and at our ages, I don't think there should be restrictions or conventions or traditions or any of that old stuff. I sincerely loved Kanji, Brent, but I loved Freddy, too. Still do. Both of them."

I reached out to take Brent's hand, and was relieved when he let me do that without pulling away. Then I was determined to remain silent and wait for him to continue.

"Naturally, I was raised to believe in marriage, and that meant it was couples only," said Brent after we'd spent some time just staring out the window at the hills beyond Elk Island. "Couples," he repeated. "Not trios, or quadruplets, or however many you want to gather together at one time."

"Open relationships don't mean weekly orgies," I countered.

He looked me in the eye. "What you're proposing is quite unconventional, from my way of thinking, and it might take some time for me to wrap my mind around it—if ever."

I nodded, but kept my tongue still.

"I don't want to be anybody's back-up boyfriend."

"I totally understand, Brent, I do. And right now we don't even know if Freddy's coming back." I couldn't bring myself to say 'alive.' "But I do know that if or when he returns, I want him in my life." I paused and took a deep breath. "But I also want you in my life, as well."

"Sylvia, Sylvia, Sylvia," Brent said my name over and over and it sounded like a long, sad sigh. "What am I going to do with you? You're like a throwback to the 60s. The summer of free love, and communal living, and all that."

"Your thinking is not all that far off, Brent. Remember who my mother is."

We both smiled.

"Leftover hippies," Brent said, chuckling. "God bless them."

"I think maybe they had it right," I said. "Open relationships mean no secrets and no sneaking around. If everybody knows there's no expectation of exclusivity, then it's not called cheating. No secrets, no shackles—just one big, happy family."

"I hear what you're saying," said Brent, "and I'm not totally opposed to it. Not exactly. It's just outside the norms of what I've always believed." He shrugged, sighed, and thoughtfully looked out over the bay. "But what does an oyster know?"

"Does that mean you can't change? Or that you refuse to?"

"That means," said Brent, "that if it's what you want, then I'm sure going to make every effort to make it be what I want too. But—"

"But?" I prompted him.

"But no threesomes, okay? I'm drawing the line right there."

"Deal!" I said. And we laughed like the weight of the world had just been lifted off our shoulders, because in a very intimate way, it had been.

Brent pulled me closer to him on the window seat and kissed me. It was soft, and tender, and at the same time demanding and delightful. "Oh Syl," he said, "you're just like a kid who wants to have her cake and eat it too."

"You say that like it's a bad thing." I giggled and snuggled in closer for another quick kiss. "But now you've mentioned it, I am getting rather hungry."

"Your wish is my command," said Brent, getting to his feet. "So unless you feel the urge to cook, I'll go pick up take-out. So what'll it be? Chicken, ribs, or pizza?"

"Shouldn't we ask the kids what they want?"

"Nautika and Cliff are having dinner over at Lorraine's," said Brent. I noticed he said Lorraine's and not Lorraine's and Kanji's, although I knew Kanji was staying over there more nights than not. "They're looking to order some new kinds of merchandise for the farm store online. Nautika texted me earlier we'd be on our own for dinner."

"Well in that case…" I smiled. "I'd like a pizza with the works, except for mushrooms—cause I'm allergic. And bait—I don't think anybody should put bait on a pizza!"

"I must be missing something," said Brent, brow furrowing.

"Anchovies," I explained. "Please don't let them go anywhere near our pizza with those stinky little fish."

"Oh! Right! Got it! No anchovies!" He put on his jacket and pulled his pickup keys from the rack inside the door. "I'll call in our order on the way and I should be back from Ocean Crest in 30 or 35 minutes, tops."

"Sounds great. I'll set the table."

Brent paused at the door and looked back at me. "This feels way too comfortable," he said.

"No," I replied, shaking my head. "It feels exactly right."

"That too," he said. And he was gone.

I'd just gotten the plates out when the land line rang. Since there wasn't anyone else to answer it, I was going to let it go to voice mail, but suddenly thought it might be Brent had forgotten something, and picked it up.

"Do you want to know what flavor of ice cream I want for dessert?" I asked, without even saying hello.

"Sylvia?" said a voice that sounded like someone who'd just finished running a marathon. He hurried on, not waiting for me to confirm who I was. "Sylvia, this is Wayne Korski." As if I wouldn't have recognized that heavy Russian accent. "There's been a ransom call."

CHAPTER 17

"Sylvia? Are you there?"

"Wayne? Yes, this is Sylvia. I'm here. Have you called Sheriff Donaldson?"

"Of course. He was my first call. Or rather, he called me. They traced the kidnapper's call, but naturally, it is to a burner phone. You are the second person to know because he asked me to have you meet him here in my office so we can arrange for the money transfer before the bank closes at 6:00, and it's almost 5 o'clock already. Time is of the essence, Sylvia. The sheriff said for you to come here right away. Can you do that?"

"I... uh..." I looked around for something to write on so I could leave Brent a note.

"Sylvia," continued Korski, "the kidnapper asked for you to personally be the one to get him the money if you ever want to see Freddy again."

Freddy! My heart leaped to my throat. "Yes. Of course. I'm on my way."

I scribbled "Explain later. Save me some pizza" across the festival events map we'd been laying out. Then I went in to get my shoes, draped my lucky Maui silk scarf around my neck, and pulled on my burgundy summer windbreaker.

I grabbed the Mustang keys from their hook by the door. I wasn't sure if I'd be back by dark, but I knew I'd be safer in a car than on my bike, and since, as the sheriff had pointed out, my bike doesn't have saddlebags, I'd need the car to carry the ransom money in—or did I? Korski had used the words "make the transfer." Did that mean I wouldn't actually be coming in contact with either a bag filled with millions or the kidnapper? Was this going to be an authorized electronic transfer and not a face-to-face encounter? One could only hope.

Some kind of sixth sense kicked in when I got to the casino parking lot, and I decided not to park in my reserved spot up close to the main door. Instead, I went on by and around the back to Mercedes' motorhome and parked the Mustang next to her rig.

Merc would be over at the casino playing dinner music for the elder crowd by now, so I didn't bother knocking on her door, as I knew she wouldn't mind if I parked there. I just had a creepy feeling the kidnapper might be watching for my car, and I didn't want to give him the satisfaction of seeing me rush to the rescue. Keeping it out of sight, as the sheriff had suggested, suddenly seemed like a good idea.

I hustled across the parking lot, weaving between lines of cars. I took a quick look at the front of the building and didn't see the sheriff's Interceptor out there yet, or maybe he'd also parked in a more discreet location.

I opened the side door, stepped inside and punched in the code for the back elevator. The door opened immediately, so either someone had recently left, or the car had been sent down empty so it would be waiting for me.

And in the scant moments it took for the elevator to arrive at the fifth floor, my Crime TV saturated brain started doubting everything that was, or appeared to be, happening.

Why had Korski called me, instead of Sheriff D calling me? How did he know where to find me? Of course, the sheriff could have told him, but why hadn't he given Korski my cell number instead of Brent's land line number? And wasn't it just too convenient Korski called mere minutes after Brent had left the house? And why was Korski so out of breath when he'd called? And finally, why hadn't the sheriff parked over at Mercedes' if he didn't want to park out front?

I dismissed that last question when I realized the sheriff might have been at the other end of the peninsula when the call had come in, and perhaps he simply wasn't here yet. Willoopah was much closer, so of course I'd arrived first.

Korski was standing in the hall next to the open door of his office when I bounded from the elevator. "You must hurry," he said. "The kidnapper said if you did not get him the money today you would never see Freddy alive again, and we are running out of time."

I entered the office, and at least one of my fears, which I hoped was totally unfounded, was confirmed when Sheriff Donaldson was not there waiting.

Korski had a savings account transfer slip made out for Ten Million dollars sitting on his desk. "Sign here," he said, handing me a pen. His name was already on the first signature line.

"Wayne! The bank in Ocean Crest doesn't have that kind of money in their vault, even on deposit days from the casino. Even if they called in an armored car to bring it in from all the other banks in their network, this is too short of a notice. Did you tell the kidnapper that?"

"I tried to," said Korski, "but he wouldn't listen. He said large sums can be transferred from one bank to another electronically, and not to worry about it. He did not want to risk us giving him marked bills from either the bank or the casino vault, but of course you are correct neither the bank nor the casino has that kind of cash all together and it would take time to physically gather it from many places."

I looked closer at the check. "Where's the bank number and the account number for the transfer?"

"You are to take my realtor's cell phone into the bank with you," said Korski. "And he will text with all the information needed. You will relay the information to the teller and she will give you a receipt for the transfer from the casino account."

My eyebrows shot upward. "From just the casino's one savings account?"

"Mr. Morgan is a very rich man. Did you not know this?"

I shook my head. "I hadn't really thought much about it," I answered honestly. "So we don't know if the kidnapper's account is offshore, in the Cayman Islands, in a bank in Switzerland, or anywhere else in the world."

"It is really none of our concern. We must get Freddy back at any price."

"But shouldn't we wait for the sheriff?" I asked.

"Why?" countered Korski. "He is just going to tell you to go ahead and sign it and I'll take you to the bank. You will go in alone and the transfer will be authorized when you get the text. There is nothing the sheriff can do. But we must hurry. The clock is ticking."

Reluctantly, I took the pen and wrote "S.L. Gardner" on the signature line. Korski swooped up the check and scowled at it. 'S.L. Gardner'?"

I shrugged. "It's my legal signature. I never changed my married name back to my birth name after I got my divorce."

"But this is not how you signed the checks here last week. Last week you wrote 'Sylvia L. Avery."

"Yes, that's right. I use a different signature for the different accounts. This is a special safeguard Freddy put in, so in case my personal identity was ever stolen, the largest casino account would still be inaccessible."

Korski nodded thoughtfully. "Come. We must go." He led the way to the back elevator, which quickly took us to the ground floor. Walking around back, he clicked the button on his key ring and the lights flashed on a big, black Lincoln Town Car.

I hesitated, thinking back to the security tape I'd seen where Korski had gotten into a little white Honda Civic. "I thought you drove a smaller, white car."

"Usually, yes, that's the car I drive to work. But when I'm out showing clients real estate, I like to drive this one. It's much more comfortable and professional."

The hair on my arms started standing up and waving in unison the moment I opened the car door. Something definitely smelled bad. I mean, really bad. Bad like the strong and pungent Russian cigarette smoke that nearly billowed from the car when I opened the door. I balked at getting inside, and abruptly, rather involuntarily, backed up.

And suddenly, Korski was right behind me. He grabbed me by the hair, yanked my head back, and held a cloth filled with what I could only assume was chloroform over my mouth and nose. According to Jimmy, chloroform's full name is trichloromethane, but they never use that on television, so I took his word for it.

I'm afraid although I tried to hold my breath, I couldn't kick Korski in the groin while he was behind me, and I wasn't able to put up much of a fight.

"You're just too smart for your own good, Missy," he hissed in my ear. "Now the bank will be closed before I can get there, and I'll have to wait to get my money until tomorrow morning."

The last thing I remember before everything went dark was the fact that I really, really hate being called Missy.

Sheriff Carter Donaldson had just finished patrolling the full length of the paved access road between the port docks in Unity and the bars, restaurants, charter fishing offices, and other shops lining the walkway. He looked longingly at the Pier 103 tuna boat turned restaurant tied up at the last dock. He licked his lips, wishing he hadn't stopped to chat quite so long with Rich Morgan and Nova Johanssen at the top of the ramp leading down to where their boats were tied up.

The best little fish and chips stop on the peninsula was now closed for the day, and as the sheriff turned to start his walk back to the Interceptor, he made up his mind to have a double-patty patty melt on rye in the upstairs bar at the *Can't Fathom It*. He wasn't going to be going "up north" to see Mercedes this evening, and just the thought of those grilled onions oozing out of the sides of his sandwich had the sheriff salivating.

And then his private cell phone rang.

Sheriff D continued walking while he took a quick look at the display. It was from Brent's land line, but it could be Sylvia calling. He considered that since the call hadn't come in through his dispatcher, it probably wasn't an emergency, so he started to let the call go to voice mail. But on second thought, maybe it was just something quick and easy and he could handle it and go on upstairs for dinner.

"This is Sheriff Donaldson."

"Hello Sheriff. It's Brent Booi. Thanks for taking my call."

"What can I do for you, Brent?"

"I went to Ocean Crest to pick up pizza, and when I got back the house was empty. Sylvia left a note that says, 'Explain later. Save me some pizza.' But Sheriff, she's been gone a couple hours, and I started wondering if you had anything to do with her leaving so abruptly," said Brent.

"She's not with me, if that's what you mean."

"Oh." Brent's hopes fell. "Well, she took her car. Could you put out an APB or a BOLO or something? As you well know, her car's pretty easy to spot."

"I can't do that," said Sheriff D. "She hasn't been missing for

24 hours—unless there's a sign of a struggle?"

"No, nothing like that," said Brent. "But Sheriff..." Brent knew he was asking for something the sheriff wasn't likely to give. "What about putting out a Silver Alert?"

The sheriff snorted into the phone. "Sylvia would kill both of us for that. We only use Silver Alerts for missing senior citizens with Alzheimer's, dementia, or other mental disabilities." He sighed. "Isn't it possible she just decided to go home and sleep in her own bed tonight?"

"She knew I was coming right back with pizza," said Brent.

"Oh, right. Syl wouldn't suddenly decide to leave with pizza on the way." Sheriff D sighed. "Look, I can have my deputies keep an eye out for her car. Even in the dark, that SYLLEE license plate sticks out. But other than that, our hands are tied until it's been 24 hours."

"I understand," said Brent. "I would call her mother to see if she's heard from her, but I don't want Meredith getting freaked out for probably nothing."

"Good thinking," said Sheriff D.

"But Sheriff..." Brent choked on the words. "I've got a real bad feeling about this."

"Thanks for calling," said Sheriff D. "You did the right thing. Now I've got another call coming in, and I need to take it."

Without waiting for an answer, the sheriff took the call from Mercedes.

"Hey, sweetheart. Nice to hear from you."

"I didn't call just to exchange pleasantries, Carter, but thanks." Mercedes then got straight to the point. "I'm worried about Sylvia. I got home from playing the early birds dinner crowd tonight and her car is parked here next to my motorhome."

"And?"

"And she's not in her car—unless she's in the trunk—and I

called her cell phone and it went straight to voice mail, so I went back over to the casino and asked Tim and Jack to locate her for me."

"You know you're not supposed to use the casino security cameras just to find your friends," Sheriff D interjected.

"That's exactly the point," said Mercedes. "We didn't find her on any of the casino cameras. Tim and Jack checked every angle of every public area, and there was no sign of Sylvia."

"Hmm…" Sheriff D pushed his Stetson back an inch on this head and scratched his scalp where the sweatband rubbed. "Maybe she's up signing some checks for Korksi," he said.

"She just did that a couple days ago," said Mercedes. "Signed off on a whole month's worth, and wasn't planning on going into the office again anytime soon."

"I see…" said Sheriff D. But before he could say anything else, his phone beeped.

"Mercedes, I hate to cut you off, but I have another call coming in. I'll get back to you later, I promise."

"Of course," said Mercedes. "But Carter— I've got a really bad feeling about this."

Sheriff Donaldson said a quick good-bye and pressed the green over red button. "Hello, this is Sheriff Donaldson. How can I help you?"

"Hello Sheriff D," said Jimmy. "It's Jimmy."

Sheriff D looked longing up at the two-story restaurant and bar and sighed. "What's on your mind, Jimmy?"

"I know you've got a bunch of tech guys—and/or gals—who get paid to do this stuff for you, but I found some information when I did a deep dive into the dark web on Wayne Korski that I think you might need sooner rather than later."

"I'm listening," said the sheriff.

"Wayne Korski, the last name ending in an 'i' was born

Ryszard Korsky, the last name ending in a 'y'," Jimmy began. "He was born in the Ukraine and there's a long rap sheet implicating him in crimes including stolen car parts and so forth until the guy just disappears from the Portland scene in the mid 1990s.

"Julio said I should call you right away in case it's important, or your own techies missed it. If you already knew, I'm very sorry to have bothered you."

"No, Jimmy, that's quite okay," said Sheriff D. "I'd rather have too much information than let things slip through the cracks of any case, but especially this one."

"You're welcome," said Jimmy. "Do you think this info will turn out to be important?"

"Sorry Jimmy, it's an ongoing investigation, and…."

"I know the drill, Sheriff D," said Jimmy. "I tried to call Sylvia to share my findings with her, but her phone went straight to voice mail. Do you happen to know where she is right now?"

"No, Jimmy, I don't, and gosh dang it all, I'm getting another phone call! Thanks for calling, Jim, I appreciate it. Gotta go!"

"Okay Sheriff, but I've got a bad feeling about this, and—" Jimmy didn't have time to finish his sentence before the call was disconnected.

"This is Sheriff Donaldson. How may I help you?"

"Hiya, Sheriff D. How ya doin'? It's Patrick O'Leary. I mean Patrick Paulsen, but not that one who ran for President, I'm the other one. Remember me?"

"Yes, of course," said the sheriff. He rolled his eyes and rocked back on his heels. "I believe you also went by the name Paranormal Patrick when you met Nadine on that online dating app. But I hope this isn't just a social call, Patrick, because I'm right in the middle of something that might be important."

"No prob, Sheriff. It's just that something wonky is going on in my neighborhood, and being the good citizen that I am, I thought I should report it right away."

"There's a dispatch number to use for those kinds of things, Patrick." The sheriff was beginning to deeply regret the number of people who had his private cell number today.

"Yeah, but then I wouldn't get to tell you firsthand why I think you need to get here right away and the dispatcher, although I'm sure she does her very best, might not be able to relate the true seriousness of the problem in order to assist you in deciding to hasten your arrival."

Sheriff D sighed and stared up at the stars just starting to appear in the evening sky. "Have you been smoking weed tonight, Patrick?"

"Uh, yeah, of course!" said Patrick. "It's legal now, you know."

"Yes, I know." Sheriff D shook his head. "Now just please get to the point and tell me what you think is going on over there, and if I think it's warranted, I'll come over there myself, but please, Patrick, try to be as concise as possible."

"Okay. So I'm part of this unofficial Neighborhood Watch over here—I'm trying to get the neighbors together to make it an authorized group—and I've been keeping an eye on this one guy—I think he's a realtor—who's been keeping an eye on a vacant house that's for sale just a couple doors down."

The sheriff's sigh was deeper this time. "Go on."

"Well, today he came to the house twice. Once this morning, and once just now, which isn't his usual routine. This morning it was in his white car, and tonight he was in his black one. As far as I know, he's never been over there twice in any one day until now."

"But it's certainly not a criminal offense," said Sheriff D, "to drive different cars, or to stop at the house twice in one day. Perhaps he is just being diligent."

"Yeah, but something didn't feel right. So after the car left, I cut through the Stephenses' backyard to take a closer look at the place. But the dogs—Hans and Stella—they kept trying to follow me, so I had to go put them in the greenhouse with Goodie. Unfortunately, when I went back, I accidentally discovered a dumpsite for human waste."

"*A WHAT?*"

"I guess maybe the toilets aren't working in the house. Or maybe the water was turned off, along with the electricity. But somebody's been dumping urine and fecal matter out along the rosebushes," Patrick explained. "And it was pretty nasty stuff I stepped in."

"Whew," said Sheriff D. "For a minute there, when you said 'human waste' I thought…"

Patrick laughed and then hiccupped. "Oh, sorry, Sheriff. No, it wasn't body parts, it was just poop."

"And while I certainly agree that it's highly unsanitary," said the sheriff, "so far, your trespassing is the only crime I've heard being committed."

"But wait, there's more!" Patrick giggled. "Gee, I sound just like those infomercials, don't I?"

"Focus, Patrick, focus."

"Yeah, so I went around to the front porch and I found the ashtray the guy uses when he's over there tucked underneath the steps. The cigarette stubs are filterless, but maybe you can get some DNA off them or something."

Sheriff D was beginning to get a headache—probably from low blood sugar—and rubbed his forehead harder, hoping he'd soon be done with this phone call and be able to go enjoy that patty melt. "Patrick, why do you think I would want this guy's DNA?"

"Goodie said to call you when I told her I thought the

cigarettes were made in Russia. We think it might be the casino CFO over there, cause he's a part-time realtor and also Russian."

"Patrick!" Sheriff D raised his voice. "Being Russian is also not a crime!"

"But I'm telling you, Sheriff, there's something wonky," said Patrick. "The guy hasn't shown the house to a client in weeks, and yet lately he's been going over there almost every day with a fast food bag or donuts or something. I think the guy is up to no good, like maybe sex trafficking."

"*SEX TRAFFICKING?*" Sheriff D's eyebrows skyrocketed. "And you think this because he's Russian?"

"Well, Goodie and I saw this documentary on the PBS channel, and—"

"*STOP*, Patrick! Just stop!"

"Okay. But Sheriff…"

"Let me guess," said Sheriff D. "You've got a bad feeling about this."

"Right on!" said Patrick. "And it's really harshing my mellow."

"Okay," said the sheriff, and he drew a deep breath. "Just stay inside your house and I'll be right there. I'm sure we can restore your mellow in a matter of minutes, and then I'll be on my way."

"I'm not inside our house right now," said Patrick.

"Then where are you?"

"I'm up on the roof in my tsunami evacuation raft."

Sheriff D did a hard eyeroll that did nothing to help his headache. "Just stay put until I get there, Patrick. Can you do that for me?"

"Sure," said Patrick. "No prob. But Sheriff?"

"Yes, Patrick?" Sheriff Donaldson said, with as much patience as he could muster.

"Goodie's out in the greenhouse around the back. She's got

the dogs and the scarf with her."

"What scarf?"

"The one I found along the side of the front porch over there when I examined the ash tray," said Patrick. "Goodie thought it looked like the one Sylvia was wearing when she stopped by here on her bike the other day."

"*JUST STAY PUT!*" Sheriff Donaldson disconnected the call and broke into fast trot along the waterfront, with only one thought racing faster than he was: *Way to bury the lead, Patrick. Way. To. Bury. The. Lead.*

CHAPTER 18

Freddy awoke with his head pounding. He wasn't lying on the mattress, he was slumped against a wall. His blindfold was on, and his hands were bound behind him. He struggled to remember what had happened.

The last thing he clearly recalled was his kidnapper had brought donuts. Freddy had assumed it had been morning, as the donuts were fresh. He hadn't eaten them all, maybe about half, because he never knew how long it would be before his captor returned with more food.

This time, though, his captor had surprised him and returned more quickly, but he hadn't brought anything to eat. Freddy recalled being instructed to put his blindfold on and turn away, as usual. But then, after his hands had been bound…

What the hell had happened? Why was he not on his mattress? Oh! He suddenly remembered the hand over his mouth and a disgustingly pungent, sweet smell. Chloroform!

But why had the kidnapper knocked him out? Had he gotten his money? Had Sylvia followed his directions and delivered it to him? Was the kidnapper preparing to let Freddy go? Maybe he'd just left the door unlocked this time so that Freddy could get out on his own once he came to. That would give the kidnapper a head start and be safer for all involved.

It wasn't easy to get to his feet with his hands bound behind him, but Freddy managed by pushing his shoulders against the wall and bracing himself as he shoved back with his legs. Then he inched carefully around the room with his hands feeling along the wall, hoping he wouldn't trip over anything new Mr. Falsetto had added "while he was out." He was glad he'd paced the room so many times before. Now when he came to the door, he sent up a silent prayer before attempting to turn the handle.

But the handle didn't turn; the deadbolt was firmly in place. Freddy's swirling thoughts cascaded downward. He sat back down with his back to the door to think. As far as he could tell, there was nothing good to be made of his current condition or circumstances. Something must have gone terribly wrong with the kidnapper's plan.

I awakened in total darkness with my hands bound behind me, by what I assumed was a zip tie. I'd never had my hands zip tied before, but this is how I imagined what an imprisoned person's wrists must feel like. At first, I thought I might be locked inside a car trunk somewhere, but I dismissed that thought when I realized I could quietly extend my legs without bumping into anything.

I lay still, listening for any clue that might help me figure out where I was. I gently turned my head and the padding beneath my cheek felt like a bare bed mattress. It smelled vaguely of men's cologne, or aftershave, or deodorant, or sweat, or all of them combined.

Although I couldn't see anything in the darkness anyway, I closed my eyes and allowed myself just a moment to imagine my head was lying on Freddy's chest. Tears streamed down my cheeks, and I sniffled.

"Who's there?!" a man's voice called out. "Is there someone there?"

If it were possible from a lying position, I would have jumped straight into the air. I knew that voice, as sure as I knew the sound of my own voice, but I was also pretty sure I might be hallucinating. "I must be dead," I whispered aloud.

"Sylvia? *SYLVIA?* Is that you?"

"Freddy?" I didn't totally trust my ears, and was afraid this was some sort of a trap, so I tried to think of something Freddy would know, but an imposter most likely would not. "What's my mother's cat's name?"

"Your mother has three cats," the voice replied. "Harlan, Chuckie, and Bob."

"*FREDDY!* It really is you!" I started crying harder, couldn't use my hands to wipe my face, and my nose began to run mercilessly.

"It's okay, Sylleegirl," said Freddy. "We're together now. We can figure this out."

I nodded, then realized how dumb that was. "Are your hands tied?"

"Yes," said Freddy. "Are yours? Are you on the mattress?"

"Yes, and yes."

"Stay put, but keep talking," said Freddy. "I'm on my way."

"Are you hurt? How long have you been here? Do you know what time it is?"

I could hear Freddy scooting on his butt across the room, punctuated by a few grunts as he tried to hurry. "You don't have to hurry," I said. "I've got a feeling I'm not going anywhere for awhile."

I could tell he was very close. He sat still for a moment, and I think we were both just breathing in the air we now shared for the first time in six months. Then he leaned toward me, and his head connected with my chest. His sigh was so big, so long, and so full of satisfaction I thought he'd expelled more air than a man's lungs could hold.

For a few moments, neither of us said anything. I think we

were just reveling in the fact we were together, and for the time being, apparently all in one piece. There was a strong sense of intimacy, there in the dark, his head against my chest, just breathing.

Then Freddy said, "No, I'm not hurt. I don't know exactly how many days I've been here, but I think about two weeks. And not only do I not know what time it is, but I also don't know what day it is, or if it's morning or night."

He paused, then asked, "Why do you want to know the time?"

"It was dinnertime when I was abducted," I answered. "And the bank doesn't open until nine in the morning. So I'm hoping I wasn't unconscious more than an hour or two."

"Because?" Freddy prompted.

"Because I sort of signed a transfer voucher for ten million dollars from the casino, and when the kidnapper tries to convince the bank teller to make an electronic transfer into whatever account he's got set up, wherever and whatever kind it is, all hell is going to break loose."

"You 'sort of' signed a ten million dollar transfer voucher?" asked Freddy.

"Something wasn't adding up," I began. "So I signed the check with 'S.L. Gardner,' my married name, trying to buy a little more time. I figured once the money had been transferred, your release was definitely in question, and I wanted to do what I could to keep you alive."

"That's actually pretty smart," said Freddy, nodding.

"Not that smart," I confessed. "I'd had thoughts about using myself as bait of some sort, but the plan was what you'd call half-baked, and I hadn't told anyone about it."

"What are you saying?" asked Freddy.

"I'm saying I didn't get abducted on purpose, this wasn't a planned event, and nobody—specifically meaning not even the sheriff—has any idea I'm missing." I paused and thought of Brent and the pizza, and Mercedes and my car. "Well, nobody knows it yet, but even then, they won't know where to start looking."

Freddy's head was still against my torso, and when he nodded, his head rubbed on my breasts. What a time for me to start feeling the feelings I was suddenly feeling! I quickly chastised myself and refocused.

"Syl?" Freddy said. "I think I've figured out who the kidnapper is."

"You mean you didn't know?"

"Not at first. I must have been drugged, because I haven't a clue how I got here. The last thing I know for sure, is I was in my suite doing paperwork, and drinking coffee, and the next thing I know for sure is I woke up here.

"But I've been building a profile of the kidnapper, and I'm pretty sure now he's working alone and that it's the guy over at the *High Tide Burger Bar*."

"*WHAT?!*" I wanted to bust up laughing, but Freddy was totally serious.

"You know the one I'm talking about? Built like a brick outhouse. Stocky, thick neck, lots of tattoos. He would have been strong enough to carry me in here, for sure, even without help."

"But what makes you suspect him, other than he's a guy with brute strength?"

"I've been subsisting mainly on mini-tsunami burgers, and there are never any pickles on them. The guy at the *High Tide* knows I hate pickles and he never even asks what I want on my burgers anymore, he just knows."

"Oh, Freddy…" I didn't want to burst his investigation bubble, but he had to know, and I figured sooner was better than later. "It's not the burger guy, Freddy. It's Wayne Korski."

"Korski?" Freddy sounded genuinely surprised, then

dejected. "Oh. Well. Are you sure?"

"Yes, Freddy, I'm very sure. And I'm sorry. I know you vetted him yourself, but I'm 100% certain. One hundred percent."

"I truly thought the guy was clean," said Freddy. "I must have missed something when I took over the casino. I thought he was just an accountant working for the wrong guy at the wrong time and I didn't want him to have to pay with his job if he was clean and it wasn't merited."

"I know. And we're still not sure of his motivation." I paused, then continued. "Didn't you recognize his voice?"

"The guy who comes in uses a high, squeaky voice, like he's imitating a woman. I started calling him Mr. Falsetto."

"Oh, right. Cause if you had heard his voice, you certainly would have known who it was, despite the fact he's lived in the U.S. for the past 30 years or more."

"I'm surprised the cigarette smell on his clothing didn't tip me off," said Freddy.

"Don't give it another thought. You were focused on survival, and by not seeing him, or hearing him, you survived. I'd say that was a win."

"Some investigator I am, huh?"

"It's different when it's personal," I tried to console him. "A lot of your objectivity goes right out the window. But let's get back focusing on Korski. Did you find any evidence of him working with the Russian mafia to install hacking devices on *Spartina Point's* slot machines?"

"Oh lord," said Freddy. "If he was doing that, then I really screwed up big time."

"So you didn't suspect him of this fraud, or confront him, or anything like that?"

"I'm confused," said Freddy. "Was he hacking the machines or not?"

"We're not sure. It's just one theory. Sheriff D, Jimmy, Kanji, Brent and I were looking for possible motives, and…" I trailed off. "Well, as of this afternoon, motive is still unclear."

Freddy sighed. "So the Brain Trust replaced me with Brent."

I ignored him and stayed on topic. "I think Korski may have been skimming for some time.'"

"What makes you say that?"

"Tell me about the North Beach Peninsula Mentorship Program."

"Oh, that. Korski set that up as a 501c3 nonprofit," said Freddy. "It's just one way the casino can give back to the community and get a tax break at the same time. He said he got the idea after I hired Tim and Jack to work for me in January."

"Korski told me you'd set it up."

After a short pause, Freddy said, "Oh shit. So you think he's been skimming $10,000 from me every month for the past six months?"

"That's my current theory. My best guess on the motivation behind your kidnapping is he got tired of nickel and diming you and was going for the big payday."

"Ten thousand a month isn't exactly nickel and diming." Freddy sighed. "I'm so sorry about all this, Sylvia. I trusted when I should have been more suspicious. And now you're right in the middle of this too."

"But two heads are better than one," I said, trying to cheer him. "Surely we can put our heads together and come up with some kind of plan before he comes back."

"What makes you think he's ever coming back?" asked Freddy.

It was a sobering thought, and one I didn't want to think about right now. "Freddy?" I said, "There was no sign of a struggle in your suite, no blood or DNA or anything."

"The best I can remember is I was doing some paperwork, nothing out of the ordinary. And then I wasn't."

"So you don't know your entire suite's been trashed?"

"Trashed? What do you mean trashed?"

"Oh boy, I hate to tell you this, but your suite has been wrecked like a bulldozer went through it two or three times. All the drawers are emptied on the floor, the couch cushions are slashed, the papers on the back of your wall picture frames are ripped open, the bed mattress and pillows too."

"What do you think Korski was looking for?" asked Freddy.

"I was hoping maybe you could fill that part in," I said. "There was no sign of forced entry, so we assumed he'd used your own keycard so the break-in wouldn't be noticeable to anyone passing by the room."

"Hhmm," said Freddy, thinking hard. "Suite 552 belonged to my Uncle Harry before me. So it's possible Korski was looking for something that might have been left behind."

"The Brain Trust went down this road too," I said. "Stocks and bonds, cash, blackmail photos, keys to safety deposit boxes. We got nothing concrete."

"But why wouldn't Uncle Harry have taken something he thought valuable with him?" asked Freddy.

"Because he thought he was coming back," we said, nearly in unison.

"So if it makes you feel any better about your trust in judgement about Korski's character, I think now that we've talked, maybe he just wanted you out of the way for a day or two so he could look for—whatever—and then return you to your room, and he'd keep working there and never be suspected until he resigned or something in a few months, or years."

"Which would be why I've been here so long and he hadn't asked for a ransom."

"And waiting for me to return and then kidnapping me probably wasn't a part of his original plan either. Just bad timing on my part."

"Or good timing," said Freddy. "I think he was getting desperate to come away with something for all his efforts, and your signature makes it still possible he would not be suspected, and we could go along as if there'd been an outsider orchestrating all this."

We fell quiet for a few minutes, then Freddy said, "I guess we're just going to have to wait to ask Korski those questions after he's arrested."

"I like the way you think," I replied.

We sat in silence for awhile, just thinking our own thoughts until Freddy cleared his throat. "Sylvia?" he began. "I'd like to talk about our future, if we still have one."

My fight or flight response kicked in, and I immediately saw both the irony and the humor in my current situation. I swallowed hard. "Of course we still have a future."

"I wasn't talking about dying," said Freddy. "I was asking whether or not you thought we could still have a relationship. After you ran off on New Year's Eve—"

"I'm very sorry I did that," I said, interrupting him. "It wasn't fair to you, or to Kanji."

"Have you spoken to Kanji?" asked Freddy.

"Of course," I replied. "I told you he was there for Sheriff D's Brain Trust gathering."

"But have you talked to him about—you know—about where you two stand?"

"Water under the bridge," I said. "I know he's with Lorraine now, and I'm very happy for him—for them both."

"I don't know what got into me." Freddy sighed. "I kind of thought I knew you didn't want to ever get married again, even though we hadn't exactly talked about it, but when I found out from Mercedes that Kanji had a ring, and was planning to propose on New Year's Eve, I panicked and went out and bought one too."

"So that's how that all transpired." I figured I'd deal with Mercedes later. How dare she know what Kanji's plans were and tell Freddy but not me? What kind of a "friend" did something like that? But just as quickly as I got mad, I realized she had probably been in a tough spot too, with her bosses both vying for me to commit at the same place and time.

"I'm sorry Syl. I shouldn't have backed you into such a public corner like that."

"It certainly complicated things, Freddy, but your explanation makes total sense now."

"So are we good?"

"Good?" I asked. "Maybe. Maybe not. It's been six months, and lots may have changed."

"My feelings for you have not changed," said Freddy. "I love you just as much now as I did in December—and November, and October, and September, and August, and— Oh Syl, I've loved you since practically the first day we met."

My heart swelled when he said that, my eyes teared up, and I was actually grateful we were talking quietly in the dark.

"I love you too, Freddy," I began slowly. "But I know how much you love kids, and I thought by now you might be dating either Tim's or Jack's mother. Or maybe you'd found someone younger, closer to your own age, to have kids with."

"Seriously?" asked Freddy. "Working with youth is important to me, for sure, but I'm just as happy I don't have any children of my own to deal with." He sighed. "And you're still the only one who has ever worried about our age difference."

I decided I'd better jump in with both feet, and avoid any perceived 'sins of omission' to have to answer to later. "Since I've

"He wasn't thrilled, but he took it better than I thought he would."

"Well, I'm not exactly thrilled either," Freddy began after a short pause. "But if we come out of this alive—"

"When," I interjected. "When we come out of this alive."

"Okay, fine. *When* we come out of this alive, I want you in my life, in any way you're comfortable."

"I'm not comfortable with secrets and lies and sneaking around, so I needed to be upfront about this, Freddy. With both of you.

"And I appreciate that," said Freddy. "So if you want to spend time with Brent out in Willoopah, go right ahead. Just plan on spending at least the same amount of time with me."

"Absolutely," I said, "and the same amount of time alone, too." I used my chin to turn his head enough so I could bend down and kiss him on the lips to seal the deal. It wasn't exactly how I'd imagined our reunion kiss, but at the same time, it was perfect.

"Glad that's settled," I said, coming up for air. "So now we've figured out the who, Korski, and the why, money."

"And also the what, kidnapping, and the how, by drugging me," said Freddy. He paused. "There must have been something in my coffee that night. Maybe in my creamer. I don't know. Did the sheriff check for drugs in the creamer?"

"I don't think so. It's something we'll have to check into once we get out of here," I said.

"So how about the where," said Freddy. "Do you have any idea where we are, Syl?"

"When I opened his car door to go to the bank with the bogus voucher, I was struck by the pungent smell of his Russian cigarettes," I said.

"Yeah, they're pretty strong," said Freddy. "When I first met him, I thought he was a pot smoker."

"Exactly what I thought," I said. "So yes, I do think I know where we are, and if the self-appointed Neighborhood Watch and Tsunami Warning System is on duty, the cavalry will arrive in the nick of time to rescue us."

"I'm not sure what any of what you said really means, but what's this 'in the nick of time' all about? You mean sometime before we both starve to death?"

"I don't know," I admitted. "In a Hallmark movie, you can set your clock by it. The rescuers always come through exactly when there seems to be no hope left for the good guys."

"I hate to tell you this, Syl," said Freddy. "But this isn't a Hallmark movie."

"Nevertheless," I replied. "I'm putting my money on the cavalry to save us." And to myself I thought, *I just hope the cavalry's not too stoned to be paying close attention.*

CHAPTER 19

"Cavalry or no cavalry," said Freddy, "we have to be ready for whomever and whatever comes through that door."

"Agreed," I said.

"So, your hands are tied?" asked Freddy.

"If they weren't," I said, "I'd have wrapped you in a hug the moment you wiggled your way across the floor to my side."

"I hoped that was so," said Freddy, "but I asked again to be sure. And you're blindfolded?"

"No."

"No?"

"I already knew who'd abducted me, so I guess there was no point in covering my eyes."

"Hhmm," said Freddy. "I don't suppose it matters, cause once he goes into the bank to make the transfer, pretending he's the designated courier for the kidnapper, he's going to be madder than a swatted hornet's nest. He'll either come busting in here, guns blazing, or just leave town, leaving us here to rot."

"I think there are definitely third and fourth options," I said. "What if he thinks he can hold you at gunpoint and force me to sign another transfer slip? He might think there's still a chance he could make some form of his plan work."

"You're right," said Freddy.

I laughed. "I wish I had that in writing."

"We get out of this alive, Sylleegirl, I'll put anything you wish in writing."

"Anything?"

"If I say yes, you're going to get highly motivated, aren't you?" asked Freddy.

"I don't know how much more motivated I could be than in a life-or-death situation, but sure—I'm going to brainstorm my tail off here working to figure out how we can both come out of this in one piece."

"That's my girl," said Freddy. "Now what's your option four?"

"Now that Korski's going to have to go on the lam and permanently hightail it off the peninsula, he could just get into the casino vault and take whatever he could carry."

"That's also true," said Freddy. "But with the number of security cameras down there, most likely Tim or Jack would see what he was up to and call the sheriff right away, even though Korski has the combinations and passcodes and wouldn't be setting any alarms off."

"Oh! I forgot about Tim and Jack!" All kinds of bad thoughts hit me like a thunderbolt.

"Don't worry," said Freddy, "they've been well trained not to intervene in the event of a theft in progress. They know to lock themselves in the security office, call the sheriff, and stay put!"

"Okay, good." My heart rate slowed considerably.

Freddy started rubbing his face along my leg.

"Freddy! What are you doing?"

"I'm trying to rub the blindfold off. I'll be able to think better without it."

I chose not to challenge his critical thinking skills at that moment. "Okay, so you'll get your blindfold off—and then what?"

"I'm hoping Korski was so rattled when he had to bring you here he didn't think to take the LED emergency lantern with him when he left."

"Okay. Mattress, lantern… What else do we have to work with?"

"There's a folding chair and a make-shift porta potty and nearly a case of bottled water." Freddy succeeded in slipping out of his blindfold, not that it did any good. "This morning—at least I think it was this morning—he also brought a bag of donuts."

As if on cue, my stomach growled.

"Now let me just roll over here and see if I can connect with that lantern."

From what I heard, I assumed Freddy was lying on the floor, moving his leg slowly like the beam of a lighthouse, back and forth, then scooting forward a foot or two and doing it again. On the third or fourth try, he found what he was looking for.

For the next few minutes, I couldn't imagine what he was doing, other than making grunting and groaning noises that were almost obscene. And then the light dawned. Literally.

The bright LED light illuminated the entire basement, and I had to squint hard in the sudden brilliance.

"Let there be light," said Freddy. Then he turned to look at me, and I saw his face for the first time in nearly six months.

And for several minutes we just sat and looked at each other, both of us with tears streaking our faces, but no way to wipe them away, even if we'd wanted to.

"I'd like to say you're looking good," I said.

"We both know that would be a lie," said Freddy. "But you look good, Syl. Really good. That tan you got in Maui looks really great on you."

"Thank you. That's kind of you to say." I looked at him fondly, but was too choked up to say much more. "So…" I began. "What do we do now?"

Freddy scooted over to the folding chair and knocked it over with his shoulder. It fell between us on the indoor/outdoor carpet, and Freddy turned his back on it. "Be my eyes back there," he said. "Guide my hands to the end of one of the chair legs."

I felt like we were at one of those team-building seminars in which there are a number of trust exercises to perform with a partner. But it wasn't long before Freddy had the rubber stopper off the chair leg, and with continued help from my vocal directions, was able to use the raw metal edge of the chair leg to saw through his zip tie and free his hands.

"Well, whaddya know?" he said. "It worked! I'd been thinking about doing that for some time, but I couldn't test the theory until I was sure I really needed to do it. You only get one chance at something like that, and I was biding my time, waiting for the perfect opportunity."

After that, it was only a matter of a few more minutes before he freed my hands, too, and we fell into a long-awaited reunion embrace. And for quite a while, time stood still.

But eventually, I eased my grip. "Freddy," I said, gently pulling back enough to look into his beautiful deep brown eyes.

"Yes, my Sylleegirl," he said, his voice husky with emotion.

"I'm sorry, Freddy, but I need to pee."

Freddy erupted into laughter, and I joined him. Here we were, perhaps facing our last few hours together, and something as dumb as a natural biological function had ended the amazing moment we were sharing. Oh, the humanity!

Freddy pointed to the potty chair over in the left-hand corner. "Help yourself."

I looked at him, aghast. "At least have the common courtesy and decency to turn your back, Deputy Morgan!" And thankfully, he did.

I'm still not sure how long we'd been in that basement. Maybe it was less than an hour, maybe it was several hours, but I can't be sure. We had established a plan of action, which I preferred to call The Attack Plan, and were just waiting, waiting, waiting, and it was driving me crazy, crazy, crazy. Or crazier, as Freddy would say.

And then, without warning, we heard a series of footfalls crossing the room above us. Freddy put his finger to his lips. "There's more than one of them this time."

Crap. I wasn't sure we were armed well enough to take just Korski by himself, and now he'd brought along reinforcements. We heard the sound of several pairs of feet lumbering down the stairs. Closer. Closer. My throat tightened, and my heart began a rapid pounding inside my chest.

"On three," whispered Freddy.

Someone was fiddling with the exterior deadbolt. Freddy was poised to one side of the door. "One," he silently mouthed. "Two." Without a sound, I read his lips.

I flipped the switch on the emergency lantern to the flashing red strobe setting. Freddy thought it might be enough to temporarily confuse and distract Korski, but during our rehearsal preparations, I'd thought it just looked like a disco ball stuck on one color.

"*THREE!*" he shouted as the door swung wide.

The door went one way, and Freddy swung the folding chair from the other side like it was bases full, two out, full count, and the entire outcome of the World Series was up to him.

"*COWABUNGA!*" We both screamed at the top of our lungs, and I just kept on screaming, as I hurled bottles of water high over Freddy's head, as fast and as furious as I could, one after another, hoping to bean the first or second guy through the doorway.

It was slightly demeaning, and definitely a blow to my ego, to be removed from the front line action at the doorway. After all, I'd been hired as a bodyguard when the movie crew had come to town last summer on the strength of my one class in kickboxing. But Freddy had been adamant, so there I was, pitching 16-ounce water bottles like hand grenades.

I was semi-hysterical and screaming like a Commanche—which Freddy told me was okay for me to say, because he's one-eighth Native American and me having his permission keeps it from being politically incorrect or racist or anything like that.

And just as quickly as our life-or-death skirmish had begun, it was over.

I fell to my knees, buried my face in my hands, and began sobbing incoherently, even as relief flooded through every cell of my body. Freddy crouched down beside me, put one arm around me, and with his other hand, switched the lantern back to regular light.

Though I'd prayed for the cavalry to arrive in the nick of time, it certainly had been a long shot, and even now I wasn't totally sure I wasn't hallucinating.

First through the door had been Paranormal Patrick, brandishing a powerful flashlight. He was followed closely by Sheriff Donaldson, with his gun drawn. Bringing up the rear was Goodie, armed with a gardening trowel, along with Hans and Stella, waving their plumy tails, happy as they could be just to be included in the parade of rescuers.

Everyone began talking at the same time until Sheriff D whistled for silence.

"First things first," said the sheriff. "Does anyone need immediate medical attention?"

We all shook our heads.

"Good." The sheriff holstered his gun. "I'm parked behind Patrick and Goodie's garage, and we cut through the backyards to get here, just in case Korski returned before we had you liberated. Do you have any idea if he plans to return tonight?"

Freddy and I shook our heads.

"We're not entirely sure he's ever coming back," said Freddy. "I'm sure right now he's feeling pretty cocky, but in the morning, when he gets to the bank in Ocean Crest, he's going to find out Sylvia pulled a fast one on him, and he's not going to be able to get any ransom money transferred to his secret account after all.

"At that point," Freddy shot a look my way, "he might come back to kill us both, or he might try again to get the double-signature access to the casino accounts, or he may just leave town with his tail between his legs."

"That last one is an unlikely option," said Sheriff D. "He's got too much time and trouble invested here, and he's going to want something for his efforts, whether blood or money."

We both nodded in agreement. It was a sobering thought, but I knew from our conversation while we waited for something to happen, it wasn't the greatest of Freddy's worries.

"And at this point," said the sheriff, now vocalizing Freddy's biggest fear, "we don't know if Korski was working alone, for his own economic interests, or if the Russian mafia is involved, has hacked into the slots in the casino, and has in other ways infiltrated our community."

"Whoa," said Patrick, "that's a lot of bad stuff."

"That's quite an understatement, Patrick," said Sheriff D. "But the bottom line here is we can't wait to see what Korski's going to do. We have to go on the offensive, get out of here and go find him, ASAP."

"Count me in," said Freddy, immediately stepping forward.

"Now, Son," said Sheriff D, "You're in no condition to go anywhere but the hospital right now, and that's exactly where you're going."

"I'll drive!" said Goodie, happy to be able to contribute more than moral support to the rescue effort.

"Thank you, Goodie," said Sheriff D. "I was hoping you'd volunteer."

"But Sheriff," said Freddy, "I'm a trained law enforcement officer, and you don't have enough manpower at the moment to take Korski down, with or without his team of goons."

"Ooo! Ooo! Ooo!" said Patrick, waving his hand in the air. "You can deputize me, Sheriff! I'm the unofficial leader of the Neighborhood Watch around here, so I know how to help!"

The sheriff put his hand on Patrick's shoulder. "Not this time, Patrick," he said, shaking his head. "You and I both know you couldn't pass a UA at the moment."

"UA?" asked Goodie.

"Urinalysis," Freddy, the sheriff, and I said in unison.

"I'm kinda stoned," said Patrick, giving Goodie a lopsided smile and shrugging.

"So it's up to me," said Freddy, nodding his head.

"Son!" barked the sheriff, but not in a real bad way. He pointed to Freddy's feet. "You don't even have your boots, much less any strength about you." And before Freddy could raise another objection, the sheriff said, "And that's final."

Freddy trusted when six-foot, four-inch, Sheriff Carter Donaldson, his towering height not including his Stetson, said something was final, it was final, and he fell silent.

"Good," said the sheriff. "Now who can tell me where we might find Mr. Korski right at this particular moment?"

"What particular moment is this?" asked Freddy. "I kinda lost track of days, and nights, and Sylvia arrived unconscious and stayed that way for awhile, so fill me in."

"It's Tuesday night," said Sheriff D. "About 10 p.m."

Freddy nodded. "Most nights I'd say he'd be at his condo up on Pacific Bluff. But tonight he might want to stay at the casino to be closer to the bank in Ocean Crest when they first open. He doesn't know Syl's signature on the transfer voucher won't pass inspection, and he doesn't know we've been rescued, so he's not going to suspect anything's gone wrong with his plan."

"Except his first plan was to get Freddy out of his suite while he looked for whatever he thought might be in there, his second plan was to send me into the bank to personally authorize the transfer while he waited in the car," I said. "But that was before I smelled the pungent Russian cigarettes in his big, black car and put it all together."

"And got yourself kidnapped," said Freddy.

"And got myself kidnapped," I echoed. "So this is actually Korski's third plan, but in my defense," I scowled at Freddy, "I also got us both rescued, don't forget!" I put my hands on my hips and glared at him.

"How do you figure you got us rescued?" asked Freddy. "It's not like you purposely got abducted and left a trail of breadcrumbs or anything."

"Oh, isn't it?" I raised one eyebrow. "Didn't I tell you I trusted the cavalry would arrive in the nick of time and save us? Didn't you believe me?"

"Seriously?" asked Freddy. "You want me to believe you got kidnapped on purpose without the forethought to wear a tracking device or have someone ready to follow you?"

I looked at Patrick. "What tipped you off?"

Patrick bobbed his head. "I saw that the guy came back a second time today. Well, I didn't actually see him arrive, but I saw his big, black car was in the driveway when I went up to sit and watch the stars come out in my Tsunami Warning Lookout Station."

"There's a raft on his roof," I quickly said aside to Freddy.

"So's when I saw him leave, I decided to investigate," continued Patrick. "And that's when I found your scarf."

"My scarf?!" My hand flew to my throat.

"And I took the scarf to Goodie, and she said it looked like the one you were wearing when you came to see us a couple days ago."

"It was!" I choked out. "Only I didn't know I'd lost it until just this minute!"

"So you accidentally lost your scarf," said Freddy, "and now you want to claim responsibility for our rescue?"

"I thought Patrick might have seen Korski carry me in," I explained.

"Nevertheless, you're both safe now," said Goodie.

"And bickering like an old married couple," said Patrick.

"But back to the point," said Sheriff D, "you think Korski's at *Spartina Point*?"

"That's my best guess," Freddy replied.

Sheriff D got out his cell phone. "Who's on security tonight?"

"Tim and Jack should be working there together until 11 o'clock," said Freddy. "Then Bill and Bob come on."

"Bill and Bob? My reserve deputies? They moonlight doing security at the casino?" But without waiting for an answer, the sheriff called the casino's security office, identified himself, and told Tim to put his call on the speaker so Jack could hear him too.

"This is very important," said Sheriff D. "Look at the parking lot monitors and see if you can locate Wayne Korski's vehicle. He may be driving his white Honda Civic, or a black Lincoln Town Car."

"He's here in the Town Car tonight," Tim said immediately. "I was watching when he got here about three hours ago. I was surprised, because he parked that big, black car of his right up front in one of the boss's parking spaces."

"Some nerve," muttered Freddy.

"Good!" said Sheriff D. "Now listen carefully, and don't ask questions. I want you two to go out and stick a knife in one of his tires. Hell, stick a knife in all of them—but don't get caught. Then get back inside and call Bill and Bob and tell them to come to the casino right away, but to wait discreetly in the parking lot until I contact them on the radio. Got it?"

"Got it," the boys answered.

"And if you happen to run into Korski, do not engage. DO. NOT. ENGAGE. You got that, too?"

"Yes, sir!" Tim said.

"We're on it!" said Jack.

The sheriff hung up and turned to Goodie. "You'll get these two to the hospital to get checked out?"

"Of course," Goodie answered.

Then the sheriff turned to Patrick. "I can't deputize you, but if you'd like to ride along, I think you've earned the right to see this through."

Patrick brightened. "You mean ride along, like in the front seat? I've never ridden in the front seat of a patrol car before."

We all laughed.

"I'll even let you run the lights and siren until we get up past Ocean Crest."

"Cool beans!" said Patrick, bounding up the stairs ahead of us. "I'm riding shotgun in a police car! This will be way cooler than anything I've ever done!"

I reached over and took Freddy's hand. "Oh, I think leading the cavalry in our rescue is probably the coolest thing he's ever done, but let's wait to throw him a parade until after Korski's safely behind bars."

Sheriff D paused and turned back to us before following Patrick up the stairs. "I can't tell you how good it is to see you, Freddy." He nodded. "And you, too, of course, Sylvia. But I don't know what I'd do without my number one deputy."

"No worries about that, Sheriff," said Freddy. "The only place I'm going—after the hospital, of course—is to see if there's any place still open where I can get a 16-ounce double-shot espresso cappuccino with hazelnut flavoring. I barely survived here without my coffee!"

The sheriff pointed to the pastry bag on the floor next to the mattress that both dogs were eagerly sniffing. "Speaking of dinner," he said, although we hadn't been, "if you've got any donuts left in that bag, I'd be happy to take them with me. I haven't had anything to eat in quite awhile."

Freddy happily tossed him the bag, and for my part, I kept from saying a single word about cops and donuts and hazelnut flavored coffee.

I could tease them both later, if I still wanted to.

CHAPTER 20

The Fourth of July's weather turned out to be one of the warmest days thus far this year on the North Beach Peninsula, and there was no need to hurriedly move our festival plans over to the casino, thankfully.

There was a fly-over by Coast Guard helicopters to kick off the parade through downtown Ocean Crest, and I clapped and cheered the loudest when *The Veiled Rainbow* belly-danced their way down Bay Avenue.

For this occasion, *The Veiled Rainbow* had set aside their usual rainbow-hued costumes and they were flipping their hips and snaking their arms down the parade route wearing red, white, and blue coin belts, skirts, turbans and harem pants.

Jimmy and Patrick, also decked out in appropriate attire, carried the group's name sign out in front of the troupe. Patrick had declined being the Grand Marshal in the parade, citing the fact he was only doing his part for community welfare, and didn't want to call too much attention called to himself in the hopes the paparazzi would leave him alone.

Meredith, Nova, Goodie and Orpha followed the banner on foot. Lester, along with charter boat captain Rich Morgan, who is also Freddy's father and now officially Nova's boyfriend, came next. They each had a handle of a crepe paper decorated wheelchair which carried the troupe's portable sound system.

It was almost funny to see the ladies doing traditional belly dancing moves to the strains of *America the Beautiful*, but I didn't complain. I was just glad Rich and Lester had found a way to provide the music for the troupe while also keeping a wheelchair close by in case 90-year-old Orpha Starr needed somewhere to suddenly sit down during the parade.

But Orpha, heart stents and all, was in great shape, both physically, and perhaps today even mentally, and when we got out to Willoopah to the *Diamond Booi Oyster Farm* for continued festivities, she kept everyone gathered around her camp chair in stitches.

"Now I'm not saying there was anything going on between Principal Anderson and her remodeling contractor," Orpha was saying as I pulled my chair over to join them, "but I'd bet my boots he was nailing more than just the two by fours over there."

And when that laugh subsided, she continued, "I can't say as I blame Maggie. If I were a few years younger, I'd have ripped his clothes off myself." She paused. "Of course, they would have had to be those tear-away Velcro clothes—and not new Velcro, either, cause that stuff sticks too hard for most anyone to unfasten—so for the sake of argument, let's say if he'd been wearing old Velcro, he'd have been mine!"

Orpha was really on a roll, and I was happy to see her having so much fun being the center of attention and "holding court" with her friends.

Felicity and Mark showed up, and I was glad Orpha was through talking about the principal's extra-curricular activities by then. No sense spreading gossip to two of the high school teachers about their boss, just in case they hadn't heard it already.

I'd been in phone contact with Felicity several times in the past week, but like quite a few of us there, I hadn't seen her engagement ring yet.

"Congratulations you two!" Orpha piped up. "Why don't you take the ring off, Felicity, and pass it around so we can see it up close and personal? I'm sure none of us would accidentally drop it in the sand and lose it."

I think that got the biggest laugh of all, and it made my heart happy to see everyone in such high spirits, despite the fact someone—namely me—hadn't thought about getting a liquor permit until it was too late to have one approved.

"We're thrilled for the both of you," Meredith said to Felicity and Mark. She was sitting between Orpha and Lester, holding Lester's hand. Then she turned to Orpha. "Now don't you go messing with that ring, Orpha. Mark needs it to make an honest woman out of Felicity."

"That's such a ridiculous saying," said Orpha. "Ain't no woman, deep down, who's totally honest, whether she's married or not. Why even I've lied, when it was absolutely necessary. Like when Bill Number Two wanted to know my true age. And did I ever tell any of you how Bill Number One actually died?"

It was a deer in the headlights moment, and I had to think fast to get the subject changed before she could utter another word. Thankfully, and I'm calling it Divine Intervention, the band chose that exact moment to start doing sound checks.

"I heard you got a new hip while I was away, Orpha," I shouted over the sound of the musicians tuning up.

Orpha's curly, over-permed, gray Brillo-pad head bobbed up and down. "Yep, I got a smoking hot new joint that can't wait to get out there to dance!" She pointed to the cleared sandy area in front of the bandstand and beamed.

"Did I hear correctly that Miss Orpha is in need of an immediate dance partner?"

We turned to see Kanji and Lorraine approaching us with their camp chairs.

"Just the man I was looking for," Orpha crowed. "I want to test out my new hip—if it's okay with Lorraine that I get the first crack at you today, Kanji."

Lorraine laughed. "I signed up for first shift at one of the barbecues," she said. "So be my guest!"

Kanji set down his chair and gallantly extended his hand to Orpha. "If you would be so kind as to do me this honor, Mrs. Starr?"

"Cliff!" Nautika called out. She waved her arms over her head to get his attention, and exaggeratedly pointed several times to Kanji leading Orpha to the makeshift dance floor.

Cliff immediately picked up on what was going on, and got his band to quickly launch into Lee Greenwood's *God Bless the USA*, an appropriate patriotic song for the occasion that was also slow enough for Kanji and Orpha to dance to.

Kanji held Orpha close and they hugged and swayed so tenderly, none of us could look away. I shot a glance at my dear friends gathered around, and was relieved to see I wasn't the only one getting misty. In fact, there wasn't a dry eye among us.

I turned to Nautika. "So much for you getting to kick things off today by singing *The Star-Spangled Banner*."

"Oh, we'd already changed up the order of things," said Nautika. "I'm going to sing it just before the fireworks start instead. You know, kind of like introducing the rockets' red glare?"

"Sounds absolutely perfect," I said.

The barbecues were busy all afternoon keeping most of the crowd filled with oysters, corn, and garlic bread. For people like me who don't care for the shellfish, hotdogs and potato chips were also available, and there were platters of watermelon wedges on ice piled high on the picnic tables near the dance floor.

Brent was in charge of keeping a continuous supply of oysters ready for the grill masters whenever needed, and he'd enlisted

Freddy's help to drive the totes from the warehouse to the picnic area. At first it made me nervous to have them working together, but soon I realized it made sense for them to get to know each other better, since we were going to be somewhat significant in each other's lives for many years. At least I hoped so.

For the *North Beach Blues'* last song of the first set, they started playing Golden Earring's song *Radar Love* from the early 1970s.

"Uh-oh," said Nautika. She stood up and started rubbing her baby bump. "I think Cliff's playing this song on purpose."

I followed her gaze, and saw him grinning just for her, his dimples giving away the fact he had an ulterior motive for the band's song selection.

It wasn't until they came to the drummer's solo that I understood what Nautika had meant. Cliff went all out with his red, white, and blue LED flashing drumsticks and really wailed on the drums. And just a few measures into it, Nautika started laughing and grimacing at the same time.

"The baby has been kicking me like crazy whenever they've practiced this song. We're betting he's going to be a drummer, just like his daddy."

"He?" I asked.

"Or she," Nautika corrected herself. "We're still not going to find out ahead of time. We're enjoying this pregnancy the old-fashioned way, and the gender of the baby will be a happy surprise, no matter which way it goes."

We exchanged a smile, and Nautika said, "I suppose I should wait for Cliff so we could ask you this together, but we've already agreed we'd like you to consider being a godmother to our child."

"Of course," I said without hesitation. "I'd be delighted."

"Wonderful," said Nautika. "That makes me very happy. Now that Cliff's band is taking a short break, I'm going to go tell him the good news."

I sat alone for only a minute before Freddy and Brent joined me. Brent pulled up the chair Nautika had just vacated, and Freddy repositioned a nearby empty one to sit on on the other side of me. Both men seemed to be in extremely good moods.

"You know that fable about the scorpion wanting to get to the other side of the river, so he asks the frog for a ride on his back?" asked Freddy.

"Uh, yeah," I replied. "As I recall, it doesn't end too well for either of them, as the scorpion stings the frog and they both drown." I scowled. "So why are you asking about that?"

"At the end of the fable," said Brent, "the frog asks the scorpion why he stung him, and the scorpion says he couldn't help himself, it's just his nature."

"Sorry. I'm still not connecting the dots," I said, looking from one to the other of them.

"Well," said Freddy, "we've accepted being a free spirit is just in your nature."

"It's not that either one of us isn't good enough," said Brent. "We're both plenty good enough to be your boyfriends."

Freddy nodded. "And we both knew you were a scorpion before we got involved."

"A commitmentphobic scorpion," added Brent, his head bobbing up and down.

I started to squirm, sitting there between them. They'd obviously been talking about me, maybe most of the afternoon, and I got that old uncomfortable feeling of being trapped.

Freddy leaned across me and spoke to Brent. "I think she's breaking out in hives."

Brent nodded. "I guess I owe you a soda."

"Hey!" I started to stand up, but they each reached out and restrained me.

"I thought you'd be happy we're getting along so well," said Brent.

Freddy shook his head, as in disbelief. "Boy, Syl, you sure are hard to please."

I also shook my head. "I certainly never thought you two would join forces to gang up on me like this."

"We're not ganging up on you," said Brent. "Not really."

"Good!" I said, "because I've decided to go back to Maui for a month or two, and I don't need either of you, or both of you, trying to convince me not to go."

I expected an argument, but I think I'd caught them both by such surprise they were speechless.

"Don't worry, you'll know exactly where I am, and I promise to leave my phone on this time," I began. "It's just that Rick could really use my help on the *Cherokee Rose*. He's got a lot of trips scheduled, and he hasn't found anyone to replace me."

I looked from face to face, but their mouths were still hanging open. "It's only for a month or two, I promise. Well, unless one of you goes and gets himself kidnapped while I'm gone."

"That was a low shot," said Freddy.

"I agree," said Brent, nodding.

"I thought you guys weren't going to gang up on me."

"Korski is in prison, at least for the next 20 or 25 years," said Freddy. "He confessed everything. He was working alone, with not even a peripheral affiliation with organized crime. So there's no indication the Russian mob even knows that Spartina Point exists."

"I supposed that's one of the advantages at living over here at the end of the world," said Brent. "We're not even on the mafia's map."

"When Korski worked for Uncle Harry," continued Freddy, "he was promised a good-sized chunk of change for keeping the casino's accounts pristine clean, neat and tidy and looking like a legitimate business in case of any federal or state audits or investigations. But those promises he was made never had time to materialize."

Brent nodded. "Uncle Harry had actually shown Korski a black velvet pouch of stolen diamonds, and promised him he'd get a healthy cut when enough time had passed they could be taken out of the country and fenced."

"Out of the country? Like maybe to Russia?" I asked.

"Maybe," said Freddy. "But since no diamonds were recovered after Uncle Harry's helicopter crash, Korski had his mind made up the diamonds had been left in Uncle Harry's suite. They weren't in the casino vault, he'd already looked, so unless they'd already been sent overseas with a courier, he figured they had to be in that room somewhere."

"He's been biding his time," said Brent, "but when the first anniversary rolled around since Freddy took over, his frustration level grew."

Freddy nodded. "I watched the sheriff interrogate him—Oh! And by the way, Syl, the Sheriff sends his regrets for not being here. He said to tell you someone has to keep the tourists in line down on the beach in Tinkerstown. It's a real wild west show down there."

I nodded. "I figured as much, but now please, let's get back to Korski's interrogation. Tell me everything, and don't leave anything out."

"Okay," said Freddy, "Since you've been busy up here, I guess I owe you the whole story. At one point in the sheriff's questioning, Korski broke down and cried. He said he thought when Uncle Harry died, he might be in line to inherit the place. He didn't know Harold Rodman the Third had a nephew— namely me—who lived locally, and he was sorely disappointed to discover he wasn't going to be living the good life he'd been promised anytime soon."

"I kinda feel sorry for the guy," said Brent. "He got left out of the will, and six months later, he devised a pretty ingenious way to try skimming his way to major wealth, at $10,000 a month, with that bogus charity."

"But he got impatient," said Freddy. "He did say he never meant to hurt me. That in fact I'd been really good to him. But he was told the value of those diamonds were worth somewhere in the neighborhood of the $100 million dollar diamond heist in Antwerp in 2003. Korski figured if he could just get me out of my suite long enough to find the diamonds, he could return me the next day and no one would suspect him of any wrongdoing.

"And as for you, Sylvia," said Freddy, "he wanted to apologize for having to involve you. He hadn't ever planned to trade me for ransom, but when you returned, he saw an opportunity to at least come away with something, then head back to Russia as quickly as possible."

"But now he's of no concern," said Brent. "And we can all live happily ever after."

"So don't worry; neither one of us will be getting ourselves kidnapped while you're gone again," Freddy concluded.

Wow! When I looked from one to the other of them as they spoke, I got the feeling I was watching the making of one of the world's greatest bromances.

"But what about the diamonds?" I had to ask. "Since Korski didn't find them, where do you suppose they are?"

Both men shrugged.

"Sheriff D says it's most likely they were long gone before we closed in on Uncle Harry's drug-running ring," said Freddy. "And it's unfortunate, but now I'll need to get a new CFO vetted and hired for the *Spartina Point Casino and Resort*."

"Yes," said Brent, "but this time you should try to hire a someone who's not going to hack your slot machines, or skim from your charities, or end up kidnapping you."

"Ok, Ok, I'm sorry I brought up the kidnapping," I said, laughing with both of them. "And I'll definitely be back before Nautika gives birth. In fact, if one of you wants to, you can come visit, but you'll have to book your own room, as Evie doesn't allow overnight visitors."

Freddy started digging in his jeans' pocket. "I've got a quarter right here."

"For what?" I asked.

"So we can flip a coin," said Brent, without missing a beat. He looked at Freddy. "Heads, I'm buying a quart of SPF 50 suntan lotion, and tails, you can go right ahead and order yourself some flowered swim trunks online."

Freddy nodded and flipped the quarter high into the air.

As the three of us watched the quarter twirl its way up and start back down, I couldn't decide which side I was rooting for. I guess what I had really wanted was for the men to be smart enough to suggest taking turns visiting me in Lahaina.

I reached out to grab the coin in mid-air, but I missed, and it landed in the sand at our feet with its edge sticking straight up.

"Hey!" said Freddy, "Whaddya know?"

"I guess we'll both be taking a vacation to Maui," said Brent.

My smile was ear to ear. "The Universe always knows best. I'll be looking forward to seeing you both on the *Cherokee Rose* later this summer. You two can figure out how to split the time, but don't tell me who's coming when. I want it to be a surprise."

"Sylleegirl," said Freddy, shaking his head, "every day with you brings another surprise."

"And there's absolutely nothing wrong with that," said Brent.

I couldn't have agreed more.

ABOUT THE AUTHOR

Tsunami Warning is Jan Bono's sixth and final book of the Sylvia Avery Mystery Series set on the southwest Washington coast. She's also written five collections of humorous personal experience stories, one self-help weight loss book, two poetry chapbooks, and one book of short romance. In addition, she's penned nine one-act plays, and a full-length dinner theater play. Jan has written for numerous magazines ranging from *Guidepost* to *Star* to *Woman's World* and has had more than 45 stories included in the *Chicken Soup for the Soul* series.

See more of Jan's work: www.JanBonoBooks.com